# THE HOUSE ON
# LAKE MAGGIORE

# THE HOUSE ON LAKE MAGGIORE

K. S. HANSEN

iUniverse LLC
Bloomington

# The House on Lake Maggiore

*Copyright © 2013 by K. S. Hansen.*

*All rights reserved. No part of this book may be used or reproduced by any means, graphic, electronic, or mechanical, including photocopying, recording, taping or by any information storage retrieval system without the written permission of the publisher except in the case of brief quotations embodied in critical articles and reviews.*

*This is a work of fiction. All of the characters, names, incidents, organizations, and dialogue in this novel are either the products of the author's imagination or are used fictitiously.*

*iUniverse books may be ordered through booksellers or by contacting:*

*iUniverse LLC*
*1663 Liberty Drive*
*Bloomington, IN 47403*
*www.iuniverse.com*
*1-800-Authors (1-800-288-4677)*

*Because of the dynamic nature of the Internet, any web addresses or links contained in this book may have changed since publication and may no longer be valid. The views expressed in this work are solely those of the author and do not necessarily reflect the views of the publisher, and the publisher hereby disclaims any responsibility for them.*

*Any people depicted in stock imagery provided by Thinkstock are models, and such images are being used for illustrative purposes only.*
*Certain stock imagery © Thinkstock.*

*ISBN: 978-1-4759-9859-7 (sc)*
*ISBN: 978-1-4759-9860-3 (hc)*
*ISBN: 978-1-4759-9861-0 (ebk)*

*Library of Congress Control Number: 2013912934*

*Printed in the United States of America*

*iUniverse rev. date: 08/19/2013*

# Dedication

*To Judy Freeland, my sister, best friend and confidant. What would I have done without you all these years?*

*But evil things, in robes of sorrow,*
*Assailed the monarch's high estate*
*(Ah, let us mourn!—for never morrow*
*Shall dawn upon him desolate!)*
*And round about his home the glory*
*That blushed and bloomed,*
*Is but a dim-remembered story*
*Of the old time entombed.*

*And travelers, now within that valley,*
*Through the red-litten windows see*
*Vast forms, that move fantastically*
*To a discordant melody,*
*While like a ghastly rapid river,*
*Through the pale door*
*A hideous throng rush out forever*
*And laugh—but smile no more.*

**"The Haunted Palace"—Edgar Allan Poe**

# CHAPTER 1

I am a testament to the fact that there are variant types of love affairs. I've had my share of the usual, been approached and invited to the not so usual, but it is a much more extraordinary love affair I am thinking about tonight. The love affair of a place—a place so profound, so inconceivably beautiful that your eyes and heart become prey to defenseless enraptures. My encounter and involvement devoured me and affected me so deeply that I was left feeling as though I had just been through the turmoil one might experience being part of an all-encompassing, heart rendering and at times, tumultuous affair with the love of your life—one that was stimulating and breath taking at the onset, but if unhappily ending, leaves you devastated and wallowing in a debilitating sadness. I put myself through an emotional wringer and I was physically and mentally exhausted. What was to be a wonderful experience eventually became convoluted and swallowed into a dark sorrow.

My experience with Lake Maggiore in Northern Italy sent me onto a very long journey. The voyage there was not all that long, but my experience there and journey back was an arduous effort. I fell in love with this beautiful place that is the closest I believe one can get to paradise on earth. After my first visit, the memory stayed so indisputably in my mind that I could think of little else. The beauty of this place could not leave my mind and I had too many pensive moments thinking about Lake Maggiore and before I knew it, those pensive moments began to control my life to the point of impeding my normal work functions. When I began to work, or picked up a book to read, or sipped a glass of wine, my mind wandered back to not only that beautiful place, but one lonely, neglected, shamble of a house that sits on the shore. I felt as though I had left a part of me there and I was no longer complete. Just thinking about it and knowing it existed made me feel a need to be there, and to perhaps rescue it, and maybe make it love me back. I had to return and satisfy the magnetism that drew me to that beautiful place; the paradise I found seemed to have a hold on my heart.

When I sit and think about it, I can pinpoint the beginning of this journey, the very moment when my mind told me it was to begin. I was no longer going to ponder a decision to return, or rationalize over the logic. It was a certainty that I would return. Somehow I was going to go back and experience what it would be like to live there, to be within the walls of that pathetic villa and to cry with it. There was clearly one particular moment when the continual niggling in my mind finally pushed at me so endlessly that I knew I had to do something and I was about to make a decision that would change the course of my life. When that reality finally hit me, I accepted it with open arms, because it was a time in my life when I had reached a cross road. My direction became blurred and I was at my most vulnerable. I needed something the help me set new goals and create a clear direction.

I awoke one morning and realized my life was too programmed, predictable and lonely. My husband passed away three years prior and it was a long recovery for me to get beyond that. We had been married twenty-three years. My daily efforts were a routine mechanization of processes: working, going home to a lonely house, dinner alone, another glass of wine, mindlessly watching late night TV with my thoughts elsewhere, and then the next day begin it all over again. I may have wanted my distance from people for a while and preferred to be alone, but when I felt like it was time to reach out to someone, it was almost too late and too much time had passed. Time had created a schism in my friendships, left me with a life of solitude and it was difficult to figure out how to change it. Finally coming to terms with John's death and perhaps being over the mourning, I realized loneliness was my nemesis. My daughter lives on the east coast and we talk often by phone, but only see one another about twice a year. She alone would fill that void if only she were near, but she has her own life to pursue and we are as much a part of one another's lives as possible, but she is there and I am here.

I realized that my life was no more than a footnote to those others that were supposed to love me and to care about me. I had been pushing the thought away and in my mind made excuses for everyone because they were busy. They all seemed to be entrenched in their own lives and problems and for one reason or another, all were wallowing in their own pathos. The pathos then became mine and I noticed that no one ever called to see if I was fine, or inquired about my wellbeing, but called instead to tell me about what was going on in their life. If I initiated the calls, I became their audience and their support system and if my calls became a little overdue no one was beyond scolding me about it. All my conversations with family and friends were always about them, never about me. I had my own struggles, trying to keep my business afloat, earning a living and striving to make ends meet somewhere in a comfortable and reasonable place and keep my head above water. No one cared and I felt downhearted and disappointed. I realized that with John's passing, I was truly alone and my struggles were my own. I had no one in the wings giving me encouragement or showing they cared about me or giving me reinforcement. It was always just John that did that, and that was one of the many things I noticed the most after his passing because we were so connected to one another's life. I felt a tremendous void with his absence.

I was always strong and independent and maybe that was the reason; everyone knew I could take care of myself and there was nothing to worry about so they chose not to be concerned, but in doing so, they showed me they also did not care. Perhaps that was my fault because I gave the impression that I was a rock and would never falter. However, at that time in my life, I was feeling much more uncertain about my place in life and needed someone to understand, and moreover, needed someone to talk to—to listen to me.

This feeling of being abandoned left me feeling sullen and too reflective. I had to stop thinking about my situation and do something about it. I believed that perhaps an adventure was what I needed to get me out of my funk. And so, I booked a trip to Northern Italy to give me the divergence I needed and to hopefully lift my spirits.

That first trip to Lake Maggiore served the purpose, but gave me so much more. I truly fell in love with Northern Italy and all the disappointments in my personal life seemed to just fade away. I was far enough removed from my dismal existence at home. My discoveries took precedence and I became absorbed in all the beauty and culture that is the essence of Italy. I spent several days in Milan and then went on to the little town of Stresa on Lake Maggiore and there, I found paradise.

My thoughts of Lake Maggiore and how much I loved my visit there that summer never left my mind. After returning home my old problems were still there and when they began to make me feel a bit down, I thought of that beautiful place and those thoughts made everything bright and cheerful again. I became overwhelmed with the thoughts of being there and found myself staring into space daydreaming about it. Soon it began to cause me many sleepless nights and pushed everything else aside.

I took many weekend getaways to my cabin in the San Jacinto Mountains near Palm Springs, two hours from Los Angeles. One particular weekend I recall sitting in my cabin at the top of the mountain, waiting for the snow to begin, stoking the fire in the fireplace to rid the cabin of the chill it acquired in its idleness since I was last there. I kept walking to the window to see if the snow had begun to fall, as was predicted. I was relieved that it hadn't begun while I was making my drive up the serpentine road carved into the mountain. I thought about what I should have been doing because of the approaching holiday season, and yet, I reminded myself that I came there that weekend to escape that thought—to rid myself of the guilt I felt by not doing the tedious tasks of shopping, addressing Christmas cards, decorating a Christmas tree, and baking cookies. I was ignoring it all and none of that was going to happen for me. Since my daughter was unable to get away long enough to come home for the holiday and I couldn't take enough time from my work to go visit her, we both decided Christmas that year was lost.

A melancholy had come over me and I was overcome with vexing thoughts of the day in June of that year and my trip to Stresa when I sat on the terrace of my hotel room looking out at the placid Lake Maggiore. Perhaps it was the juxtaposition of the situation that made me remember. In reality that night I was after all, sitting alone waiting for a pending snow storm, dark winter skies hanging low, and dampness all around, about to be snowed in for days looking at nothing but the inner walls of that cabin.

I studied the painting over my fireplace, which I believed to be a scene from somewhere in the Alps—tall snow covered mountain tops reaching into a flaming chatoyant sky, green velvet canyons flowing into a frothy creek cascading rapidly over large boulders, and a small cabin nestled into the side of a murky cliff, with a veil of water falling next to it gently, mingling with the rushing creek below. A stream of smoke climbs from the chimney of the cabin, windows luminous with a glow from inside, and all mingling in the amber and mauve dusk settling over the scene. The imagined life inside that cabin wasn't much unlike mine at that moment, I was certain, with candles and the fire in the fireplace lighting the interior. I was mentally taken away and I recalled visions of that other, most beautiful day in Italy. My thoughts of Lake Maggiore brought sunlight into my mind's eye, reflecting the Alps onto the mirrored surface of the beautiful lake, with the heady fragrance of camellias and wisteria in the gardens all around me. Perhaps it all existed just beyond the mountains in my painting, on the other side of the Alps.

My biggest conflict in life was always dreaming of another place, always finding comfort and satisfaction waning all too quickly from a current situation, and then planning my next house, and even when I was young it was the next love affair, another trip or adventure to feed my impatient nature. My restlessness brought too much confusion into my life. I could not be complacent, idle or bored—I just would not allow it. But after marrying John, I felt more grounded and somehow he was reinforcement that the restlessness I felt was energy that could be redirected and be a positive thing. With his death I lost my ever constant reinforcement and the direction in my life became skewed. In order to deal with the void I was feeling, I had to have a list of things in front of me, waiting to tackle, things to learn, things to pass along and be archived in my past and stepped over to get to my future. Being busy kept me from thinking too much, but I was running in too many directions and not accomplishing anything. So I would go to the mountain cabin and try to unwind and rethink my life, to dissolve all that restless nature and sit still for a while, and enjoy the present. It became my sanctuary where I would be compelled to just relax, listen to the silence and let my thoughts run wild in my mind until they were exhausted and my head finally cleared.

As it was, weekends were all I could take. Come the third day, I found myself bored and feeling shut in and then I closed the house and headed back down the mountain and onward to my condo in Los Angeles and again engaged in my hectic life there as an interior designer. There I would once again be intermingling with the thousands of other people on the freeways, rushing from one place to the next, juggling my time only to fall into my bed at night exhausted, but somehow I felt natural living that way, as unhealthy as I knew it probably was, and also as life shortening.

Perhaps it was my big mistake of the year: going to Stresa on Lake Maggiore. My soul found a new home and my life made a drastic change. My soul and my heart stayed in Italy and I sat there one weekend in that mountain cabin in Southern

*The House on Lake Maggiore*

California and felt as if I was an empty vessel—just a body—no heart, no soul, no more me. I missed those parts of me and my sought after solitude became overwhelming and I felt too cut off, and much too alone. I found peace and quiet especially difficult to adjust to and I realized I wished for the company of another human being, another voice, someone to spend time with and to cook dinner for and share time, but that night it was me I was missing. And yet, I asked myself: did I really want to reel it all in again and be that person I was before experiencing the emotions that stirred within me when I sat on that terrace of my hotel room in Stresa, looking at that magnificent body of water and the Alps? It changed my life and it was that night remembering all that while in my mountain cabin in California that I realized I was truly a different person, void of my heart, the engine that made the channels of my arteries pulsate that kept this body seeking another breath to keep me alive yet one more day.

I felt I must rejoin myself and in order to do that I must go back to Italy and Lago Maggiore. Only then could I hope to understand what it was that pulled me back to that place, that confused my mind and would not allow me to forget its beauty and why it seemed to call me. I was not able to return to my usual and predictable life, as it was before I set eyes on its magnificence, and I needed to know what power that place had over me. I knew I would have to go back to Lake Maggiore again. I wrestled endlessly with the idea, but there was more to the decision.

There was a business opportunity that presented itself, but as time passed it seemed more unrealistic and I wasn't certain how to pursue it. I was so driven and my imagination got the best of me trying to figure out how to make it happen. The more time that passed, the less likely it was that this could happen and the opportunity would have to belong to someone else. The challenge in my mind was the magnitude of the adventure and I had a reasonable fear of the unknown. I was fearful and anxious as to what this venture would entail, if I could indeed make it happen.

As wonderful as it is to live on the peak and view the world from that mountain and sleep among the treetops, I wondered if that cabin in the woods was what I still wanted. That cabin on the mountain was my ultimate dream a year prior and I was not in want of anything else. And then I visited Lake Maggiore and my inner self set higher standards of what I must see to witness the glory of God's most incredible accomplishments. My vision of the tall cedars and pines of the San Jacinto Mountains became clouded and altered with the vision of the Alps and the Savoy Mountains on the other side of that Italian lake, dotted with the enchanting Borromeo islands with their beautiful Italian gardens. It was all wonderful and beautiful, but it was much more than trees and beautiful gardens. It had an aura about it, just hovering over the lake, mingling in the sweet smelling blossoms of the gardens, an aureole that wraps itself around you and you not only see the beauty, but you feel it almost in a spiritual way.

My love affair with Italy had gone on for several years. Our first trip to Italy only made me want more. After John died, I took a short trip alone to Italy, but it was a rather sad trip because I was overcome with thoughts of how much we enjoyed seeing Italy together. I visited the northern lake area and saw Lake Garda, Lake Orta, Lake Como and Lake Maggiore, Italy's second biggest lake. The area lies within the two regions of Lombardy and Piedmont. The northern tip of Lake Maggiore is in Switzerland and the Alps reflect so beautifully on the lake's surface. Centuries ago the dynasty of the Borromeo family of Milan, brought their wealth to that area and built palaces and gardens and it eventually came to be known as Lake Maggiore. Ernest Hemingway used it for the background of his story "Farewell to Arms." Napoleon visited, Byron wrote poems about it, artists painted it, and through the centuries it became a favorite stopping off place for royalty. It has the reputation of being an unforgotten paradise because when you first see it, you can never forget it.

Having had a small taste of Stresa once before, on my visit last summer, I decided to spend more time there and get to know it better. I toured Italy and ended my trip there. Milan is within an hour's train trip so I would return to Milan to fly home. When I arrived the terrace of my hotel room became a sort of nirvana as soon as I stepped onto it. The shores of the lake are graced with beautiful villas and the town of Stresa has wonderful boutiques and restaurants and many tourists pass through this charming little town while visiting the glorious lake regions. I remembered that afternoon, how I sat for hours being bathed in the warm sun, sipping the white fruity wines made from grapes grown on the glacier carved slopes of the nearby terraced mountain, and I let my mind go where it wished and I became embroiled in the visions before me.

Time escaped and I lost track of everything real and present and when I finally realized the sun was setting, I retreated to my hotel room and as if in a trance, walked forward toward the mirror above the dresser and realized I had been in the sun too long. My face reflected the heat of the day and I felt the sting of my sun drenched taut skin. My eyes struggled to focus in the darkness of the room after looking out at the silver reflection of the sun on the lake for so many hours and they began to sting and tears poured fourth burning oblique paths down my cheekbones.

The dilemma of what to do to make that face more presentable sent me into panic because the task seemed too impossible to accomplish. Soon I was to join new acquaintances for dinner and I had to pull myself together.

I took the train earlier that day from Milan and after I arrived I quickly settled into my hotel room and then I took a walk along the Strada Sempione, the avenue along the shore of the lake and happened to pass by a Villa that sat forlorn and abandoned. This was my first acquaintance with the house that would become so important to me. I stood for quite some time looking through the iron gates at the pathetic shadow of a house that at one time must have been magnificent. It was a ragged outcast of blatant negligence, but the magnificent architectural splendor could not be hidden. The house was grand and it broke my heart to see its misery as it sat in its nakedness staring out at the lake. Visions of what might have been its history took over my thinking process and I stood for some time, looking at this house thinking about what it must have been like in its full splendor—the elegant social affairs and parties held within its walls, the children that may have been born and lived there, the lives that may have ended within its embrace. Truly, that house at least represented someone's life. It represented their happiness, their existence, and their most important memories, and perhaps their sadness, which spoke most loudly. That afternoon it seemed to bend with the humiliation of the despair that cried out from its cracks and flaws.

    I stood on the sidewalk in front of the house, looking through the intricately coiled and rusted iron gates. As I peered up the long drive through to the house and into the large window at the front of the house into the interior, I could see a magnificent staircase with a mirror at the top that reflected the grand room at the foot of the stairs, and the lake across the street from the house. How many wonderful grand entrances were made while entering the room at the foot of that staircase when the house was in its prime? One could only imagine watching the mistress of that incredible house descending the elaborate staircase to meet her awaiting guests, and the relationships that represented the society during the time in history when the house was in its prime and most important relevance. And now, emptiness and no one except the rodents or other creatures that inhabited this wonderful house could bear witness to any spirits that may remain there, to tell its story, and I was certain there was a remarkable story. This house could only have an incredible history and could not be just another house. It had character, purpose, meaning, and I was so sure it held the dreams of the souls that may still linger and in my mind I thought I could hear the breath of those long lost souls calling out from behind the blistered walls.

    As I stood watching the palm trees and bushes surrounding the house caress and gently kiss her facade from the slight breeze off the lake, a man approached and stood behind me at my left shoulder. I noticed his shadow before he spoke and for some reason I was not startled by his appearance. It seemed natural to me that anyone passing by would stop to look at the house.

"She was once the beauty of the shore, albeit of course for the Borromeo palace on the island across the strand. I knew her when she was at her best." I slowly turned and looked into his eyes, brilliantly blue and intensely focused on the house. He then turned his attention to me and looked so deep into my eyes that it gave me a sense of uneasiness for just a fleeting moment.

I remember my comment. "It is such a beautiful house. I can't believe no one lives there. It seems like such a shame that it is empty."

"Its emptiness is fitting because I believe it would be impossible to live there now. I believe it is a busy place, but of a business that we cannot see. I think there are many souls that still live within the walls of this house and it has proven to be a fact, for anyone that has tried to inhabit this house has found it to be impossible to coexist with the voices that come out of the walls," he said with almost a breathless whisper.

His knowledge of the house intrigued me and I wanted to hear more. I probably sounded a little over exuberant when I asked if he had been inside the house.

"Yes, many times, but it was a very long time ago. The house has been vacant for many years, but I remember it from my childhood. My father was some sort of business associate of the owner. They had grand parties and celebrations here and I came at Christmas with my parents. The adults were always asked to bring their children. It was like a fairy tale to see how beautiful the house was at Christmas. See that tall bank of windows at the front of the house? There was always a wonderful Christmas tree in front of those windows. The lady of the house had no children of her own, and took special pleasure in decorating and entertaining to make it especially exciting for the children." He became quiet for a moment and I could see he was reflecting on favorite memories of his childhood.

"I imagine that every time you pass by this house, you must think of those happy days of your childhood."

"I don't pass this house that frequently any more. I no longer live here, but I feel something pulling me back every now and then and I return, not especially just to see the house, but to visit friends. But I find I cannot resist taking the walk here to the house and looking at it and just reflect on those days." He turned and looked out at the lake. "My father and I used to go out on the lake in his boat. It was wonderful to sail on this lake, looking at the beautiful shore, and to go to the islands. That was so long ago. I now live in Lugano, Switzerland, not that far from here." His tone changed and became more uplifted. "You are American, right?"

"Yes. I'm just here for a few days."

"You're on Holiday, I assume?"

"Yes. I've been here once before, just briefly and wanted to see more of it, so this trip gives me a few days here. I've been traveling through Italy for two weeks."

"How lovely. I think you will see no place lovelier than this. Where do you live in America?" he asked.

"Southern California, Los Angeles really and also a small place near Palm Springs."

"Oh yes, very lovely place, also quite mountainous in that area. I've been there. May I ask, are you traveling alone?"

"Yes. I'm taking trains all the way through Italy, but my trip finishes in a few days. I'll take the train to Milan and then will fly home from there," I answered.

"Well then, perhaps I can invite you to join me and my friends for dinner this evening. We can tell you more about this lovely house."

I didn't hesitate for a moment. "Yes, if you're sure I'm not imposing. That would be very nice." With that, we exchanged names and pleasantries and decided to meet at a little cafe in the town center at seven o'clock. I was anxious to hear more about the house and his memories. With what he had already told me, I was drawn into the image of those days so long ago when that house lived.

*The House on Lake Maggiore*

This gentleman's name was Adam Trafino and as he said, he lived in Stresa when he was a young man and he came back to Stresa often, mostly to visit lifelong friends. Adam looked as though he was in his late sixties, very distinguished looking with a full head of beautiful white hair. Looking at his eyes one could see the look of an intense man, perhaps quite intelligent, very observant and also quite thoughtful; that is to say, he was always thinking about something, even as he spoke. He had a busy mind, and as I came to know him better, I came to realize he also had a busy spirit. He was seldom idle and I'm sure his mind was seldom quiet and unoccupied. I found him charming and he had an engaging personality, which held my full attention and one could not help but find him interesting and actually intriguing. It was that summer and the months that followed, that Adam and I became very good friends.

Adam's friends, Mary and Paul Montclair, joined us at dinner. Paul and Adam were boyhood friends and Mary and Paul, who had been married for over forty years, had an apartment close to the city square in Stresa and when Adam came to visit, he always stayed with them. Adam's wife died seven years prior, but from what he said, his life was quite full and he was quite active in his children's lives as well as his grandchildren.

Adam introduced me and told Paul and Mary how he met me standing in front of the abandoned villa, which triggered an interesting conversation about their childhood experiences at the house. Both Paul and Adam had many memories of their young life in Stresa and recalled being brought to the house for Christmas and Easter holidays by their parents. They remembered how magical Christmas was in the house and how lavishly the home was decorated. The parties were always on a large scale, with at least fifty to perhaps over a hundred people there, all dressed formally. At Easter they had an Easter egg hunt in the yard and served lots of food and sweets. Adam seemed to have more detailed memories than Paul.

"The people that owned the house were Mr. and Mrs. Contrelli. I recall my parents telling me a little about her. Mrs.

Contrelli was brought to the house by her husband soon after the end of the war in 1945, as his bride. She was German and he met her while in Germany. He had some sort of business, which no one was certain of, but it was questioned by many as to what he could have been doing in Germany during the war, other than some clandestine support for the war effort. It was a bit suspicious, but for whatever reason he was there, evidently he had taken ill at that time and met Mrs. Contrelli in a hospital while recuperating from surgery, fell in love and married her. His name was Pietro Contrelli who was supposedly a wealthy financier. He built the house in the twenties for his first wife who apparently died of heart disease two years before he married his new wife. The new Mrs. Contrelli merged herself quite easily into Pietro's life style and became well acquainted with the local society. She was not easily accepted, because she was German and relations between Germany and Italy were quite strained at the end of the war. But she worked hard for acceptance and she probably gave those lavish parties in an attempt to win people over. My parents didn't tell me very much, other than their speculation, but I was a young boy and wasn't really interested in knowing much about her, but I enjoyed the parties," said Adam.

"Well, I think my parents talked more about it to me," said Paul. "My mother was a bit of a gossip. I remember her saying that nothing dissuaded Mrs. Contrelli from wanting to be part of the social scene and she pursued every avenue she could to become accepted. She was in her glory when there were lots of people around, and then after a few years, Pietro succumbed to cancer and died. She was left alone in the house and seemed to disappear. There were no more parties, and no more Christmas celebrations that I can recall. No one heard much about her and they wondered what happened to her after that. I remember my mother talking about it saying that Mrs. Contrelli probably backed away from people because she knew it was Pietro, her husband, that people liked and without him, she wasn't important. I think she remained in the house and lived a quiet and private life and I think she married again, but what happened to her after that is lost in everyone's memory. From time to time there were small notices in the newspaper about her or what went on in that house. Evidently a couple people died in that house, but I can't recall who they were or the circumstances. I just remember my mother mentioning it to me. She thought the house had a curse on it. I was a young boy with other things on my mind, except for the part about the curse on the house. I began thinking it may have been haunted and it certainly gives that appearance now, don't you think? Well, in time people stopped wondering and just figured she left, and probably returned to Germany."

"Yes, I remember one year returning from school for a holiday and the house looked so run down and I thought it looked like it was haunted. My mother told me that someone had died there, but I don't recall the circumstances either. It just seemed to become more neglected as time went on and I figured that no one lived there because it was haunted. You know, young boys love that sort of thing," said Adam with a laugh in his voice.

Paul and Adam talked about the house and how they remembered it and the longer they went on about what they knew, the more intrigued I became. We talked long after dinner, and lingered over coffee. I enjoyed meeting them and by the end of the evening I felt as though we had been friends for a very long time.

I was totally titillated and determined to see the interior of the house, and so, feigning a potential buyer, the next morning I went to the realtor's office and inquired about it. Apparently it had been quite some time since anyone showed any interest in the house and they were all too happy to show it to me, believing me to be a prospective buyer. I didn't want to discourage the realtor into thinking otherwise, for fear she may not be so willing to take me to the house.

The real estate agent's name was Maria Virregio, who spoke with a beautiful Milanese accent, in perfect English. She was quite accommodating and I immediately took a liking to her. She didn't know much about the history of the house, but pointed out fascinating architectural features and shared some of her ideas and visions of what the possibilities were to bring the house into repair.

The massive old carved wooden door had warped through years of un-use. It took both of us, challenging rusted hinges, to push the moaning door, but in feeble dispute it finally opened and we entered the entrance hall. I stood for a moment looking up at the souring ceiling in the entrance hall and a gallery beyond the entrance, and then the large living room to my right, which was brightly lit with the morning sun streaming in from the tall windows. The faded carpeting in the room laid almost colorless like death from years of being swathed in unshielded sunlight. The entrance hall opened into the long gallery running the length of the house and ending at a solarium at the opposite end. The open door created a disturbance of the vacuum sealed house and sent dust hovering in the light from doorways opening into the wide gallery. The air in the house was stale and smelled musty and probably had no fresh air filtering through for quite some time.

As we walked through the entrance hall, we entered the gallery with doors leading off into the various rooms. We went through the elaborate pillared gallery and then down two stairs to our right into the large room that I saw from the street through the two story tall windows. The view of the lake was incredibly beautiful on that lovely summer morning and the sun shone on the lake like diamonds twinkling on its surface. The ceiling in the room met the second story of the rest of the house and from it hung a huge chandelier wrapped in paper for protection. There was a balcony looking out over the room at the top of the winding staircase that descended into one section of the room, adjacent to a massive fireplace. I could see a stain on the outside walls where water must have been leaking for quite some time from the roof. The floors in the entrance hall were wood and led to marquetry marble inlaid in multiple colors in the gallery and in the living room the floors were a beautiful wood under the carpet. I noticed some water damage on the

*The House on Lake Maggiore*

floor, which had buckled in parts and scuffed quite badly, but nothing that couldn't be fixed and brought back to a luster. My mind immediately gave in to decorator mode and I imagined the extraordinary possibilities of what this house could be once again. The room was quite large and the tall palladium windows had wrought iron filigree ornamentation at the top of the arched frames allowing sun to cast lace shadows across the floor and onto the wall where the fireplace stood. Two sets of French doors opened to a private walled patio, quite grown over with weeds and moss. Another set of French doors opened into the gallery on the other side of the fireplace. Through those doors one would go across the gallery to the large dining room with another chandelier, all wrapped and covered in paper and plastic for protection. The solarium at the end of the gallery had windows on all three sides. I imagined the sun would shine in quite brightly if it weren't for all the overgrown shrubbery outside blocking all the windows. I thought it would be a good place for entertaining, serving wonderful dinners and I imagined that there might be a good view of the lake from the side windows.

    The door next to the dining room off the gallery also had beautifully carved French doors opening to a wonderful library with another smaller fireplace, coffered ceiling, shelf lined walls and time-dimmed wood paneling that could easily be refinished. Walking through the dining room gave entrance to an extremely large superannuated kitchen with a wonderful breakfast nook nestled into a curved window niche. The kitchen was designed for function and probably used by professional staff only and never entered by the inhabitants of the house themselves. The bay windows looked out to the rear of the house in the yard choking with overgrown tangled trees and climbing vines tying everything together into one mass of vegetation. Untamed Bougainvillea bloomed everywhere and almost created a sort of umbrella over the wildness of what may have once been a beautifully orchestrated and laid out Italian garden. A walkway attempted to cut a path through the dense shrubbery and then disappeared into a green mass of oblivion leaving it quite impassable with the bramble bush enveloping the garden. Somewhere beyond the entanglement of vegetation and at the end of that overgrown path were the remains of a carriage house, which at one time served as the garage. It looked as if it had been years since the building could be entered because the roof had caved in and the building was more or less a pile of rubble.

    We went back through the gallery and ascended the winding stairway past the mirror at the top and entered a hallway with French doors opening into rooms on either side. The hallway ended at a round stained glass window, which was quite beautiful and almost in perfect condition with beautiful colors from the light shining beyond it casting jewel like reflections onto the floor. The hallway then continued to the left, which was over the dining room, kitchen and library on the first floor, and lead to other bedrooms and bathrooms and a small room that looked as if it were a storage room for linens. There were eight bedrooms in all, and five bathrooms, all in dire need of updating. My head spun with ideas and the possibilities of how beautiful this home could be with lots of work, a good designer's imagination, and of course a lot of money. The largest bedroom faced the side of the house and had a terrace with a breathtaking view stretching across the lake, up the main street of Strada Sempione along the shore and of the Alps across the lake. The room had an adjoining bathroom and a sitting area with a marble surround fireplace. I couldn't imagine living in such a house and awaking each day to the beauty outside those windows and terrace. As beautiful as the structure of the house was, it was quite shabby and run-down, but I was able to see beyond that dreary façade and grime and envision the treasure beneath.

    Maria shared my vision of the possibilities of this house, but quickly brought me back to reality with the huge price tag and pointed out the cost of repairs and updates. She knew little about the history of the house and said that for the seven years that she lived in Stresa, the house remained empty and held little interest to potential buyers, perhaps because of the amount of work to bring it up to date, and the price. As out of reach as the price was, it was even more startling to think of the price in American dollars. The boilers had to be replaced, so there had been no heat in the house for many years since the last renters left. There were wiring problems and the roof leaked very badly and needed to be replaced. It was truly neglected over the years and in shambles. Maria said the house was owned by a bank and although she was not certain of the circumstances, she guessed that the bank would be anxious to unload it and would probably agree to drop the price. The house had renters in it for many years, but because of the fact that there was no heat and the plumbing was bad, the house was no longer habitable. It was sort of a white elephant and its destiny was strangled by zoning laws because it was a historical site and who ever bought it had to keep it a home, not a hotel, or condominiums, which probably contributed to the fact that this left a very small arena of potential buyers because it would be an expensive property to maintain, because of overburdened taxes.

Although the property was extremely expensive, I could not resist trying to imagine a way to buy it, just to bring it back to life and then sell it at a profit. As a designer, I could see how wonderful that house could be once again. I had been involved in helping clients buy very expensive, although substandard properties and renovating them to resell for a profit, so it wasn't completely impossible to find financing for this endeavor. I knew I would try as hard as I could to come up with a solution, and from that day forward, I could hardly think of anything else. I knew it was quite in fashion for wealthy Americans and British to buy property in Italy for investment purposes, so I would do my best to explore the possibilities. I was in no position to make any definite promises, but told Maria that in all honesty, it would be difficult, but not impossible to find this solution, and there was no way I could purchase the house myself, but I would stay in touch with her and go home and try to figure something out. She was agreeable and told me she would also let me know, in the unlikely event, if another potential buyer presented an offer. I left for home the next day and for all the hours on the plane heading to California, I could think of little else except that house on Lake Maggiore. It was a designer's dream to renovate a beautiful home such as this.

And so those lonely weekends in my mountain cabin, I day dreamed about Lake Maggiore and that house. There was some part of me that never came home and I felt I had to go retrieve it, or complete the meaning of the event and try to understand why both the place and that house impacted me so emphatically, but as time went by, the possibilities of returning began to dissolve into a hopeless fantasy.

# CHAPTER 2

So there I was back in my mountain cabin thinking again about the house on Lake Maggiore. My mind could not stop thinking about renovating that house. I sat in the peaceful seclusion of my little cabin, watching the tree tops move gracefully with the wind and listening to the birds, but in my mind, I was walking through each room of that house, examining every detail, as my mind had recorded them. I went from the gallery to the solarium, back into the large front room, and then across the gallery again to the beautiful library, back out to look at the tall windows in the front room and the wonderful view of the lake. I didn't want to forget one detail and I imagined myself walking from room to room, up the staircase, looking down from the balcony at the room below and the lake across the street and I listened to my footsteps as I walked. I so wanted to be there.

I was determined to find a way to make it happen and while being fairly well connected to other designers, design studios, and publications, I went to work immediately to try to find financing for this house. I thought if I set my mind to it, I could find a solution. The plan was to renovate the house and turn it around for a profit, document the processes, and produce a good article for a designer publication. While I feverishly began the task to find an investor, I stayed in touch with Adam by letter. He promised also to see what he could do to find investors.

Several months passed after returning to California and I had come up with nothing and began to give up on the dream realizing it was just too preposterous. I sat in that cabin with my disappointment, depression, and feeling my dream fade away. On one particularly dismal weekend I realized I had wasted enough time thinking and dreaming impossible dreams and decided I had to let it go. I might as well have stayed in the city for the time I wasted staring into space, while my mind took its house tour. But then there are times when you think the bottom falls out of your world, some miracle out of nowhere presents itself with new options and new dreams.

When I returned to Los Angeles, I had a phone message from Maria, the realtor in Italy, asking me to call her. When she told me another party had inquired about the house, my heart dropped even further with disappointment thinking that it was now in someone else's hands and my dreams of renovating it were over. Then she said the gentleman that asked to see the house is an investor and had an interest in renovating it for resale. She told him about me and he thought perhaps an arrangement could be made that he would finance the home and work that needed to be done and I would work for him handling the renovation and design. He asked Maria to get in touch with me. After talking to her, I decided that maybe Adam could become an intermediary and see if this was a good possibility, since he was already there. He got in touch with the investor who was eager to discuss the matter with us and suggested we schedule a meeting in Milan.

I can't describe the euphoria I felt at the possibility that my dream of renovating that house might happen and that someone else would fund the project. After the disappointing months of not making any headway with raising the money and giving up on the idea, I could not believe this was happening and I was immediately ecstatic at the possibility. I had Adam get specifics about the proposed meeting and when he got back with me about an actual date for later in January, I booked my flight.

The day I arrived Adam met me at my hotel where we had dinner and then he surprised me with tickets to that night's opera. I will remember that evening forever because it brought me into a new world of culture. I have long been a casual fan of opera, although I had never seen a production such as that night at the famed La Scala Opera House. It was a beautiful production of Tosca, and Adam was a wonderful host. The evening was so amazing and truly an introduction into a life of culture that I loved and wanted so to be a part of. I will live with the lovely memory of that evening forever.

Adam arranged a luncheon the next day with the potential financier. He filled me in on the details at dinner that night. While we were having dinner a photographer came around to all the tables and took pictures, one of which Adam bought for me as a remembrance of what might be a very productive weekend and cause for celebration. He proposed the most sincere toast to successful new beginnings. It was really such a sweet and memorable moment.

The next day, we met our potential investor at our hotel for lunch. Bjorn Thorner is a man with a large presence, approximately six foot two inches tall, I guessed in his early seventies, with a well-kept mustache, and extremely charming. He bowed when Adam introduced us and spoke with an effective and potent Eastern European accent. We all ordered lobster salad and sipped a lovely Austrian Riesling wine while we exchanged pleasantries before the awkward subject of finances came up. He proceeded to tell us that he represented a group of aggressive and rapacious investors who invested primarily in real estate and were always hungry for their next "deal." He had done a bit of homework and after the realtor Maria told him about me, he discovered some of the articles I wrote for designer magazines and knew that I had done work for some prestigious clients and therefore, knowing I had the initial interest, thought I might have the capacity of turning the dilapidated old monster of a house around and creating a good return on their investment. There was little I had to do to promote myself or sell the idea and I believed he was as eager as I was about the project. It was agreed that he would meet Adam and I at the house to do a walk through the next day. The committee left it up to him to determine if we were right in our thinking that this renovation would be a worthwhile investment. If he agreed, he would prepare the contract, arrange for the financing and the work could begin soon after. Bjorn himself stated that this sort of real estate was being sought out by the British rich and turning the house around for a sizable profit was inevitable. I was again swept away with enthusiasm and felt like a child filled with the excitement of opening gifts on Christmas Morning.

That evening Adam and I took the train from Milan to Stresa. I checked into the same hotel I stayed at on my previous trip and I was feeling quite complete and happy again. Winters are relatively mild as the Alps protect the area, which makes it possible for palm trees and other Mediterranean plants and trees to survive the winters, although it can get chilly and at times have a light dusting of snow.

The next morning Adam and Bjorn met me at my hotel for breakfast and Maria, the realtor joined us. We discussed all the wonderful things about the house and then after breakfast made the short walk up the street to the property. We hesitated outside so Bjorn could peruse the property and take some pictures. We then walked up the long winding pathway to the entrance.

We stood at the portico and Bjorn looked up at the concrete cartouche over the entrance and pointed out the detail of the ornamentation, suggesting this was in all likelihood the family crest. Again, the heavy wooden door did not want to open and Bjorn and Adam gave it their all until it finally gave way, squeaking loudly on its hinges. The house was airless and musty with the overpowering aroma of mold, which I had noticed the first time I entered the house, but thought it became more prominent. I would undoubtedly find the source and have to deal with it as part of the renovation.

Bjorn stopped in the entrance hall and looked up at the soaring height of the ceiling and the extended span of the gallery beyond. It was truly an impressive entrance and the drama alone demanded that one would be forced to stop and take it all in before moving forward. We moved on to the gallery, which was large enough to be a ballroom. Then we went to the right through the arched entrance with ornately carved spandrels and flanked with columns on either side. We stepped down the two steps into the room and all stood looking up at the ceiling, studying the massive fireplace, the dramatic staircase, and the tall windows peering out at the lake. Bjorn shared my joy and was overcome with ecstasy as he commented on various details of the house: obliterated frescos on faded walls, the intricately carved moldings and doors, the beautiful Art Nouveau brass hardware adorning doors and windows, the serpentine float of the staircase with its intricate iron work of the banisters and the inlaid marble floors. He expounded in anaphoric bombastic comments exclaiming the obvious to us and ultimately put to shame my first response when seeing the interior and mumbling something like "wow." He stood in place and with each comment, turned a few degrees, stretched his arms to the ceiling and began to exclaim, "This house has tremendous plausible possibilities. This house has the fundamental structure it needs to be great. This house has an imposing quality that screams out to me. This house has concealed its splendor for much too long. This house will be magnificent, and deserves to be the grandest house on the lake." As he spoke, I watched him and could almost see the intense emotion he was experiencing and his eyes were alight as if they were blasting neon dollar signs. I had to turn away to keep him from seeing that I was biting my lip to not laugh out loud, but also to try to camouflage my happiness because I knew this was a sign that this was going to really happen. We became lost in our discussion, each over animated as we talked about the possibilities.

    I noticed Adam stepped aside and had not shared in our discussion. He went into the gallery and was standing there, as if in a trance. I walked over to him and asked if he was all right. "Oh yes, I'm fine. It is just that it has been so long since

I have been in this house, I am a bit overcome with nostalgia. Somehow, it seems so different than I remember, smaller, perhaps, or narrower, or something. Of course, it is so shabby. It was incredibly beautiful and decorated so well. Seeing it like this, it seems like a different place. Something about the structure is changed, but I'm not quite sure what it is, but of course, I was a very young boy and it would be natural to remember it as appearing larger than I see it now. But my, oh my, the memories this house brings back to me are overwhelming," he said. "It truly takes me back to my childhood."

I asked, "So, do you really think it's haunted?" He smiled and answered "most definitely."

Maria was continuing the excursion of the house and was leading Bjorn through the dining room and into the kitchen. Adam insisted I go and catch up with them and leave him to his old tired memories. When I caught up with Bjorn and Maria in the kitchen, he was snapping photos and making notes. I was certain that this was very positive and reinforced my certainty that everything was beginning to fall into place.

Our meeting ended with a hopeful promise from Bjorn that he would convince his other investors that this was a promising investment and he would let us know the outcome as soon as he got an answer.

It was almost two months after returning again to California that I finally received a voice message from Bjorn's office saying everything was set, the financing was arranged and all the details had been ironed out. I could plan on beginning the work within the next month, which would be early spring. The agreement stated that I would pass all my plans by Bjorn for review and approval, but I was given a free hand to do as I saw fit and they had confidence in my ability and were sure there would be minimal intervention. They would also finance my expenses during the project, which included my travel and hotel expenses, as well as a monthly income for the months I would be working there and a small percentage of the profits at the end of the project when the house sold. It was a gamble, but I knew the house would turn a good profit once the renovation was complete. I then had to make arrangements to turn my clients in California over to other designers to work in my absence and keep my business running smoothly at home. I got things in order and decided it would undoubtedly take several months so I cleared the way to be gone that long.

I was off to Italy for what I believed the opportunity of a lifetime. I would help create a fabulous house that would be sold well beyond the current worth of the depressed property. I was certain the entire experience and article I would write would ultimately give my career a nice boost.

Maria told me she had gone down to the cellar a few weeks previous and thought maybe there was something there that would help me. She brought a flashlight with her and we both began to head towards the door to the cellar, just off the hallway at the back of the kitchen. We walked slowly down the dark stairs and entered the cellar, which seemed much like entering a tomb that had been closed for many years. It was dark and humid and the smell of mold became stronger. She flashed the light into a dark corner where there stood several pieces of old furniture covered with canvas tarps. We removed the tarps to find a nice large table that would be suitable for the kitchen, along with some well-worn ladder back chairs. There was also a desk, three over stuffed upholstered chairs, and a cluster of small tables. On one of the tables were cardboard boxes that contained rolls of papers, perhaps wall paper fragments or drawings. We took them with us as we went back up the stairs and spread the papers out on the floor, happily discovering, as she suspected, within the many rolls of paper, there were blueprints of the house. Maria commented that they were very old and perhaps were the original blueprints, and there may have been updates to the house over the years so they may not be exact, but they could help somehow in the renovation.

"As much as I'd love to stay here and explore this house further, I have an appointment with a client and will leave you alone. Here are the keys, my dear. I cannot wait to see what miracles you perform with this house." With that, Maria left me and I stood there finally alone.

This was a moment I had long thought about: me being alone in the house. Standing in the immense room at the front of the house, I felt almost miniaturist and diminutive amongst the size of the room. I looked up at the ceilings high above my head and then at the tall palladium windows so badly in need of cleaning and was almost overwhelmed with the thought of the work ahead of me, but I was elated to finally be there, inside the house and now looking out onto the sidewalk where I had before stood beyond the front gate staring at the house. I loved the largeness, almost cavernous feeling of the room with the height up to the second floor ceiling. The silence of the house was immediately discernible, and I smiled as I remembered what Adam said about the voices that remained of the souls that once lived here.

    I loved the calmness and the peacefulness I felt being inside the house. Often times that was what I liked most about my mountain home—the calmness the silence rendered. When I arrived, I would pour a glass of wine or cognac and sit and just look through the windows at the treetops and enjoy the silence, or the slight whisper of the wind through the tree limbs, and let my mind wander. Being removed from the city and the constant surrounding of people and voices, I found myself feeling at peace, enjoying the clarity of my thoughts and feeling a release, as if in an attempt at cleansing my mind. A margin of solitude is a healthy existence to allow us the freedom to be alone with ourselves and our thoughts and somehow reach down inside and get in touch with our soul. I felt this same peacefulness that day, standing in that house, even though the surroundings were so foreign. The house was so much grander than anything ever before connected to my life. I was full of the sense of adventure and anticipation and so eager to begin exploring what possibilities existed with the renovation. It was from an era and a status unknown to me, but I was eager to move forward to become acquainted with this strange place. I turned slowly, looking at all the walls, the ceiling, the windows, the balcony overlooking the living room and then moved along the gallery to the other rooms and then finally up the long flight of stairs, examining everything as I went along.

    I stood at the top of the stairs near the balcony overlooking the large room below, carefully peeking with trepidation in order to not excite or antagonize my vertigo. I felt a little buzz in my head standing there, which is normal whenever I stand at extreme heights bordered by a severe periphery and I will become lightheaded when standing too near a dramatic drop, such as that balcony. I looked straight ahead and could see the lake through the tall windows. I could see the palace and the beautifully manicured ornamental Italian gardens and the Palazzo Borromeo on Isola Bella, the most important and impressive of the islands of the lake. Beyond that I could also see the adjacent island, Isola dei Superiore Pescatori, which was once a fishing village with beautiful Mediterranean structures, which included shops and restaurants. Not too far from that island is another small island called St. John, also called Islet of Toscanini because the famous conductor, Arturo Toscanini lived there for many years of his life. Still further across the lake is another island, Isola Madre.

The sun glistened on the shimmering surface dotted with white sails from the small boats and beyond the far reaches of the lake, stood the snow tipped Alps. Behind me on the wall was the huge mirror that I had seen from outside the house, tilted slightly away from the wall in order to reflect the lower part of the living room. I was anxious to see the chandelier hanging over the room, carefully wrapped and hidden under the protection of paper. It hung below the balcony level and although I had no idea what was beneath the paper, I imagined it would be exquisite, and if not, I would replace it with one deserving of its place in that room. After painting the ceiling, unwrapping the paper covering the chandelier to see what it looked like should be the next tasks, and then cleaning each individual crystal prism, and have it glisten as it was intended.

Beyond the large mirror, was an archway leading to the hallway with the rooms on the second floor opening into it. The carpet going down the hallway was worn and frayed in places, but it was mostly cosmetic and along with a few repairs, fresh paint on the walls, new carpet and flooring in adjoining rooms would bring the luster back into the house. The more I could fix, instead of replace, would help my budget. The most difficult task would be to make repairs without compromising the beautiful frescoed ceilings in several of the rooms. I would have to find an excellent artist for this work. I stood and focused into my mind's eye and visualized the ultimate look of this house, the type of furniture that should be placed in certain areas, the arrangements for sofas, chairs, tables, paintings hung in certain places, the lighting that would offset the rooms. I had many books being shipped to me that would provide references and help with the selections to be sure I was capturing the exact detail of the decor and essence that represented the period of the house's history.

The largest of the rooms on the second floor I guessed to be a master suite. It had a sitting or dressing room and an adjoining bathroom, which was quite large, as well as French doors that led out to the terrace that was over the solarium downstairs. I stepped out onto the terrace and walked the perimeter. At one end was a lovely view of the lake, and on the other end, the side yard of the house. The floor of the terrace was in need of resurfacing and had a heavy covering of droppings from the trees surrounding the house. It had a beautiful railing of poured concrete balusters and provided a nice outdoor retreat off the master suite. I imagined enjoying coffee on that terrace looking out at the lake in the early mornings or watching the sun set. My mind became lost in reverie about what life was like in this house during its prime.

Back in the bedroom I walked to a wall of mirrored tall doors that had become darkened around the edges where the silvering had worn off. The mirrors were encased in elaborate Baroque moldings and beautiful brass. Crystal handles opened the doors to reveal a huge closet beset with shelves and cubby holes that would have held hats and handbags for the lady of the house. The ceiling was dome shaped and had a painted fresco of a night sky with a constellation of stars circling the center moon, where a chandelier-less wire hung limply in space.

I went back down the stairs and the gallery of the main floor through the frescoed walled dining room on to the kitchen. It was very large, very white and almost industrial in design. It appeared to be the type of kitchen that was run by a staff, designed purely for function to provide service to large dinner parties. I imagined the lady of the house never really entered the room, unless to just direct her staff. It had a very large industrial looking gas stove with eight burners and four ovens below. The floor was wood and in bad condition, with most of the wear around the stove and sink areas. There were small white tiles halfway up the walls and stainless steel counters and sinks and the dreariness resembled more of a laboratory than a kitchen. It was in desperate need of upgrading and begged for color.

I especially liked the breakfast alcove surrounded by the tall bay windows facing the yard to the rear of the house, but the view was obliterated with overgrown vines. The yard was quite spacious and the remnants of a brick floored logia were just beyond the back door leading to the yard. A walkway beyond was covered by a pergola with dense wisteria vines draped heavily on the almost invisible frame of the trellis. Again, in my mind's eye, I could envision a beautiful logia being a great place to dine or entertain, perhaps small dinner parties at one time took place there. Maybe Mr. and Mrs. Contrelli had their evening cocktails there, surrounded by the aroma of night jasmine, gardenia and lilies. Camellias grew in a tangled mass of greenery, choking for life, but somehow surviving and their waxy leaves and lovely blossoms bobbed gracefully in the late afternoon breeze coming off the lake. I stood at the windows of the kitchen and thought this may be my favorite place in the house for now. I would bring the table and chairs up from the cellar and use the table as my desk to plan the work to be done. The light fell into the room in long straight panels and as the day progressed, the late afternoon sun washed a sort of amber veil into the otherwise sterile and lifeless room. That area in the kitchen with the bay windows, in fact ultimately became the workroom and the nucleus of the house for me and I used it for an office to plan and design on paper the first steps in launching this project.

At the end of the gallery, near the entrance hall was a lovely little powder room, which had the remnants of elegant wallpaper hanging sadly in shreds and terribly outdated fixtures. This was the only bathroom on the first floor, but positioned well and would be easily updated and look elegant again. Across the gallery from the powder room was the archway to the living room. I walked down the two steps into the living room and stood in front of the tall fireplace, the mantel measuring about a foot above my head. The fireplace was surrounded by carved marble, with columns on either side holding up the massive stone mantel. The arabesque columns were carved with ivy and other vines and small animals climbing the vines and the little faces of monkeys and squirrels looked at me from beyond their stone leaves and as I walked, their faces seemed to always focus on me. The sad faces of the impressively large lions on the andirons were in dire need of polishing. I would have the fireplace checked for safety and begin to use it to relieve the chill in the early spring months while I worked in the house, until the boilers were replaced.

I went into the library, which was entered from a set of wide arched ornately carved French doors leading off from the gallery. The room was paneled in dark wood and worn empty shelves lined three walls and it had a bold coffered ceiling with dark wooden beams. An old red oriental rug lay lifelessly in a heap on the floor and another wire, minus its chandelier, hung from the ceiling. There was a small fireplace with a black marble surround and mantle and brass sconces on either side. One small window with hood moldings over the top of the window at the side of the room facing the yard was covered with foliage from outside, obliterating any light from entering the room. I loved the architectural detail all over the house, but especially in this room. The coffered beams were offset with ornate entablatures and heavy crown moldings carved with what I guessed to be scenes from literary tales, which I would in time try to decipher. As time went on, this would become a sort of game for me. I would look at each scene and then try to find the symbolism and would determine that a story was being told as we followed each scene around the room.

There were many possibilities to bring this room to life again and it might be one of the first rooms where the work should begin. Because of all the wonderful wood in the room, I envisioned an English manor or pub representation to keep

*The House on Lake Maggiore*

the masculine effusion intact. A black iron chandelier, heavily adorned with crystal prisms and small black silk shades would be perfect. I stood silently for a moment, again closing my eyes to listen for those nebulous voices Adam mentioned, and imagined the interpretation of the room in its time, and what quiet souls of the bibliophiles lived and loved the room and searched the shelves for their favorite books. Perhaps many snifters of brandy were enjoyed while fictitious characters stirred the imagination of the cloistered occupant and I don't think I imagined the venerable aroma of tobacco that may have seeped into the woodwork. Every room I entered rendered another image of the history and life that had once existed within the surrounding walls.

    I walked back into the gallery, or long hallway, past the next room, which was the dining room and to the solarium where the hallway ended. I entered the room through glass paned doors with tarnished, but beautiful brass hardware. This was the room beneath the terrace that extended outside the master suite on the second floor. There were windows on three sides of the room, which would make the room quite sunny and pleasant once the overgrowth was removed outside. I imagined the room being a sort of garden room, much like Palm Court in the old Plaza Hotel in New York in its grand bygone days, with lots of plants, maybe wicker furniture and I thought it to be another wonderful place to dine. I would imagine in the winter the room might be a bit too cold and may even be closed off during some months.

    There was no escaping the fact that the house was sorrowfully in need of repair and the closer I looked into corners, the more I realized that it would be a massive job. There were water marks on the walls and ceilings, which suggested leaking pipes within the walls and the wallpaper in some rooms hung in shreds and some of the warped woodwork needed to be replaced. The age of the house, coupled with the years of neglect assured me that the problems that were visible might be minor compared to what might be found inside the walls.

    I realized that several hours of my exploration had passed since Maria left me alone in the house and darkness was beginning to fill the rooms. It was a stirring afternoon of living with imagined thoughts of an age unfamiliar to me. It was late afternoon and I wanted to never leave, but there was no electricity in the house and I had to be sure to leave before dark. I would postpone having the power turned on until an electrician could survey the wiring because I didn't want to risk an electrical fire. As time went by, I knew that everything had to be done in Italian time, not in my time. It got done, when someone got around to it and never was anyone quite as enthusiastic as I.

It was time to leave, but I didn't want the day to end. I backed out of the house slowly, closing the massive door behind me using two hands, ever so excited to return the next day and begin scoping out my plans for the renovation. I stood on the pediment covered portico studying all the facets of the elaborate entrance, especially the intricately designed cartouche ornament with the initial C in the middle, obviously as previously determined, the Contrelli family emblem. The entrance itself was a neoclassical design with an elaborate architrave molding surrounding the door and caryatid columns supporting a mantel over which the cartouche rested. The door itself was heavily carved and had heavy brass hardware. A chain that once held a lantern was in place, minus the lantern, but the wiring was there, so a new fixture would be in order. It was an impressive entrance and with a good cleaning, and refinishing of the door and hardware it would eventually be a grand entrance to the fabulous house I envisioned.

My company at dinner that night was a pad of paper I used to draw floor plans, wrote notes of things I needed and wanted to do, made lists of things to buy, repairs I noted while exploring the house, and discussions I would have with the architect and contractor that were to meet me on the next day at the house. Bjorn contracted the architect and crew he used on previous projects. My head was filled with ideas and as is my usual nature, I would dive right in and waste no time in my progress. I was highly motivated and anxious to begin to see the fruits of my labor pay off and the beauty of the house come shining through.

It was as if there was a clean slate and the possibilities were endless, but of course I had just so much money to work with and at times, would have to force myself to scale down my vision. I had to plan wisely and try to stay within Bjorn's estimated budget if possible, but he even knew it was an estimate, and if need be we should go over and not skimp on important things. It all had to be managed carefully and monitored to be certain I stayed close to my allotted budget so as not to eat into the profit, but Bjorn agreed it had to be a grand house and if he had to go ask for more money, he would.

The next day I woke early, dressed quickly and hurried out of my hotel room, stopping to pick up coffee and pastry to take to the house. All the way to the house, I still couldn't believe I held the key in my hand and I was eager to get to work. It was all too good to be true. I entered the house again and sat on the stairs drinking my coffee and eating my pastry, just looking around the entrance hall and reviewing my notes from the day before. More notes came to mind and I entered them in my notebook, ideas I had, things that needed to be done, resources I needed to line up, and supplies that needed to be purchased. I worked on my notes while waiting for the architect to arrive. I wanted to be ready to get our plan into action and begin the work as soon as possible.

Adam was due to come for a visit that day also and I looked forward to seeing him, and I'm sure he also looked forward to inspecting the house further. I telephoned him the day before telling him that I had arrived and had the keys to the house, and also gave him my mobile phone number.

When Vito Prevarra, the main architect and contractor arrived with his assistant, I walked them through the house and shared some of my ideas with them. We went down to the cellar and decided to bring the furniture up into the house. We put all the furniture, the table and chairs, the desk, and the upholstered chairs in the kitchen. I planned to have the chairs redone and they confirmed that the structure of the chairs was intact and some new stuffing and new upholstery fabric would bring them back to life, and perhaps the kitchen table and chairs could be refinished and still be quite attractive and serviceable. For the mean time, I wiped down the table and chairs so I could put them to immediate use as part of the kitchen office so we had a place to work. There were other things in the cellar that I needed to investigate, also under tarps. There were some old paintings, more chairs and smaller tables and commodes that could also be refinished. I was overjoyed to also find several boxes of books, perhaps some that would ultimately give me the story of the carved moldings in the library. Besides utilizing whatever I could find within the house, I would be buying other furniture and antiques as my budget allowed.

As we walked through the house, Vito took notes and estimated how many people he needed to bring in to help with the work. The first priority would be the electrical wiring and plumbing, the chimneys for all the fireplaces in the house, and the roof.

We sat around the kitchen table with the blueprints and they agreed, some newer structural changes had been made to the house since it was originally built. They found the blueprints interesting and recognized the name of the architect printed in the corner, who was quiet well known in the period between 1890 and the 1920s for the Liberty Style, which the blueprints confirmed, was the style of the house. The style was quite unique and stressed asymmetrical, curvaceous designs based on organic inspirations, such as plants and flowers and used materials like wrought iron, stained glass, tile and hand-painted wallpaper, which were all evident within the house. They stressed, and I agreed, it would be important to not stray from the architectural style of the house, as we were working with classic art and the interior design should complement the same style.

Vito and his assistant brought some tools onto the service porch behind the kitchen and then left to begin acquiring the additional tools and supplies they needed and told me they would return the next day with a crew and would begin work. He had a plan in mind and a good idea of where the work should begin.

As they were leaving, Adam walked up the drive and I introduced them all. After a friendly exchange of conversation, Adam and I entered the house. As I became busy telling him what the contractors and I had discussed, he again paused in the gallery and was distracted.

"Adam. What is it? You have the same look on your face as you did the last time you entered the house." I could tell something was bothering him.

"I don't know what it is. I just remember it looking different—bigger. Some things are the same though, like the stairs, and the hallway. I remember when I came here with my parents, Mrs. Contrelli always wanted to talk to me, separate from the other people. She took me by the hand and walked me through the gallery to a small room. She would close the door behind us so we were alone and then she had me sit on a stool as she talked to me," he said, still with a look of bewilderment on his face.

"Was it the library? It's not a very small room though." We began to walk through the gallery towards the library. We stopped at the entrance to the room and commented on the elaborate paneled details.

Adam said he didn't recall that room at all. "No, I'm quite sure I've never seen this room. Maybe she only allowed certain visitors to enter certain rooms. This is a beautiful room. I can't wait to see what you do with it."

"I know. I have lots of ideas, but want to keep it dark and masculine. I love all the wood paneling and the moldings. Maybe I'll put some dark velvet furniture, or leather in here. I think this room will be fun to work with. But you're sure this wasn't the room you saw? There are no other rooms leading off that main hallway, other than the dining room and solarium."

"No. It was a much smaller room, sort of like a pantry. It had high white cupboards in it. Oh well, it doesn't matter. Perhaps I am imagining this. As I said, I was a very young boy. Also, maybe walls have been moved through the years. It's not important."

"Maybe it was a small closet or something. Over the years there may have been changes made and maybe they eliminated some closets over time. What did she talk to you about in that room? Do you remember?"

"She asked me about my friends, the games we played. Things like that—it's hard to remember now, but it was mostly small talk. Sometimes she gave me a toy. She always wanted to embrace me. I didn't mind talking to her, but I was uncomfortable with her hugging me. Don't get me wrong. She was never inappropriate. It seemed like she was overly interested in me—my life—what I was like, more so than the other children, which was a little disconcerting to me because I saw her so seldom. I never knew why and as I got older and thought about it, I was very curious about her fascination with me. I mean, why me? I was only a small boy and my life wasn't very interesting. I think all my life whenever I thought about it, that sort of bothered me—not knowing why she was so attentive to me at these holiday gatherings, but then the rest of the year, I never saw her. But it was only when my parents brought me here for holidays. Never any other time, and always when there were many other people in the house. She never came to visit us. I don't remember seeing her act that attentive to other children—it was just me. Maybe I should have been flattered, but she was a strange woman. I asked my parents, but they gave me no satisfaction from my questions. They dismissed most discussions about her and just would say, 'she likes you. There is no harm in that, is there?'"

"It's sad really, when you think about it. Maybe she was unable to have children of her own and she took a fancy to you. Poor woman. Maybe she did have a child of her own after that. Do you recall ever hearing about it?" I asked.

"No, I don't remember anything more. I know Mr. Contrelli was quite a bit older than her, so it might not have been possible for her to have children, and I don't know what happened to her after his death. It's all a vague memory. As time went on, my parents sent me to school in France and I lost track of her

# CHAPTER 3

I flew from Los Angeles to New York, and then directly to Milan. My excitement about seeing the house again made the flight torturous in length. Every time I closed my eyes to try to sleep, I visualized the house and my anxiety kept me awake and wired the entire trip. Upon arriving in Milan, I rented a car and within an hour arrived at Stresa. I checked into my hotel and immediately called Maria, the real estate agent and set up an appointment with her for later that afternoon. After freshening up and stopping for a bite to eat, I went to Maria's office. The financing had been taken care of and there were papers I still needed to sign. She also had a package for me from Bjorn's office, which contained a checkbook and credit card, furnished by the investors giving me access to all the funds I needed to cover expenses. We finally concluded the business part and left for the three block walk to the house.

Again, the dreadful door was difficult to open, but both Maria and I leaned heavily and gave it a forceful push and it finally opened. I stood for a moment taking it all in and just looking at the size of the house and the obvious abuse from years of neglect, I felt overwhelmed with the task before me with the renovation. I was excited, but also a bit apprehensive about the magnitude of the job, and realized it was more than I had ever taken on and the work to turn the house around would indeed be a huge challenge.

all together, and the people at this house. I asked my mother once and she told me that her husband had died and she came and went from time to time, and no longer lived full time at the house. Everyone lost track of her and turned their attention elsewhere. No one seemed to care and it all just became unimportant. Everyone thought she was strange and really stayed away from her. It was her husband, Mr. Contrelli that people liked, and respected. Once he was gone, no one really cared what happened to her. As time went on, she was not even a memory to the society that lived here."

As we talked, we began to walk through the dining room into the kitchen. Upon entering the room, Adam changed the subject and commented on the furniture I had brought up from the cellar and we began talking about what might be done with the various pieces. The subject of the former lady of the house became lost as we discussed the kitchen and the possibilities for remodeling.

Adam left early that day and we agreed to meet for dinner at seven. I was very impressed with Adam. It was not just the charm and charisma of such an interesting man that pulled me emotionally towards him, but the stories and memories he told about the house on Lake Maggiore. His fascination of the house soon spilled over into me and I became enchanted. I wanted from that point on to know more about the former owners and the events that took place over the years. I soon became embroiled in his memories and the nostalgia that I could clearly see he relished in talking about. He kept me always wanting to hear more.

I sat down at the kitchen table and again studied the blueprints spread out before me. I was curious about Adam's memories of the house and realized that perhaps his recollection served him well and, as testament, it seemed to agree with the blueprints. Something was a little different than it currently appeared. He recalled a room that resembled a pantry, and clearly there was no pantry. I thought maybe the kitchen had been enlarged or perhaps there had been other updates made to the house and the blueprints may have been the original structure. Doorways weren't the same, it seemed. There may have been multiple renovations and clearly the small wing that was the solarium had been added, which also added the terrace off the large bedroom upstairs. I walked through the house and looked at the blueprints as I walked through the gallery. A doorway shown on the plan was now just a solid wall. I walked back through the dining room and kitchen to the yard and studied the plans. I noticed that the windows shown on the plans may have been covered over with vines, but where were they inside the house? I began to pull at the heavy ivy vines and saw an outline of what was newer brick and mortar tracing the outline of a window frame. I went back into the house to the service porch where the contractor had left his tools and found what looked like large sheers that might cut through wire and went back into the yard and began to cut more of the vines away and there I could see even more evidence of what was once a set of windows, only visible by a trace of color difference in the brick. The original bricks were weather worn and showed signs of fading whereas the alternating brick was not as worn, but still looked as though they had been in place for many years, if not decades and had also been shielded from weather by the heavy vines. The blueprints showed there should be windows at that position.

I went back into the house into the gallery and studied the walls and tapped on them. Sure enough, it sounded as if there was an echo behind the wall. I thought about waiting for the workmen to come in the morning and have them break through the wall, but decided I was too curious to wait that long and decided to take matters into my own hands. I believed the windows would have been between the kitchen and the library and could not understand why anyone would have closed them off.

I found a sledge hammer on the service porch and with a little trepidation began to pound the wall. The old plaster gave way quite easily and with just a few swipes of the hammer, I broke through the wall. I kept working at it until I had a hole in the wall big enough to stick my head through. I poked the flashlight in and illuminated a dark vacuumed sealed off area, very narrow in size with very tall cupboards. This had to be the small room Adam remembered. I hesitated for a moment, afraid of what might be within the dark space, but then leaned forward further into the room with the flashlight in front of me and saw that it did look like a butler's pantry, an elongated room with shelves and cupboards on either side with a small carriage light hanging from the ceiling. I stepped back and tore more of the wall down to create an opening large enough to step through. Once inside, I could see on the back wall of the room new brick that matched the outline of the windows I saw in the rear of the house. I walked back into the gallery and then to the kitchen. After studying the wall in the kitchen running parallel to the pantry, I surmised that the kitchen must have been renovated and the wall where there was once a door was now a row of cabinets dispelling any trace of a once existing entrance to the pantry. I guessed that the room appeared to have been sealed many years ago.

I went back to the opening from the gallery and again stepped into the room. There was a small step stool in the corner of the little room. I opened one cupboard hesitantly and saw a stack of books, mostly written in German and some Italian language books and a couple of very old and worn cook books. I then opened a drawer and found tarnished silverware, serving pieces, ancient kitchen utensils, a few time-faded photographs, and a few empty envelopes post marked from Germany after the war. I continued to look through the cupboards and found crystal goblets covered with years of dust, china, and musty linens. It all seemed so strange to me that someone would seal off a room, leaving things inside, which made me even a bit more apprehensive when opening the doors to the cupboards. My imagination got the best of me and I had visions of perhaps finding old skeletal remains in this room, which now seemed like it could have been a tomb. I was a bit uneasy because the room was dark and the day was nearing end, which left little sunlight outside this dark room filtering into the house and the battery of my flashlight was beginning to fade. I decided I had to wait until morning to finish exploring the contents of the room.

    I took the small bundle of photographs and stuck them into my bag, closed the house for the night and returned to my hotel room. I couldn't walk fast enough because I was eager to study the photographs once I got to my hotel room.

    I spread the photos on the bed and saw many containing groups of people, and some of children, perhaps one of which might be Adam. I then remembered I was meeting Adam for dinner and I was full of dust from breaking through the plaster wall and had to hurry to shower, fix my hair and pull myself together. I decided to covet my treasure and keep the secret of what I had found to myself and not tell Adam. I wanted a better look at the photos as well as a better look at the room the next day. I hoped to surprise him properly with something interesting about my findings. It was difficult to not mention it during dinner, and also to not seem too eager to finish our meal together. I couldn't get the photos out of my mind and looked forward to returning to my hotel room to study them in more detail.

    Our discussions during dinner avoided the topic of the house and the renovation, instead with Adam telling me a little about his life. I felt I was becoming very fond of him. Listening to him speak stirred thoughts of my father and I think that may have been my initial attraction to him. He reminded me of my father in many ways: his sensitive nature, intelligence, and even mannerisms. I had a pleasant comfortable feeling being with Adam. He told me quite a bit about himself. He was a college professor before he retired, teaching science. He married his wife the same year he graduated from the University of Geneva and then he went on to seek a Ph.D. in Science at Oxford. He and his wife had three children: a son and two daughters. His son and one daughter live in Milan and another daughter lives in Geneva and all three children had a higher education and successful careers. Adam was no slouch, but I knew that from the day I met him. I think he was probably a wonderful father and husband and it made me think how lucky his wife was to have such a good man for a husband. Adam asked about my life and my daughter. It was a very pleasant evening and once we pushed aside the mutual interest of the house and its esoteric charisma, we found there was still much to talk about. I enjoyed the conversation so much I almost put the entire episode of finding the secret room out of my mind. It was good to think about other things for a change.

Later that night, once back in my hotel room, I studied all the photos and the handwriting on the photos and envelopes, which were written in German. There were photos of small groups of people. They stoked my curiosity enough to make me wonder who the people were and if the Contrellis were in any of them. Given the age of the photos, I imagined many were long gone. All my excessive thinking about the photos and that little room made me want to return to the house in the morning before Vito was to show up, so I could search for more things. The anxiety also wouldn't allow my mind to quiet down and I barely slept at all.

Once at the house the next morning, the sun was shining brightly through the gallery, which allowed more light to filter in through the opening I made in the wall. I found a beautiful box inside one of the cupboards made of dark burled wood, perhaps walnut, with an ivory inlay and a brass lock, with the key still in the keyhole. The wood was worn to a beautiful patina, which looked as if it had been handled for many years. On closer inspection the box was an old lap desk with glass bottles for ink in small little compartments, separated by another covered part, which might have been a place to store pens. When laid flat, the writing surface could be lifted with a small leather tab where there was additional storage containing a few more photographs. As I looked at the contents I had to wonder how long it had been since these photos were handled, and how long the box had been hidden inside this secret room.

I brought the box out into the kitchen and placed it on the table and spread the contents out in front of me. Inside were a few photos of people, which looked like it might have been during the 40s and 50s, by the style of their clothing. Some of the photos had names and dates on the back. One photo was a group of soldiers that appeared to be wearing German military uniforms. There were many other pictures, but there were no names or dates on the back of the photo, but all looked like German soldiers. The empty envelopes had a German postmark. I decided that I would have to go buy a magnifying glass in order to study the photographs more closely. I got carried away with my treasure and decided I would put it all away before Vito arrived and get back to it later. I put the lap desk and other things in one of the kitchen cupboards.

Vito arrived early in the morning before his crew showed up. I was embarrassed to show him what I did, but explained that I could see there was an obvious space unaccounted for between the kitchen, dining room and the library. He looked at the hole in the wall and then at me and raised an eyebrow and smiled. He muttered a few words in Italian while shaking his head, "L'OH il mio dio! Donna Americana pazzesca," as he stepped through the hole in the wall. I later looked it up in my Italian/English dictionary that I carried with me faithfully because I was determined to learn the language, or at least as much as I could. I thought it was best to not let on that I knew what he said: "Oh my God! Crazy American woman." After all, I probably did appear to be a crazy woman. He looked around for a moment and then came back into the hallway and stood there, scratching his head in deep thought. I followed him through the dining room into the kitchen and watched him as he studied the cabinets on the wall adjacent to the little room. I wasn't sure what he was looking for. His hands ran across the moldings and inside the shelves and suddenly, there was a loud click. We both looked at each other in great surprise. I'm sure my mouth fell open when I realized what had just happened. He pressed a button that released a latch and the panel of the cabinet slowly sprung forward, opening the

*The House on Lake Maggiore*

entrance to the little room. He fingered his moustache for a brief moment, as if pondering what he was about to say. "Seniore, there is no mystery. I believe the owner felt the room was better accessed through the kitchen, but needed the additional storage so they covered this entrance with shelves. Pretty clever I think, no? Perhaps the people that lived here after the original tenants moved out just did not know there was a latch here to open the room. This door may not have been opened for many years! It is "oscuro" (obscure) and unless a person say, such as you, were overly "curioso," this could easily be overlooked. It really is kind of funny, don't you think?"

"I have to say, I feel a bit foolish. It never occurred to me to look for another entrance. This opening was well hidden. I can't believe this. It is a clever use of space to have a cupboard instead of just a door, but it is a tricky access and a lot of bother to enter the pantry this way. Wouldn't you think the new tenants would have wondered about the space between the kitchen and the library, being unaccountable? It just stayed locked up there for years, like a tomb." I looked at Vito for some sign of agreement, or understanding, but he shrugged his shoulders and smiled at me. It seemed to me that by his expression, he thought I was a hopeless fool and was probably wondering what would lie ahead for him, working with me. Somehow I had to redeem myself in his eyes.

"Well the walls of these older houses are much thicker than they are in newer houses, and it is a small narrow room. Probably no one really thought about it." He entered the pantry and looked around, while I stood at the doorway just peering in after him. After a few moments he pointed out that some of the electrical wiring and plumbing had been changed in the past, probably to accommodate upgrades made to the kitchen in an attempt to make it more modern. He thought at one time, the room contained a sink and was used for things other than a pantry, perhaps a laundry room. Finally he agreed that two entrances to the pantry were a good idea because china and table servings could be accessed and brought to the dining room from the gallery pantry door without having to go through the kitchen. A door from the gallery would also provide another entrance through the pantry into the kitchen, without having to walk through the dining room so he would be sure to put a door at the place where I had made the opening in the wall. We would remove the cupboard with the secret latch and put a frosted glass door in its place leading to the pantry, which would also allow natural light into the pantry from the kitchen windows. All the wiring would have to be replaced and a new light fixture needed to be hung. They would leave the bricked over windows intact and not risk damaging the structure of the outside or interior walls.

Vito and I sat at the kitchen table going over my list and soon a crew of workers showed up and joined us. I told him one of the very first things we needed to do was refinish the entrance door to the house and make it easier to open and also stop it from making such a horrible noise. After that they agreed the most important task at hand was to examine the electrical system before we had the power turned on, to see where we needed to replace wiring, upgrade outlets and light switches, and add new electrical outlets and light fixtures. They would soon need the power in order to use their power tools.

The plumber also had a list of tasks that were priority items, such as checking the plumbing in the entire house, remodeling all the bathrooms, replacing toilets and adding showers and new tubs where needed. Within two hours of discussions, Vito gave his directions to the workers and they set out to begin working. I heard them speaking in Italian as they walked through the gallery and stopped to look at the gaping hole in the wall. Vito relayed the story about the crazy lady and their failed attempt to hide their snickering ensued. They stood and commented about that hole for quite a while, each offering an idea about what to do about it. I created quite a fuss and this was just two days into the project.

I was finally left alone in the kitchen at the worktable and my eyes again looked up towards the pantry. At last, I had good daylight coming in from the kitchen through the open door, as well as the large opening in the other wall from the hallway, so I brought one of the kitchen chairs into the small room with me and stepped up to look into the taller shelves. There were large soup tureens, platters and other serving pieces that matched the china, as well as some silver pieces, elegant, but black with tarnish. I would take them all out and clean them and wash the linens. The linens were of a very high quality and most had a monogram of C, obviously for Contrelli. With each monogram I ran across in the house, it made the original owners more predominant and important. In another cupboard I found a couple bottles of wine and a bottle of cognac. I was certain the wine had turned to vinegar, but the cognac would be fine, and might be worth something, seeing as it was quite aged. There were still shelves higher up that I couldn't reach. The room was indeed a tomb and once the latched door closed, the room and its contents were hidden and long forgotten. Whoever cleared things out of the house, never thought about this room and it remained sealed and overlooked all these years.

Adam called on my cell phone and I told him that I had something to show him at the house. Later that afternoon when he arrived, I told him I had a very big surprise for him. I walked him through the gallery toward the dining room and stopped at the hole in the wall leading to the pantry. His eyes widened as he listened to me, quite captivated at my story about how I broke through the wall. I took him back through the dining room into the kitchen and showed him the cupboard in the kitchen that opened into the pantry. We walked over to the table where I had spread the contents I found in the pantry and briefly looked at the photos and then walked over to the open door of the pantry and with some trepidation, stepped inside. He stood for a few moments with his hands in his pockets looking around and then noticed the small stool in the corner.

"Well, I guess I did remember correctly. Look, there is the stool she had me sit on when she brought me in here. It is all clear now in my mind. She would lean against the cupboard over there and smoke a cigarette while we talked. I recall the small light hanging from the ceiling. I think I looked around the room quite a lot, just to avoid eye contact with her. Yes, this is the room. So it was always here; just walled over. What on earth was the reason for this, I wonder."

I told him that Vito speculated that the door from the kitchen took up too much room, so they replaced it with the shelving to match the other cupboards and installed the latch that released the cupboard to swing open and become the door. I showed him how the automatic latch worked and if one didn't know the latch was there and that it was a door, it blended in with the other cupboards lining that wall. So any new tenants never discovered that the cupboard opened into a pantry. We had no explanation why there was no hallway door, which did show on the blueprints.

Adam stood in amazement just looking at it and I knew he was reminiscing and searching for memories of those old days when he was a small child and led by the hand into the dark pantry by Mrs. Contrelli. Finally he spoke. "Goodness. It gives me a chill to think I stood right here in this little room as a child so many years ago. It's as if I dreamed it, but I do remember it, so well. I think I was about five or six years old, but it went on for a few years, maybe until I was ten or so. Every Christmas she would comment on how much I had grown since she last saw me. What was it all about, I wonder. Maybe it was nothing more than a childless woman, taking a fancy to a little boy. Who knows! I've spent too many years thinking about it."

We came back into the kitchen and to the table where I had strewn the photos. He picked each one up and turned it over to see if there was some sort of caption, or names written to identify the people in the photo. He picked through them carefully, as did I.

"I don't recognize any of the faces." He paused for a moment and looked at me. "Diana, these military men are in SS uniforms. You see the double lightning strikes on the collar? It signifies the emblem of the SS. I can't imagine what interest these were to anyone that lived here. But of course, that was a long time ago. Well, who knows where these people were before they lived in this house."

"What do you mean? Mr. Contrelli was certainly Italian, right?" I asked.

"Well yes, but he did marry a German woman. I remember my parents saying he brought her back here from Germany after the war. I wondered why he was in Germany. I don't see any photos that resemble Mrs. Contrelli, but who knows what her history might have been. These SS men may have been her friends in Germany."

I was becoming even more curious about these people that lived so long ago in this house. "Mrs. Contrelli? Well, she also could have been married before she married Mr. Contrelli. Maybe her husband was an officer in the army and died in the war. It is interesting that nothing here seems to relate to Italy, or Mr. Contrelli."

Adam shuffled through the photos and envelopes on the table. "Yes, that's true. Look at the envelopes; they are all postmarked from Germany. There's nothing inside the envelopes. They are all empty and addressed to C. Contrelli. The return addresses are various places in Germany. Also, some of the photos are of little children. I can't tell if I am in any of these photos, but possibly I may be."

I recall the conversation that afternoon so clearly and how we dismissed our curiosity for the time being. However, we came back to the same questions many times: Exactly what was Mr. Contrelli doing in Germany during the war and who was he? We left for dinner that night and speculated endlessly over our meal about who the characters were in the pictures.

The next day I went to a store in the village and bought a magnifying glass in order to look more closely at the photos. When I returned to the house I noticed one of the workmen had brought a ladder into the little service room behind the kitchen. I dragged the ladder into the pantry and climbed up to the top shelves. I found a paper bag in the very back of the shelf, but the rest of the shelves were empty. When I grabbed it, I was a bit alarmed because there was something heavy inside. The bag was wrapped and tied with twine. I took a scissors and cut the twine and unwrapped the paper. Inside was a cloth bag with a drawstring. I opened the bag and inside was a revolver. I continued to rifle through the drawers where I found more loose photos. I gathered them up and brought them out to the kitchen table, along with the revolver and again had to put it all away as Vito was due to arrive and I wanted to covet my found treasure.

Soon Vito's team of men arrived to begin work. We all went into the kitchen to talk and plan the day's work. I talked about some of the ideas I had, and also shared the list of what was obvious that needed to be done, such as the plumbing, clean and test the fireplaces, fixing the plaster, removing wall paper, refinishing floors, demolishing the bathrooms and removing old fixtures, taking up old carpet and either getting it cleaned, repaired, or replaced, cleaning the chandeliers and light fixtures, and painting walls. We walked through the house together pointing out areas where repairs needed to be made. We all agreed there were no walls that needed to be removed, so structural changes would be minimal, but the bathrooms, and of course the kitchen would be gutted and rebuilt. Vito laid out his plans and directions and within no time at all, the men had scattered and began working. Scaffolds were assembled in the living room and dining room to begin working on electrical wiring, repairing plaster, cleaning or hanging chandeliers, repairing the ceilings and light fixtures. After they left the kitchen, I walked over to the cabinet with the secret lever and pressed it to open the pantry entrance. I remember standing in that dark room thinking about Adam being in this room, as a child with the woman of the house. He would be here, sitting on this stool while she talked to him. I imagined the windows were still there that looked out into the yard and imagined the room filled with linens, china, crystal and silver. Maybe it was a laundry room, as Vito suggested because of the small sink and faucet. There may have been some sort of washing machine at one time, but there was no trace of its existence anymore and it looked like that was all moved to the service porch.

Vito knew someone that reupholstered furniture and called them with my cell phone. That afternoon they came and we met in the kitchen and looked at all the pieces and agreed I would come to their shop the next day to look at fabric samples and they would begin the work recovering the upholstered pieces, as well as begin refinishing the wooden pieces. They took all the pieces away with them, just leaving the kitchen table and ladder back chairs.

Adam began to come to Stresa more often than before because of his interest in the house renovation, but only stayed a couple days at a time when he visited, and we talked on the phone during the time he was gone so I could give him updates as to what was happening. He was interested in the progress of the house and how things were moving along. He returned to his home in Lugano, Switzerland and then came to see me every other week or so and we would always walk to the village for a nice dinner. His visits were always something to look forward to and I so appreciated the company and our friendship was developing into something very nice.

The work moved along slowly, but at times that was in my favor because it allowed me time to change my mind, or be certain I made good decisions. It was important to me that the renovations brought the house back to its original splendor and not stray too far from the fundamentals of the era the house represented and its design. Adam recalled some of the original décor in parts of the house and gave me some hints and ideas about what to look for as far as design, furnishings and also color.

Upon his visits our conversations always drifted back to the history of the house. It may have been his wish that as the work progressed, the house would resemble more of what he recalled and it would in fact jar his memory and provide more details of what it was like in those old days. Time and time again Adam and I would sit at the kitchen table with the photos and look at them with the magnifying glass when the sun came into the room the strongest so we could study them carefully. Some of the photos were taken from a distance and the faces were too small to see them well. He kept coming back to certain photos where he believed he may have seen himself as a child. He said he would search through his own things, left to him by his parents, to find photos of him as a child and bring them on his next visit, which he did and as we looked at them and compared the faces, we thought we may have recognized him in a group photo, along with other children.

Within a few days of the onset of the work, Bjorn called to ask how things were moving along and said he would be in Milan for two days and he would take a train to Stresa so we could talk about the planned renovations. I was satisfied that sufficient work was underway so he would see things were moving along. I always wanted to be sure to keep him informed of the progress and also to let him know if I ran into any snags that he might be able to help me work through. He was very good about assuring me he would help in any way he could and wanted to stay in the loop. I knew he was a valuable asset and anything that needed to be done, if I couldn't figure a way to make it happen, he always seemed to be able to have a solution. At times language for me was a bit of a barrier, and he spoke many languages so he was a big help with communication. He had a way about him that made people listen and people understood that if Bjorn wasn't happy, it was serious. He earned the respect of all of us and also the fact that he held the purse strings let us all know who was really in charge.

When he arrived at the house we sat in the kitchen and I went over the list of what had been accomplished, the status of ongoing jobs, and what was going to happen in the next week or so. After that discussion I told him that I had a real surprise for him. I walked over to the cupboard and lifted the latch and the door gently swung forward. His eyes opened wide in amazement and he was quite intrigued with my story about finding the pantry and thought I was quite resourceful in breaking through the wall and making this discovery. He had noticed the hole in the wall in the gallery, but thought that it was part of the plumbing or electrical repair. We had a good laugh about Vito finding the latch in the cupboard in the kitchen that simply set the opening in motion after I had broken through the wall. He walked around the little pantry and opened and closed a couple of the cupboard doors. I told him of the things I found, some of which I left in the cupboards, like the china and flatware. I brought him back to the kitchen table and took out the beautiful antique lap desk and the photos. While he looked through them, I opened a bottle of wine for us.

After I poured the wine, I opened the drawer to the kitchen table and took out the little bag that held the pistol. "Well, I saved the best for the last. Take a look at this. I found this in the back of one of the top shelves."

"Well, well, what have we here?" Bjorn was giddy with pleasure at this and he giggled a bit. He opened the pouch and pulled out the revolver and said, "This is a German Lugar. My goodness. Look at this, Diana! It's incredible!" he said while examining it carefully. He turned it over and then reached for the magnifying glass on the table and looked at it carefully. "It has the initials of CD engraved onto the handle. Hm, this is very interesting." It was apparent that Bjorn was no stranger to guns by the way he opened the chamber carefully and inspected the gun thoroughly. He then put it back in the pouch. "Let's leave all this here for the time being. I think I would like to research all this a little closer, but for now, hang on to this and keep it in a safe place so none of the workmen find it." I said that I was using a cupboard to put some of my things and thought it was safe enough. I told him that I had a bit of curiosity burning inside of me about the original owners of the house, and thought that knowing something about them might help me with a vision of how I wanted to decorate and try to keep the style similar to the opulence of the original decor, but of course updated. He agreed and thought maybe we could both work on researching the old history of the house and how it looked before it fell into ruins.

"I think I will take this little business card though and try to figure out if this person still exists, or if they know something about the people that lived here. It's some sort of doctor in Switzerland, who is probably long gone, but you never know." I told him that would be great and I was eager to also know if there was any remaining connection to the original owners of the house.

"But Bjorn, I have one more surprise." I went to the cupboard and got the bottle of cognac I found. He was ecstatic.

"Well, this is by all means the most special treasure." He studied the label on the bottle carefully and with approving rise of one eyebrow, he said, "Let's keep this for our final celebration when the house is complete. I think it would be a good way to toast the new life of the house."

# CHAPTER 4

While in the cellar one day rummaging around to be sure I hadn't overlooked some other useful old furniture pieces, I found several free standing column plinths that were most likely used to hold things like statues, or plants. They were all in good shape, but I wasn't quite sure what do with them. Vito thought we should take them into the yard for now and clean or paint them and decide later how to use them. We thought they might be good in the solarium to hold plants, or in the gallery to hold art pieces. It was fortunate that items, like the column plinths, survived all those years and were obviously overlooked as having little importance to the renters that occupied the house. Perhaps they never ventured into the cellar. I believed they were the remnants of decades long past, but we would bring them back and use them somewhere in the décor.

Being an architect, Vito had a trained eye for details, and also knowledge of what sort of ornamentation suited architectural styles and what was appropriate for the style of the house. He believed the style of the house was conflicted in certain places. Although Liberty in design, there were many traces of Baroque details that might have been too elaborate for the décor, but somehow, I thought it all worked well and those things he pointed out were in my opinion, extra ornamentation that added to the architectural detail. Perhaps the builder and designer had a mind of their own and wanted custom features to give it more uniqueness.

Vito led me into the gallery, which in Italian he referred to as a Piano Nobile, to look at the columns between the gallery and the living room and gave me a lesson on the specific detail of the capitals, which were extremely ornate and had quite a lot of symmetrical ornamentation of elaborate Baroque detail. He pointed out how the ornamentation on the capitals was carried to the spandrels, also quite ornate, that appeared to support the archway leading into the room, but merely decorative. Part of the crocket detail on one of the column capitals had cracked off and would have to somehow be repaired.

Vito then took me outside and we walked the perimeter of the house and he pointed out many parts of the architectural details he found interesting. He spoke with such passion that I believed he, like I, was totally enchanted with the house. At times he stopped to pull some of the vines off the structure to see what was underneath and then he talked about what he saw. He pointed out the Churrigueresque design, which was also ornate Baroque detail cast in concrete and ran across the top of the façade near the roof, also quite hidden under the vines. The house had a small blend of Mediterranean Revival, which was a period in the early 1900s, along with the obvious Liberty Style, which was popular through the 1920s, the exact time the house was built. The blueprints we found verified the apparent style. Liberty was Italy's rendition borrowed from the Art Nouveau era. Some of the light fixtures, both inside and outside, and wall sconces were unmistakably representative of Art Nouveau. We would polish them and keep as many as we could without replacing them. I volunteered to make that one of my projects.

In architecture and painting the Art Nouveau movement took different forms in different countries, so the style varied from London to Paris to New York to Eastern Europe. The movement was popular in the late nineteenth century and lasted into the 1930s and also took on different names in different parts of the world. In Italy the movement was called "Liberty" for the firm Liberty and Company in London, which sold this kind of art for several decades. On a previous trip to Budapest, I saw a very large influence of Art Nouveau, where it is claimed to have begun. Its flowing, flowery forms distinguished Art Nouveau from contemporary architectural styles such as Art Deco. Artists created asymmetrical, curvaceous designs based on organic inspiration taken directly from nature. This was evident in the house with the carved frieze detail in the library, the entablatures and spandrels, the iron work of the staircase, as well as the fireplace surrounds and the detail over the front entrance. These details were all typical of the motif. Like Art Deco, Art Nouveau was a total style encompassing architecture, interior design, painting, graphics, fashion, furniture design and other areas. Artists used materials like wrought iron and the gate outside the drive had the many swirls and waving lines that are typically Art Nouveau in design, which complimented and blended well with the Italian Liberty style. They also used stained glass, tile, and hand-painted wallpaper, which were also evident in some of the wall coverings, which were in very bad condition and hanging in shreds, seriously beyond salvaging. The glass window at the end of the corridor on the second floor was created in the Art Nouveau motif. In design the glass of the American company, Louis Comfort Tiffany and much of the art of Gustave Klimt, Henri de Toulouse-Lautrec and Maxfield Parrish are classified as Art Nouveau, which in Germany was called "Jugendstil" and in Spain "Modernista." The basis of Art Nouveau consisted of delicate flowing and bending lines that seemed not to conform, beginning in parallel, converging and contradicting each other and then uniting. Horticulture and the female form lent themselves ideally to this new style and it was applied to many things, including jewelry, which was represented so well by the French jeweler René Lalique.

Frank Lloyd Wright style architecture was more representative of Arts and Crafts Style and the succeeding trend of Art Deco using more perpendicular lines. Art Nouveau led the way to Art Deco so it might be natural to see these styles blending due to the era of the house. Craftsman homes represent Arts and Crafts style and I was quite familiar with Craftsman design and had updated a 1930's style home in Northern California only two years before. A Craftsman revival was popular after the war and is a common style in Southern California. Art Nouveau led the way to Art Deco so it would not be surprising to see representation of both styles melding together as the propensity of styles and fashion of the time moved throughout the era that the house was built.

With all of our discussion of architecture and design that day, we agreed that in order to keep the décor as close as possible to resembling the essence of the original design of the house, we would have to search for those elements that best complemented the original style for anything that needed replacing. We would keep close to the design and remember preservation was the most important part of our renovation. Vito was very exact in his direction to me when he said, the interior decoration must harmonize with the structural design and the harmonization must have rhythm and logic throughout the house, inside and out. I had no argument with that and agreed it would be my true objective to make sure the interior suited the style of the architecture. Vito was a brick and mortar kind of guy. Structure and façade were his world and architecture was his life and I respected his knowledge and beliefs.

I, on the other hand, had the expertise of the interior of the home and my own philosophy of decorating a house. Sometimes when renovating an older home, and especially in this house, we are unconsciously intimidated over the wants of others, perhaps even the wants of dead and gone predecessors, who have a tiresome way of thrusting their habits and tastes across their successors. As much as I found myself trying to think about what this house looked like when the Contrellis lived in it, I had to allay that thinking and realize that the design can be that of their day, but the style will be of this day. No one wants to buy an old house that looks as if old people lived in it. The current trend that still celebrates the original style can work very well in making this house reflect the original design, but with all the comforts, trends and conveniences we are accustomed to today in the twenty-first century.

I thought about my theories in two ways. What if I could do time travel and go back sixty years and show up at Mrs. Cantrell's door one day and she invited me in for tea. What would I see? How would that interior clash with my look, a woman of the twenty-first century and what could we possibly talk about over tea? I would see trends in the décor that appeared old fashioned and dated. The kitchen was a classic example of what outdated exemplifies, but it was the house she, not I, would be comfortable living in. In the second scenario, what if Mrs. Contrelli appeared out of nowhere and showed up at my condo in Los Angeles. Imagine how confused she would be, especially when my robot vacuum cleaner circled around her ankles as it swept the carpet, or if I pulled the tea pot out of the microwave, or if I tried to explain to her that the furniture was placed as such, according to Feng Shui, to allow the "Chi" or energy to flow through the rooms. Imagine me trying to explain ergonomics to her, a word that didn't exist in her day. There were no slate floors, granite counters, dimmer switches on the wall, ice makers, freezers or dish washers.

I would not stray too far off track of what Vito thought was harmony, but this would be a new house and have the conveniences that the twenty-first century could afford us, no matter how intrusive and would include steam showers, spa tubs, air conditioning and modern appliances. I knew Vito and I were perfect partners and he and I might have lengthy discussions on our own particular views, but we would learn from one another, and at times one of us would compromise. I was extremely grateful to have his guidance and expertise close by to call upon when I felt I needed help with a decision; however, it is a new day and the interior work is my work. Time does have a tendency to march on and I am right on top of the latest and greatest of home conveniences.

I discovered several antique shops that handled fixtures from demolished villas and I was certain the search through the various shops would present great findings that would lend new charm to the house. Any findings would include refinishing, so I knew there was a lot of that sort of work ahead for us and I realized that the first time I laid eyes on the house. To renovate something, while not compromising the originality of it, meant we would be working in an aesthetic sense and the cosmetics were vitally important as was the priority of the comforts people of our generation enjoy and expect in order to make a house a home. The potential buyer of the house would understand the essence of the home and would appreciate design. This was not a house for just anyone, but instead it would be someone with the appreciation of the art of that era and for the effort that went into the renovation. Everything and every room had to be in conformance and the harmony of style had to flow from room to room, but it had to be a home of the twenty-first century.

The books I shipped from home finally arrived and Vito and I studied them endlessly. All the time, through all the work, the vision of how the finished home would look was imprinted in my mind. I felt fortunate to have Vito as my architect who shared the vision and had the knowledge to keep us on track in all purposes of cost, time and style.

The weeks were moving on and the work was progressing, but it seemed at a snail's pace. Nevertheless, I began to see results and every success, no matter how small, was a delight. The important work, such as fixing plumbing and wiring in the walls, fixing plaster, the roof, were all things that showed slow, but steady progress and I was overly anxious to get to the cosmetic changes, the things I could see that would show the most visible results and move us to complete a project.

All this time, other than visits from Adam, I was always alone. I had Vito and the workmen who I tried desperately to converse with and in time, my Italian language skills improved, but our conversations were awkward and always work related. I missed chatting with a friend and made up for it when I talked to my daughter in New York on the phone. I did my best to keep the conversation going and never wanted to end the call.

Vito spoke excellent English and was my intermediary when he saw me struggling to talk to one of his workers. We became good friends, but when the day ended, he was gone and I was left alone again. Adam came about every other week for a day or two, so I had a good dinner partner, but every night after working at the house, I would return to my hotel room and then go to a cafe for dinner and eat alone. The evenings were lonely and I always looked forward to getting through it and returning to the house the next day, just to be around people.

One afternoon I needed a change of scenery and a break from the house. I went to the town center and had lunch at my favorite cafe. It was a beautiful sunny day and I felt like getting out into the fresh air and away from the dust and dirt that was flying around the house due to the work. I finished my salad and was enjoying a cup of coffee, when a woman approached the table and began speaking to me in Italian. I tried to answer her, but she knew right away from my feeble attempt with Italian that I was American and as it turned out, she was also. Her name was Jean Griffith and she was from Chicago and was spending a few months with an aunt in Stresa. She said she had noticed me eating there alone before, as she did quite often, and thought that perhaps one day we could have lunch together. I invited her to join me at my table and we had a very pleasant conversation over coffee. When I told her what I was doing in Stresa, she remarked that she noticed work was going on at that abandoned villa and was very happy to see that it was being renovated. Come to find out, her aunt lived in an apartment not far from the house. Her aunt was quite elderly and knew some of the house's history. I told her I would love to meet her aunt and hear what she knew. I gave her my cell number and we left the restaurant together and walked back up the street. She said she would give me a call and I could come to her aunt's apartment and meet her. I looked forward to that and hoped her aunt could shed some more light on the house's history.

The next morning Jean called and said her aunt would love to meet me and asked if I could come for lunch that day. I can't describe how happy that made me, just knowing I wasn't going to sit in that dreadful kitchen eating the usual mundane sandwich but would meet someone new and have some interesting conversation. Just the idea of interacting with other human beings was a pleasure.

I went into the yard and picked some lilies and made a nice bouquet to take along with me. Her aunt, Irene Danzetto, lived in a small apartment just up the hill a few blocks from the house. Jean was a school teacher and had taken a leave to come and spend time with her aunt, who had some health problems. She said she spent many summers with her aunt there in Stresa. When I arrived at the apartment, Jean met me at the door. It was a small but quaint apartment in the back of a building facing the back hills. Every now and then the train would go by, which comes from the direction of Milan.

Mrs. Danzetto was seated on a sofa in the living room and seemed happy to have a visitor. When greeting her, she asked me to call her Irene. She asked where I got the lovely flowers and I told her they came from the yard behind the house. As I learned that day, Irene's hobby when younger, and when she had a home, was gardening and she had a great appreciation of flowers and plants. She was an extremely stylish woman that appeared to be in her late eighties, albeit quite attractive and I imagined when younger, she was quite a stunning woman. She was petite with a full head of very white beautiful hair, which she wore pulled back smartly in a French twist. She was made up very nicely with just a hint of blush and pink lipstick and had on pearl earrings and a string of pearls around her neck beneath the collar of her white cotton blouse. She wore a slight fragrance of gardenia and I believed she prepared herself well for her visitor, and I felt honored. She had a lovely smile and asked me to sit down next to her on the couch while Jean went to the kitchen to put the flowers in a vase. She said her hearing was not very good anymore and she wanted to be able to converse with me so I sat next to her good ear. She spoke with a voice much larger than her person, with a very heavy Italian accent and a deep throaty tone. "Jean tells me you are a decorator and you are renovating the big house on the shore."

"Yes. The renovation is being funded by a group of investors."

"What will become of the house when you are finished?" she asked.

I explained that we hoped to find a very wealthy buyer and the investors would make a good profit, and also explained that I worked for them and would make a small percentage of the profit, as well as be able to write articles about the renovation.

She sat back, sinking into the cushions of the sofa and seemed to reminisce for a moment. "I'm very happy to see it being renovated. It has been such an eye sore. I remember that house when it was so beautiful. It was quite a grand house in its day. Now it is so overgrown it is difficult to even see it from the street."

"Oh yes, I know. Pulling those vines off the house will be a big job and then the entire structure will probably have to be sandblasted. Tell me, Irene, have you ever been inside the house?" I asked.

"Oh my, yes. I was in the house on a few occasions many, many years ago after the war. The former owners had wonderful holiday parties there and invited many of their neighbors. My husband and I were newly married around that time when they began to have their parties. We used to have a house on the shore also, just a few homes away from that house. But after my husband passed away several years ago, I couldn't take care of it any longer and I just could not afford to stay and keep it up myself so I sold it. It is no longer there, I'm sad to say. The new owners tore it down and built an apartment building in its place. It broke my heart, but I am left with my memories."

Irene reflected for a moment again before speaking. "I was only in that house at Christmas. The owners were, now what was their name?" I interjected and said, Contrelli. "Oh yes, Contrelli. Mr. and Mrs. Contrelli. My memory does fail me every now and then." She took a moment to collect her thoughts.

"They had wonderful Christmas celebrations and invited all their neighbors. Other than those Christmas parties, I seldom saw them or spoke with them, but then again the following year an invitation arrived at my door, to come again to a Christmas party. It was a very nice affair and nice to see all the neighbors again. The invitation always said to dress formal. It was great fun to go shop for a new dress for that party. The house was quite beautiful inside and everyone was very elegantly dressed. It was always a splendid night."

Jean entered the room carrying a vase with the flowers I brought and Irene commented on how lovely and fragrant the flowers were and thanked me for bringing them. Then she continued with her reminiscence. "I do recall Mr. Contrelli. He was a lovely gentleman. He was some sort of financier from Milan and very wealthy. You know, the first Mrs. Contrelli died and after a short time he remarried. I think he found it difficult to live in that house alone. I remember the first Mrs. Contrelli and liked her very much. We were in a garden club together. She and I talked often about gardening and flowers. She had a wonderful garden. Isn't it interesting that these flowers you brought came from that garden? It is as if a piece of history came to visit me. I'm sure these old lily plants are still from the roots she planted so long ago. After she died, the next wife wasn't as interested and you could see that the garden was terribly neglected."

I told her how overgrown the garden was. Some beautiful flowering plants remained, but it would be a very big job to untangle it all and redo the entire yard. She talked a little about her garden and the type of plants she grew and at one time, had a greenhouse and raised orchids. She asked Jean to retrieve a photo album from a bookshelf. She thumbed through the album showing me photos of her beautiful home. It was quite obvious Irene lived a very privileged life of wealth and the house was very stately and elegant. It was such a shame the home was no longer standing. It must have been heartbreaking for her when it was being torn down.

I asked what she remembered about the new Mrs. Contrelli. She thought for a moment before answering. "She surprised me because she was so much younger than Mr. Contrelli. She could have been his daughter, or even granddaughter. He was getting up there in years and not very attractive any more, and I'm sure his illness had taken a toll on him. Of course there was no other reason for her to have married him, other than his money. I did not like her for that, but it was not my business. She was very tall and—well, I thought she was a bit odd looking. She was extremely thin with very bony aquiline facial features, but nevertheless, she was rather striking and quite sophisticated looking. I didn't think she was attractive, but the way she put herself together, I would say she was interesting looking, and, as I said, striking. If she were walking through a room full of people, they would have noticed her because she had an air about her, like a look of confidence, you know; she sort of floated when she walked. She wore fashions very well and it appeared took good care of herself and she was made up perfectly. She had rather broad shoulders and long legs and carried herself well. I felt though as if she seemed to always be posing, as if she knew someone was watching her. She dressed extremely fashionable in the latest styles, but of course, her husband was quite well to do. Her hair was always just so, as if she just came from the beauty parlor, which reminds me. Jeannie, I must get an appointment for my hair. Would you take care of that for me, dear?"

"Of course. I'll call tomorrow. When would you like to go?" Jean asked.

"Well, later this week if they can take me. I'm a horrible freight, I know. I am sorry I don't look my best, dear, but I haven't been feeling well. I'm so happy to have Jeannie here to help me. I don't know what I would do without her."

Jean returned from the kitchen carrying a tray with a tea service and put it down on the coffee table in front of the sofa. She said that lunch would be ready in a little while, but she thought we might enjoy a cup of tea first so we could continue talking. I poured the tea and handed Irene a tea cup and saucer, which she held gracefully with her slender hands and then continued her walk down memory lane again reminiscing about Mr. and Mrs. Contrelli.

"Let's see now, where was I? Oh yes, the new Mrs. Contrelli. I sometimes spoke with her while at her home during those Christmas parties, but always briefly, you know, just idle chit chat. She had many guests to tend to, but always found time to chat with me for a while, which I thought was very nice. We were similar in age, I think around our mid-twenties. I recall that she tried desperately to camouflage her heavy German accent by speaking with exaggerated pronouncement, which put a strange twist to her speech, almost as if she had a speech problem, but I think she was trying to emulate an English accent. It didn't work well. I thought it amusing and remember mentioning it to my husband. I complemented her on the decor of the house, how beautiful it was and how lovely the Christmas decorations were. You know, I was just making small talk because I didn't know her very well and I didn't know what to talk about with her. She really didn't seem to want to talk about the decor of the house, probably because it was all due to the first Mrs. Contrelli and she didn't know much about it or seem very interested. I was pretty sure she knew little about decorating. She loved to talk about books and stories and the arts and was quite well versed on literature. I was at one time an avid reader when my eyes were better. Now of course, my eyesight has failed me and I don't read as much. We got into some nice discussions about literature. She seemed to be quite intelligent."

This brought to mind the carved moldings in the library and my search to decipher the allegoric characters. "Did you ever see the library in the house? It has some wonderful carved moldings along the ceiling that I think must depict stories. Do you remember that at all?"

Irene looked towards the ceiling in a pensive moment, as if she was taking herself back into that library and paused for a moment before responding. "Well, yes I do, now that you mention it. Because we were talking about literature, she took

*The House on Lake Maggiore*

me into the library and showed me those moldings. She said they were all individual carvings depicting literary tales and nursery rhymes. The first Mrs. Contrelli contracted a sculptor to make them. The first Mr. and Mrs. Contrelli had a daughter that died at about five or six years old. She drowned in the swimming pool behind the house. After she died, they got rid of the pool. They may have just filled it in with dirt, but they didn't want that reminder in the yard anymore. Losing their child left them heartbroken. I knew the first Mrs. Contrelli, but the child must have died before I got to know her, and she never spoke about it. So the first Mrs. Contrelli had those moldings designed with stories she used to read the little girl, in memory of the child. I think they were quite extraordinary and I'm happy to hear they are still there. The artist they hired did an amazing job, I think. I imagine that was very costly, but they were really a wonderful work of art. Well, then of course, Mrs. Contrelli, the first wife, died from a heart attack, as I recall." She paused and had a sip of tea. "It was a couple years before Mr. Contrelli married again. I think he and the first wife loved each other very much. I imagine he married the new wife because he was so lonely. I don't know if he loved her, but he was good to her nevertheless. I recall complementing her on her gown and she said she went to Switzerland to shop as often as she could. She said she just adored fashion. Well, then of course after a few years Mr. Contrelli died, and she then owned the house. He wasn't well for quite some time. I believe he had cancer of some sort. Well, after he was gone the parties ended and we never heard from her again. I know she still lived there and my husband or I would see her come and go, but she kept to herself."

Just then Jean came to tell us that lunch was ready and we should come into the dining room. I helped Irene up from the sofa and we went into the dining room and continued our conversation over lunch. Jean prepared a tuna casserole and a green salad and it was wonderful to have simple American comfort food for a change. I asked Irene if she heard rumors or ever speculated about what was going on in that house after Mr. Contrelli died.

"Well, yes, I think I do recall something. Let me think for a moment." She delicately began to move her salad around the plate and took a couple small bites, then continued talking. "Someone said she remarried not long after Mr. Contrelli passed on, but I never saw the man or heard much about it, until a couple years later, his death notice was in the paper. Evidently he died in a boating accident on the lake. Then I think I heard she married again, but I lost track of her. I really don't know what happened to her after that. I really would love to know, if you ever find out, just out of curiosity. I never knew how that house came to be abandoned. I guess there were renters in it, but never for long lengths of time. I often wondered what happened to her. She just seemed to disappear. People speculated and talked about her every now and then, but in time, she was forgotten. All I recall is that the house seemed to become more neglected looking and more overgrown with vines. Such a shame!"

Soon after lunch I had to get back to the house to meet a kitchen designer so I excused myself and invited them to come by the house and see how it was progressing. It was truly an interesting afternoon and I loved all the detail Irene recalled and it set my imagination going again thinking about the history of the house, but especially the very fascinating character of Mrs. Contrelli. I made good friends that day with Irene and Jean and saw them many times during the months ahead.

# CHAPTER 5

Before even thinking about the future decor of the house, I had more research to do to keep my vision in check for the interior design. I needed to explore the area more extensively and get a better understanding of the appropriate assimilation of décor, aesthetics and culture. I invited Jean to come along on my exploration as it would be more enjoyable with some company. I rented a car and we drove along Corso Umberto, the scenic shore road to view other mansions nestled into the verdant hills embanking the lake, along through all the little communities of Baveno, Belgirate, Verbania, and up the coast towards Locarno, Switzerland on the northern part of the lake.

Mount Mottarone rises to the west above all the coastal villages and behind Stresa. We took the funicular up Mount Mottarone where there is a lovely garden and a wonderful view, not just of Lake Maggiore, but when it is a very clear day, you can see the other lakes in the surrounding areas: Lake Garda, Lake Orta and Lake Como, some fifty miles away. It is the most extraordinary view and you just want to sit for a while and feast your eyes and listen to the birds and every now and then the clanging of a cowbell somewhere beyond a small forest of trees. From that vantage point of Lake Maggiore you can see the lake dotted with the islands, and the boats going to and from the islands, leaving a pattern of lines in their wake on the glistening lake surface. We sat on a bench in the warm sun, just looking at the wonderful view. Jean was very quiet, as was I and then I wondered if she was meditating and I hesitated to speak for fear of interrupting her. The beauty from that perspective would tempt any devout person to take the moment to reflect on their own spirituality. We sat in silence for a while, each of us enraptured in our own private thoughts and then became intrigued with a small lizard playing in the flowers near the bench where we sat. I will always recall that peaceful event and how impressed I was with Jean and her sensitivity and appreciation for the splendor of the moment.

It was great having Jean along because she was much more familiar with the area and knew of places I wasn't aware of so it was like having my own personal tour guide. We took a launch across the lake, which included stops at the three main islands so I could study the gardens and the architecture. On Isola Bella, we took the tour of the palace and studied the furnishings and paintings and the colors within the wonderful Baroque decorated rooms. The large garden, the Giardino Grande is fabulous and the tour books say it is favored as the most exquisite garden. It has a huge assortment of Hibiscus perennials and the gardens are accented by allegorical statues and other decorative elements, so typical of Italian gardens. The garden has ten levels, or tiers and each tier is divided into multiple gardens with espaliers forming the grand pyramid with an esplanade at the summit of one hundred and fifty Roman pines. The gardens and the Baroque statues and topiaries gave me the feeling that I had gone back in time to another century. White peacocks wander freely and it is apparent that it is their private domain. Under the gardens is an incredible grotto that is an extensive living area to escape to in the warm summer months. The grotto walls are made of inset shells and stones that took centuries to complete. Also in the grotto are treasures on display that were pulled from the lake, like old tools and weapons that told tales of past history and perhaps battles being fought in Roman times in this area. From every part of the island is another beautiful view of the lake and the shore of Stresa with its impressive presence of large stately hotels along the shore.

I took photos and also detailed notes of everything: the tiles in the walk ways and fountains, the steps leading to small gardens, the lush ground cover with delicate pink and purple blossoms, the type of trees and plants in many of the gardens. We had lunch on the other island, Isola Pescatori looking out at another vantage point of the lake behind that island, which faced another shore across the lake. The island was once known as a fishing village and has many beautiful Mediterranean structures with shops and restaurants.

Many of the mansions along the Corso Umberto were designed with the Liberty structure, with lots of stone, pillars, loggias and gardens of centuries past. Along the coastal road are small beaches, some belonging to the homes, or hotels and some boat landings. Some homes had iron gates in front of them, as did the Contrelli Villa, but well-kept gardens and driveways leading towards the house, sometimes up a serpentine drive winding its way up the fertile hills where the homes sat, each positioned carefully to take advantage of their lake view, probably from every window of the house. Sadly so many of these old mansions were converted to condominiums and apartments and it brought to mind the photographs of Irene's house and I tried to envision what this area looked like in the early part of the last century when many of the elegant villas were in their prime. Jean pointed out where Irene's house once stood, which was now a nondescript structure of condominiums. The days of extreme wealth were long gone and taxes probably ate up most of the wealth. We could only hope there was someone somewhere in the world that could afford to buy our house, once fully renovated. As I mentioned before, those ever present zoning laws dictated that the home, because of its famous architecture and well known designer, must remain a home, and not be turned into condos, which was another reason it stayed vacant for so long. The strict standards placed on the home limited the scope of potential owners. We would search the world to find a good owner for the property. It would be a fabulous house, once complete, I was certain, but feared it may become a white elephant that no one could afford.

# CHAPTER 6

One foggy morning I sat in the kitchen beginning my day as I had become accustomed to, having coffee and a pastry I picked up at the bakery on the way to the house. By this time the ancient monster stove was working and I was able to make coffee, boil water, and do minimal cooking. The stove, or as it is really called, the cooker was a very complicated piece of machinery and I needed Vito to give me a lesson on how to use it. I sat at the large plank table in the bay window of the breakfast nook in the kitchen going over my notes of things to do and reviewing my checklists with the status of things the workmen were doing. I looked out into the yard, thinking about the possibilities of turning the mass of tangled greenery into something similar to what I saw in the beautiful sculpted gardens of the islands and realized the overwhelming work that still needed to begin. As my eyes scanned the muddled mess of the yard, I saw something moving towards the back near the carriage house, almost totally obliterated by the heavy vines clinging to everything. I watched a little longer and a woman slowly stepped forth coming further into the yard. She stopped under the tangled pergola and looked at the bougainvillea and then turned slowly studying the shrubbery and then turned and stood with her eyes fixed on the house. I'm quite sure she didn't see me at the window. I grabbed my sweater from the back of the chair and threw it over my shoulders and went to the door leading to the back patio and was about to open the door, but then noticed she had turned and was walking out of the yard. I was curious about her, but decided it was just another passer-by wondering what was happening at the house and I decided to ignore her.

A few minutes later I heard the door knocker slam against the front entry door. Before I could leave the kitchen to walk through the gallery to get to the entrance hall, the woman I saw in the yard had already pushed the door open and was standing in the entrance hall. When she saw me she became startled and apologized for entering the house and explained that she thought no one was inside. She told me she once worked in the house and was curious as to what was happening to it. I introduced myself and briefly told her about the house renovation and that I was the decorator. Her name was Ingrid Zinger and she was the housekeeper for many years. Of course my curiosity took over and a voice of its own came out of my mouth before I could guard myself and I invited her into the kitchen for a cup of coffee.

As we walked through the gallery towards the kitchen, she stopped at the conspicuous yawning hole in the wall and said, "Oh my, what on earth happened here?" I told her it was just some of the work we began and blew it off as if we were looking for electrical or plumbing problems in the walls.

"Ms. Marshall, I don't want to impose. I'm sure you are very busy," she said. I guessed she was somewhere in her eighties, very soft spoken and in a very respectful and humble manner. Her grey hair was pulled back into a knot and she wore no makeup and her clothes, although very neat and well pressed, were not stylish and appeared to be well worn. It was my feeling her life was probably never about her, but serving someone else and always more concerned about them than herself. I could tell from her appearance that this woman's life was driven by hard work. As usual, I was more than happy to have company with my morning coffee and also thrilled to think this woman undoubtedly knew quite a lot about the history of the house.

"Oh please, stay for a while and have coffee with me. I would love to hear about what it was like when you worked here." I took out another cup and saucer, from my archived pantry treasure, which now were cleaned and polished and lived in the kitchen cupboard. I poured her coffee and moved a plate of cookies toward her. She didn't need a lot of convincing and said that it seemed so strange to be inside the house again after so many years and it brought back a lot of memories. She studied the coffee cup and saucer and had a slight smile of familiarity with the china. I asked her if she worked for Mr. and Mrs. Contrelli, and indeed she had. She seemed a bit hesitant and shy at first, but soon became lost in her reminiscence and wanted to share it with me. I was only too happy to listen and could have sat there all day listening to her pour out her heart about those old days.

"I spent many years here. I worked for the lady of the house for several years. It really just gives me a chill sitting in this house, in this kitchen again. It's been many years since I've seen this kitchen, or the inside of the house. Um, the Misses, Mrs. Contrelli had three husbands, you know. I worked for her off and on through all three marriages."

"How fascinating. I have wondered about her. Please, tell me, what was she like?"

"Oh, she was a fine woman, I suppose. She was German, like me. But she was very private and wanted her distance with me and with the other staff. I think as time went on she came to trust me a bit more and became a little more friendly towards me. But she could also be, well, ah, not very pleasant. She was quite haughty and loved to order people around and fired people a lot, and many times when they really did not deserve to be treated so cruelly. She wasn't comfortable having people around, but she needed them. We were all instructed not to be in the same room as her if at all possible. She liked her privacy, and of course the privacy for her husband, Mr. Contrelli. That was her first husband."

"So, you mostly worked for her, not for her husband?"

*The House on Lake Maggiore*

"Mrs. Contrelli, um . . . . of course. Charlotte was her name, but of course we always called her Mrs. 'What-ever' because of all those husbands, as time went on, it was sometimes hard to remember what to call her; well anyway, she ran the house. I hardly ever had to deal with her husbands."

Ingrid had a tendency to speak in a choppy manner, to pause and throw in filler words while she collected her thoughts. I wasn't sure if it was because she had a difficult time with English or maybe the words in her mind were German or Italian and she was translating as she spoke. I found myself almost trying to help her form the words as I waited for her to continue and actually caught myself moving my lips. I had to check myself to be sure I didn't do that and wasn't being rude. As the conversation progressed, I think her pauses occurred because of a lack of confidence probably by conversing with people as their subordinate for so much of her life. It was a sign of modesty. I urged her to continue. "Tell me about them. What did you know about her husbands?"

Ingrid continued. "Well, the first husband, of course, was Mr. Contrelli, who originally owned the home. Ah . . . He built it for his first wife and child who both eventually died. It was sort of like a holiday home for them and he owned another residence in Milan. After his first wife died, he sold the home in Milan and moved here full time. Towards the end of the war he went to Germany and when the war ended, he brought his new German wife back with him. That's when I was hired to work for her. Then after several years, he passed away. He wasn't a well man and quite a bit older than her. I think they were married eight years when he died. He had cancer for a long time. In fact, that was why he was in Germany during the war. He knew a doctor, supposedly who was an exceptional surgeon and he had some sort of cancer surgery. As I said, they were married eight years when he died. It wasn't long after he died that she remarried. His name was Mr. Barrusta. I believe she met him in Monte Carlo. He was a race car driver, and a very handsome young man. She loved to spoil him and fuss over him and he was more her age, so I could certainly see that there was much more passion in that marriage than in the first. After a couple years he also died. He had some sort of boating accident and died on the lake." She paused for a moment and sipped her coffee and nibbled on a cookie, as if she was forming her thoughts. I was hanging on every word and just waited patiently for her to continue.

"She married a third time. His name was Mr. Strausner. This was probably her worst marriage. They argued all the time. This is when she released me. I think she just didn't want help around when there was so much arguing going on. Then she would call me again and if I wasn't employed with another family, I began working for her again, but then in time, she did the same thing and told me not to come every day. She retained me, and paid me full time, but told me to only come when she called me. She needed her privacy I think because she didn't want anyone hearing all the arguments. It was really a very unfortunate marriage, but it ended badly. I think he died during one of their arguments. I think they did get rather physical. I saw bruises on her, and him for that matter, and she just never seemed happy. She would sit and brood and she would stay in her room alone for long periods of time and have me bring her tea there, upstairs."

"So, after he died, what did she do?" I asked.

"She lived here alone and kept me on, but again I only came when she called me. She became very despondent and a bit of a recluse. She didn't have any friends and I'm sure she was running out of money. When she first came to the house with Mr. Contrelli they had many parties, and entertained, but they were his friends and people that lived close by. Those were the best years and life in the house was most active and grand. Oh, the wonderful parties! This room especially, was very active with the staff running in and out with serving trays! This was a very busy place. So after Mr. Contrelli died and she married the second husband, no one came around to visit. There were no more parties. I think she stopped trying to make friends here and just became very private. They lived a quiet life and she sort of withdrew from people. She just wanted to be with him. You see, her first husband was much older than her and this new husband was younger and quite handsome. I think she was so happy with him, but then of course, after he died she was very distraught. Well, all along she had this gentleman friend named Mr. Strausner, who later became her third husband, as I just said. He was always around, even during her first marriage, like at her parties, or sometimes just visiting her. She said she had known him for many years in Germany and they were very good friends. Well, after her second husband died, she married Mr. Strausner and I was shocked because I never suspected there was anything between them other than friendship, but then I felt that maybe this was very good for her, you know, to marry a good friend who seemed to have been very loyal and caring of her."

I was becoming spellbound as if I were a child listening to a fantastic fairy tale. "But she still didn't seem happy in that marriage?" I asked.

"This was when I was only here from time to time. At first she seemed happy, but then I think it was just for appearances sake because they argued so much. Really, it was more than arguing. They shouted at one another. This was when she told me to come only when she called me and I was sure it was because she wanted me out of the way. They were married two years. He died right here in this house by falling over the balcony overlooking the living room. She claimed he was trying to pull the chandelier towards him with a long stick with a hook on it, in order to clean it and lost his balance. Well, now I had a hard time imagining Mr. Strausner cleaning the chandelier, or anything for that matter. It was my guess that she may have pushed him during one of their arguments. The police evidently thought so also and questioned her about it, but I believe in time dismissed it as an accident. So then she was alone again. She brooded a lot and I came every now and then to help her, but she lost interest in keeping the house up. She was always in a dark mood and so sad."

Ingrid took a sip of her coffee and sat pensively for a moment looking around the kitchen. I could tell that when she first began speaking, she was just giving me highlights, but as she began to uncover her memories, she almost couldn't stop herself from letting it all out as if she had these memories locked up in her mind for many years.

"So, he died in the front room here?" I asked with almost a whisper. I was so stunned I could hardly get the words out.

"Yes, it was quite tragic. Of course, I wasn't here when it happened. He smashed through a glass top coffee table that was in front of the fireplace."

"How dreadful! At that time, were other people working for her?" I asked.

"No, she had let them all go. It was pretty obvious to me that she was running out of money. They were a rather odd lot, I have to say. Mr. Contrelli was a very lovely man, but the other two! I didn't know them well, but they were not friendly to the staff at all. We just couldn't get to know them and always wondered about them. Mr. Contrelli always made a point in speaking kindly to us and asking us about our families. But um . . . . Mrs. Contrelli didn't like it that he spoke to us. She said many times that he shouldn't consort with the help. We overheard her scolding him, but he just laughed and ignored her. After all it was his house and he lived here with his first wife for over twenty years and then she died and left him a widower. Charlotte was new here and really had no right to be so haughty, but he didn't stop her. She did as she wanted to and the staff feared her. Some of them worked for the first Mrs. Contrelli and didn't like this new Mrs. Contrelli. It was as if they maintained a sort of loyalty to the first Mrs. Contrelli and resented this new woman. Well then of course, after he was gone, she did as she wished and it was no longer a very friendly place. Some of the staff did their best to avoid her. They feared her because right away she fired those that she knew didn't like her. But, um . . . . in time she let them all go anyway, one by one."

"What kind of staff did she have before she let them go?"

"Well, um . . . let me see. She used to have a cook, and there was a butler, or gentleman's servant for Mr. Contrelli who served him for many years, even when he still had the home in Milan and went back and forth between both homes; the butler accompanied them. Of course, after he died, she let the butler go. But she also had a kitchen staff that worked with the cook, cleaning maids, usually about two or three, who cleaned all the rooms, changed the beds, did laundry and took care of the linens, and kept the silver polished. There were a lot of silver serving pieces and candelabras. That was a full time job, keeping them polished, as well as all the copper pieces that were in the kitchen. And when she had parties, she would hire more servants to wait on her guests. I was the main housekeeper so I was in charge of all the help, keeping them working and busy. And of course she had a crew of gardeners. In time, she let them go too and the garden became overgrown and just a horrible mess. She didn't care much about the garden, although she liked to sit out in the loggia with a glass of wine in the evening and watch the sunset. The first Mr. Contrelli loved to do that also. Well, as the husbands died, her needs changed in the house and she didn't need such a large staff. She lived a more simple life in time and even as time went on, she closed off some of the rooms."

"She sure seemed to have had her share of bad luck with men. So, then what happened to her? Why was the home abandoned? Do you know where she went?"

Ingrid paused for a moment and took another sip of her coffee and slowly placed the cup in the saucer. It seems she was gathering her thoughts to continue and then she leaned closer to the table to add more drama to her response. Her voice became lower and softer and she barely whispered. "Well, um . . . . it appears to me you honestly do not know. She died here also, you know. Right in this house! She hung herself in the attic. In fact, I found her. It was a day I shall never forget. I was devastated."

For the second time in just a matter of minutes, I was truly shocked and almost choked with a gasp. "She hung herself in the attic? How dreadful. That must have been horrible for you to have found her." I realized I must have had a look of disbelief and she repeated the sentence again.

"I will never forget it. It was horrible. It is the worst thing I have experienced in my entire life. You were not aware of this?"

"No, I had no idea," I answered, a bit dumbstruck and actually felt a little weak as though the blood had rushed from my head.

"I don't think I'll ever get over it. Poor Charlotte! It was a rather sad life, you know, don't you think? I've thought that for a long time. Yes, she was not a happy woman. It was like she experimented with her character, or her position here or something. One day she would be haughty, and another day she would be depressed and I would find her lying in her bed so distraught, all folded up like a child. She didn't want to talk or get dressed. She would ask me to bring her some tea or soup, but she was just so depressed. She wanted the bedroom dark and the drapes closed. She was miserable. Sometimes she would sit on the terrace off her bedroom, in a lounge chair, wrapped in a blanket, and just sit like that for hours, smoking cigarettes, and drinking tea or sherry, just staring at the lake. She smoked so much; I was always emptying ash trays. But then she would in time snap out of her depression and again start giving orders to me to do something or other. She couldn't stand to see me idle."

I was dumfounded, reeling from shock and when I tried to speak I found my voice sounded frail with a slight tremor. "I haven't known much about who lived here. It seems that any trace of them is wiped away. You certainly know more about her than anyone. Even the realtor didn't know any of this. I even went to the library in town to see if I could find old newspaper articles to try to find out more. I'm so thankful that you dropped by and told me all this. I'm so entrenched in the work of the house, but I often find myself wondering about the former tenants and sometimes I feel a sort of presence. It's hard to describe, but I am always wondering what the house was like when people lived here, and also, who they were and what they were like."

She sat quietly for a moment listening to me with an insightful smile on her face and I could see she understood what I meant about the presence I felt. "It is such a fantastic house.

*The House on Lake Maggiore*

You should have seen it when I first started working here. It was furnished so beautifully. It's so sad to see it so empty and shabby, but when I sit here I can almost hear the voices that once filled this house. I think it is understandable that you would wonder about who lived here. I almost feel that same presence. It's as if it was the old days and I would hear her yelling for me. 'Ingrid! Ingrid!' She could shout so loud. She might have been on the balcony yelling: 'Ingrid, Ingrid. I need you. Come upstairs.' I wore my legs out going up and down those stairs, so many trips a day and for so many years.

"Well I really poured my heart out, didn't I? Sorry to have done this to you and I hope I haven't upset you too much, but I haven't talked to anyone about this in so long. Just being in this house brings it all back. I walk by here some days and just stop and look at the house and think about those days. I remember this kitchen so well. Back in those first years in the house when Mr. Contrelli was still alive, it was a busy place. I think about the parties at Christmas; this place was a beehive of activity. There were people in here hustling about and preparing trays of hors d'ouvres and cocktails. It was quite a scene, but in time the cook was gone as well as the rest of the staff and I was alone to try to run this place. I was in and out of here, preparing her meals, fetching things for her, getting her afternoon tea, boiling an egg for her breakfast, trying to prepare something for her to eat. I had to manage getting all her meals for her, even though she didn't eat much. She was so helpless, especially in the kitchen. She had no idea how to work the stove. I doubt that she could boil water. She was very spoiled. But she was like a little bird and she got very thin as time went on. She said she had no appetite. Now look at this poor pathetic room, so white and sterile looking. I never realized how much it resembled a hospital with all this white tile and stainless steel counters. In those days there was life here. Life was the color. Now it's like death. I used to sit right here by myself at times, having a cup of tea and just enjoying the view of the garden through these windows. Now look at that yard. It's so over grown, it looks like a jungle. So many years passed by. It's a bit scary, isn't it, how time can get away from you? It really is sad. So many years have passed." She sat and reflected for a moment more and we both looked about the room and probably each in our own mind tried to visualize what it was like with cooks working diligently, and maids wearing black and white uniforms carrying silver trays in and out of the kitchen to serve Charlotte's guests.

"Oh my dear, look at the time. I have to go and I'm afraid I've taken up too much of your time. It was nice to be inside the house again, and reminisce like this. It brought back so many memories, some good, some bad. Some of the staff were good friends, you know. We spent years together, and this kitchen was our place to congregate. Those people made my time here a good experience. When time passed and the staff dwindled down, I missed them very much. It was a very big part of my life, you know and they were like family. So many years in this house! Well, it was lovely to meet you and thank you so much for letting me go on like this."

"It was my pleasure, Ingrid. Please come back any time, but before you go, I want to show you something." I walked over to the cupboard and showed her the secret opening to the pantry that we found. She said she recalled when Charlotte had that made. There was a door there at one time and also one leading to the hallway, in fact right where the hole that I made breaking through the wall. She used to go into the pantry all the time to put linens away and to get things from there to set the table in the dining room. She remembered when Charlotte made the changes to the room and bricked up the windows and covered over the door to the hallway so there would be more wall space in the pantry for cabinets. She said she wanted more storage space in the pantry and there was no need for that second door. She had the work done up to that point, but the new cabinets were never put into the pantry. She agreed, maybe it was better to access the room from the kitchen in order to put things away, such as the china after it had been washed. It made it more difficult to take them through the kitchen to the dining room when she had to set the table because she had a longer walk. The other door leading to the hallway was closer to the dining room. Charlotte said the windows just let too much sun in and it faded the linens and laundry, which in the early days, was also done in that room. She confirmed our thinking that the cupboard with the secret latch in place of a door was to provide more shelf space in the kitchen. After that, they built a new laundry area in the small hallway at the back of the kitchen. She wanted the laundry to be taken care of in that hallway, so the servants could access it from the service stairway at the back of that area. That way it got the maids out of the center of the house and the whole business of the laundry could happen away from her sight. They would take it out that door and hang it outside in the side yard in the summer to dry. Ingrid believed it did make more sense and it also gave them more room, because that little pantry was too small to fold those large table clothes and linens.

I told Ingrid that I think by having that cupboard put in place of the door, the new tenants never knew there was a pantry there and the room had been shut off for years. She thought that was amusing but could see how that could happen. She thanked me again for letting her go on as long as she did and for the coffee. She seemed a bit emotional and all the things she talked about were nostalgic memories for her. I think she was overcome with too much sentiment and became anxious to leave even though I told her to go ahead and look at the rest of the house if she wished. I thanked her for coming and again invited her to come back soon so we could talk some more, and also to see how the work was progressing. She thanked me and said she enjoyed our talk and would love to come again. She said she lived in a small apartment not far from the house and invited me to come and have coffee with her one day.

Just when I thought about bringing out the photos to hopefully have Ingrid identify Charlotte, she said she had to rush off. So I thought I would save that part of the conversation for the next time, even though I was anxious to put faces to the names.

For the remainder of the day I could think of nothing else except the people Ingrid spoke of and the sadness that had taken place in the house. I decided the actual legacy was justly reflected by the sad disposition of the house aesthetics. My curiosity was whetted and I had to know more. Now that I knew the stories of the lives in the house and that now had names, I went to the village library again the next morning and searched the archived newspaper articles on microfilm for any news I could find about the people of the house. I found the death notices for all three husbands. Mr. Contrelli died from a long time illness, which I know now was cancer. Her second husband died in an apparent boating accident and drowned, and the third husband's death was ruled an accident that happened in his home. There was also a very small obituary of Charlotte's death, and by that time her name was Mrs. Strausner, so had I not talked to Ingrid, I wouldn't have known about her name change and would never have found the obituary, which in itself was succinct and did not mention the cause of death.

By the time I got back to the house after my morning in the library, the workmen were already busy. There was a good sized crew and work was happening in many parts of the house, which pleased me and was also unusual. I heard men speaking Italian to one another, the pounding of tools and saws whining and it made me feel good to see so much work going on. After finding Vito in the kitchen talking to one of the plumbers we sat down to talk about the plans for the kitchen. The designer I met with earlier that week was drawing up plans and would be delivering ideas for a proposed redesign. I wanted to be sure Vito was available to review the plans with me and help decide what would be best.

The entire concept of employing professional cooks may have gone by the wayside and it was a different era. Maybe the new owners of the house would be using the kitchen themselves and maybe it needed to be more "family friendly," than was the previous design. It needed to be brought into the current fashion where kitchens were designed to be well used with new technology as well as entertaining guests. The Italians were ahead of the game with kitchen technology and I looked forward to the designer's expert input. There might be a possibility that so much space might be wasted for a new style kitchen that wouldn't be overrun with chefs and servers. Maybe we would want to use some of the space for another room, like an office or a cozier sort of family or media room. We agreed it would be important to nail down the design as soon as possible in case we needed to do any plumbing work, rewiring or moving walls. We decided to hold off on any demolition for the time being and focus on plumbing problems that needed to be fixed, rather than any new plumbing arrangements.

After Ingrid's visit and hearing everything she had to say about Charlotte and my research at the library, I felt a strange force pulling me towards the attic. I hadn't been up there yet and was now a bit hesitant about it, but decided that with so many workmen in the house and it being daylight, it would be safe to venture up there. I wasn't sure of the rodent situation in the cellar or attic and had someone scheduled for the next week to look into that. The fact that the house was not lived in for so long assured me that there was more than likely a serious rodent problem.

I went upstairs to the second floor and stopped to talk to two of the plasterers who were trying to decide the best way to repair a large crack near a doorway. We also talked about the work that needed to be done on the ceiling where there were also cracks, but we had to be sure not to destroy too much of the ceiling because of the frescos. I made a note that I needed to get an artist in who could work on any of the frescos that needed repair. I didn't dare walk anywhere in the house without my notebook because small reminders of work to be done were always popping into my head. There seemed no end to the things that needed attention. Finally after all the discussion with the workmen, I headed down to the end of the hall towards the stained glass window. The hallway continued to the left toward the additional bedrooms that were over the kitchen, dining room and library on the first floor. I thought that some of the smaller bedrooms were intended to be maid's quarters and were far enough away from the main bedroom at the front of the house near the main staircase, in order that any resident servant could not be seen as they would be using the back service stairs. The rooms were small enough that I thought they were either servant's quarters or just storage rooms. Maybe we would have to knock out some walls and rearrange those rooms to make them larger and more suitable for guest bedrooms. The larger of the other bedrooms must have been for the little daughter that had died and perhaps the small adjoining room was for her nanny.

The little doorway to the right of the stained glass window off the main hallway led to the service stairs that Ingrid talked about leading to the back hallway behind the kitchen where the maids did the laundry and the stairs going up led to the attic. I climbed the stairs very slowly and after entering the stuffy attic, just stood for a moment before moving forward.

There were a few pieces of very old furniture and some boxes, which I would have to go through. I moved with great trepidation for fear of seeing spiders, mice or even bats. I thought I should probably have brought someone up there with me, just in case something jumped out at me. I looked around and saw several dormer windows facing out to the front of the house and the lake. The view was quite lovely from this third floor of the house. I tried to visualize what Charlotte's last moments must have been like for her to die in such a way. I was certain that the untimely deaths happening in this house was the reason the house sat vacant and people feared that it may have appeared to have had a curse. Adam was right when he said that no one could live in this house with the ghosts that remained. I walked towards the dormer windows, which were covered in cobwebs and looked up. The ceiling of the attic was quite high, and had open rafters. I looked at one rafter in particular, closest to the window and thought that might be the one where she tied the rope and the thought sent shivers up my spine.

This woman, Charlotte, who I believed lived a fairy tale life, marrying a wealthy Italian who brought her into this house, and gave her a life of riches, had her fair share of grief and I felt sorry for her. How sad to think that with everything she had, it didn't seem to bring her happiness and she ended her life so horribly, and so young. From what Irene and Ingrid said, she was quite young and at the time of her death, only in her late thirties. Having stood there and thinking about her last moments, I was even more obsessed with thoughts about her, as if I were grieving for her and her unfortunate demise. Even though she lived in this beautiful house, she was not a happy person and had many unhappy years here.

After that day there were other days that I went into the attic and sat for long periods of time just to be alone with my thoughts, probably sitting on the very chair that she used when she stepped onto it and placed the rope around her neck. I could look out onto the lake from that nearest window in the attic and believe Charlotte must have looked at the lake the very moment she kicked the chair out from under her. From this window there is a wonderful view of the Isola Bella and the Borromeo palace. I felt so sorry for her sad life and thought that I might be accompanying a part of her soul that might remain somewhere suspended in the rafters, with nowhere to go, but wanting to always mark that place where Charlotte ended her life.

I looked out the window across the lake and studied the view. I wondered what made Charlotte so despondent to have taken her own life. While I could see there was much sadness in her life, losing three husbands, I wondered what drove her in that final moment to make her so unable to continue. In my thinking, no matter what demons pushed at me, if I sat there and looked at that beautiful lake and the wondrous palace on Isola Bella, wouldn't that have given me what I would need to stay alive and realize that life can be beautiful and always well worth living? What could have been so horrible that she saw no reason to go on? Perhaps it was the end of the road for her money and she had run out of options.

On one of my days in the attic, I began going through boxes, most of which were filled with old books, and old Christmas decorations. I would eventually bring the books into the library after cleaning them up. There wasn't anything else in the attic really worth saving, let alone a few pieces of furniture, some old picture frames, and well-travelled suitcases. I would have to decide what to save and what to discard.

I looked down through the attic window at the sidewalk in front of the house and saw an elderly gentleman standing there, looking at the house. I became curious about him, but dismissed it as just another interested person passing by. However a few days later I spotted the same man there again. This time I decided to go talk to him to see what his interest was about the house, but by the time I got to the front door, he was gone.

One morning as I arrived at the house the same gentleman was again standing outside looking through the gates. I approached him and asked if he was familiar with the house. He said he knew the house had been vacant for many years and was curious about the recent activity. His name was Felix Von Streiner and he said he once knew a man named Mr. Strausner who he believed once lived at the house. I introduced myself and went through what had now become my regular soliloquy defining my efforts at the house. I told him that yes, I just discovered Mr. Strausner had lived in this house and also died here. He was the third husband of the lady of the house named Charlotte. He died of an accidental fall. Mr. Von Streiner seemed like a pleasant man so I invited him in for a cup of coffee. I gave him a quick tour of the main floor of the house on the way to the kitchen, pointing out some of the changes we planned for certain areas. We sat down in the kitchen and talked over coffee and cookies. He said he knew Mr. Strausner just casually while in the army together in Germany, but had seen a small article many years ago in the newspaper that said he lived at this address. The article wasn't about him although it named him as being one of many in attendance at some sort of social event. He wanted to call upon the home many times over the years, but saw that it was vacant and now that he saw some activity he thought he would inquire as to any knowledge of Mr. Strausner and if indeed

*The House on Lake Maggiore*

this was the same man he once knew. He didn't say much more than that.

I told him that Ingrid, the former housekeeper had been by to see me and knew quite a lot about the original tenants, including Mr. Strausner. I suggested that maybe he would like to talk to her. I was also curious to know what he knew about this man named Mr. Strausner. I asked him where I could reach him and said I would try to arrange for him to meet Ingrid. I invited him to drop by whenever he wished, which seemed to please him. He wrote his name and number down on a pad of paper I had on the kitchen table. After a friendly exchange of conversation he said he would love to return again to see the progress. He was very interested to see the fruition of the work I described that was part of my plan for the renovation.

I made a note about him knowing Mr. Strausner. I was beginning to collect my notes from things I was hearing from people, to help me figure out more about the former tenants of the home only because my own curiosity was getting the best of me. Now that I knew more about the people that lived in the house, I became obsessed with the enigma of those lost souls and wanted to know more. Charlotte's persona taunted my curiosity the most, maybe because I thought she was the most pathetic. Who was Charlotte Contrelli? Where did she come from? How were these people involved in her life and why such interest and attachment to her memory? What power did she have over so many that all these decades later, they can't stop wondering about her? I spent many hours being entertained with my imagination about who they were and what they were like as I wandered through the house visualizing them living there and I felt as if I moved with their spirits.

Driven by this increasing curiosity, I continued my trips to the local library to find anything that was written about them, or the house. As I dug deeper I found more stories that casually mentioned society functions that Charlotte and her husband attended or parties they hosted. I found an announcement that Mr. Contrelli won a boating regalia on the lake in 1948. I then found an obituary for "longtime resident, Mr. Pietro Contrelli died of cancer" in 1953. I also found an announcement that "Charlotte Contrelli, wife of the late Pietro Contrelli, married well known race car driver, Vincinzo Brusta" in the same year. I agreed with Ingrid that it was interesting that she didn't mourn the loss of her first husband very long before remarrying. Then I found an obituary for Vincinzo Brusta who died in 1956 in a boating accident. She was then the widow Charlotte Brusta. I found nothing further about Charlotte Brusta in further searches. Perhaps she had become less important after Mr. Contrelli's death and as time went on, the memory of her became less important and was not worth mentioning in the society columns.

# CHAPTER 7

The service hallway behind the kitchen was a perfect place to set up a workshop for all the hardware repair work and I soon got busy cleaning and polishing old light fixtures, doorknobs, hinges and other hardware. The workmen and I created a production process to try to streamline the work. They brought the fixtures down to me as soon as they were removed and I repaired them if I could or labeled them for repair by a workman, then cleaned them and finally marked what area of the house they came from so that once the room was painted, they would be returned and reinstalled. With eight bedrooms, lengthy hallways with a multitude of lights and sconces, electrical outlets, air ducts, and light switches, this was a very big undertaking. I set up a long table made up of an old door to put all the repaired fixtures, along with their identifying tags.

While I worked in that service hallway, my mind ran away with me, thinking about how the maids would be coming and going up and down the stairs in the back hallway, working on the laundry in this room and taking it outside to hang and dry. This room was, in all probability, where they entered and exited the home. Then I thought about the gentleman's butler, probably spending time there polishing shoes for Mr. Contrelli, or the gardener coming and going through this entrance to the yard, maybe repotting plants or the cooks bringing in groceries to stock the pantry and enter the kitchen to begin their work. I imagined them jabbering together and felt that this quiet space was once a heart of the house for them and it was the people and their activities working in this space that kept the house thriving. I began putting an entire scenario together in my mind, thinking about everything that went on in that area, the only place the servants were probably sure they were safely removed from the people they served and could speak freely amongst themselves.

The pace of our work began to pick up and being busy working with the contractor and other workers, shopping for art, selecting wall paper and furnishings, left me little time to be idle, but when I was I found my thoughts always going back to Charlotte and imagining what was going on in this house over sixty years ago. At the end of the day, when the workers had all left, the house became quiet and I resumed my thoughts about Charlotte. I would sometimes pour myself a glass of wine and just walk through the house imagining whispers coming from within the walls or floating through the room telling me about the house and about her. My imagination ran wild as I stood in vacant rooms, thinking about people from the past walking through, perhaps hesitating at a table to pick up a book, or to stand by the window looking out at the lake, having a pensive moment. I studied the space on the living room floor where Mr. Strausner must have died after falling over the railing. I studied the railing and saw no telltale signs of repairs. While standing there I imagined Charlotte's voice echoing through the house calling for Ingrid from the balcony. I would wander back up into the attic and think about Charlotte hanging from the rafters. These characters became real and I felt as if I were intruding on their privacy.

I became more obsessed with the thoughts of the ancient souls, which generated more puzzling questions and it all began to nag at me until my curiosity got the best of me and I realized I was spending too much time thinking about things that didn't matter and I was too distracted. What difference did all of it make to my current situation and trying to renovate this house? New people would walk through these newly remodeled rooms making new history and I was here, working for them, whoever they might be.

Then one day I realized that I felt uneasy and uncomfortable living with the ghosts of the house. I had forgotten my life, my ghosts, and my history and maybe it was resentment I was feeling. Everything that was mine and part of my life was so lost in the past and my feeling of emptiness and desolation became apparent. I found myself thinking about John, my husband, and missed him more than ever. How I wished he was there experiencing all of this with me. My daughter and I communicated by phone and email often, but I seemed cut off from everyone else. I spoke to business partners and checked in on how things were going with them handling my clients, and everything seemed fine. No one seemed to need me at home. I began to compare my life to Charlotte's and wondered if anyone would ever seek out my history, try to find out who I was and what I was about. I started to ask myself if I was hopelessly lost and did I lose myself in the life of another woman I never knew or would never know? She was of no consequence to me. Where would my ghosts be found one day? I supposed my ambition and fruition of my dream to renovate this wonderful house would somehow put me on some small map in the field of interior decorating and create some sort of accomplishment noted by a published article. That was the most I could envision for myself and my career. But I felt like some days I was paying heavily for the experience and to make this minute remuneration happen. Those few times when I had time to think and realize how alone I was, created anxiety and a feeling that I wanted to wrap this up and go back to my life in California. Maybe I feared those unknown ghosts that lived within the walls of this house may not have been worth the time I spent thinking about them and maybe I should go renew acquaintances with my friends who were very much alive.

I was homesick and I missed my little mountain cabin and the serenity it gave me. I missed the beautiful silver squirrels that came to my deck for the peanuts they knew I had for them, and the blue jays waiting in the trees for me to open the squeaky door to the deck and also throw them a handful of the nuts. I missed living in the treetops and the smell of cedar and pine. But there wasn't much else to miss. I had created a life of solitude and peace, but in doing so had shut the world out. The loneliness I felt after my husband's death was a very long adjustment, but somehow the mountain cabin gave me the peacefulness I needed. It was a place he had never been, so there were no reminders of him and being there helped to relieve my grief. Most of the time being there, I felt I truly loved it, but I found at times it was too much solitude, too much me and then I had to escape and go back to my condo in Los Angeles and again surround myself with people, friends, clients, sometimes just people I didn't know. No, I was quite certain, no one was looking for my ghosts, or missing me, or thinking about me in wistful moments.

Whenever I had thoughts of loneliness like that, I remedied it by throwing myself back into my work. This never solved the problem, but instead helped me avert it. I had devoted no time at all to trying to get into a better social life, or joining in functions where I might meet new people. Maybe in my mind, I really preferred the loneliness and solitude, or maybe if truth be known, I might have preferred being alone or had gotten used to it without realizing it. Or perhaps the remedy made me work harder and in essence, more productive, so the remedy was really the benefit, or my nemesis.

In those empty times since John's death, I found myself still speaking to him in my mind. I believed I would never find love again and didn't make any attempts to change that. I loved my memories of him and our life, but our happiness ended all too soon. I missed him terribly and had not come to terms with how my life would change with him gone. I couldn't understand how Charlotte could remarry so soon after her husband's death and move on so quickly. I tried to solve my grieving by becoming entrenched in my work and just took one day at a time, never really making plans or thinking about the future. I just continued my life day by day. But now, living alone in a foreign country, being alone so much of the time, or being with people that were all new to me and wondering about a woman who once lived, made me think that one day this would end and I would return to that life in California where I made every excuse to avoid the circumstance of my existence and I asked myself if I wanted to continue as it was. Was I ready to open my life up to others and let someone else in? There just had to be more for me than the life I was living back there. Perhaps this endeavor was an attempt to escape the reality of my exanimate existence, but how foolish I was to compare my life to Charlotte's and maybe I over embellished what I thought was her life.

The steady queue of visitors continued and I would find people surreptitiously peering at me from behind secret places, waiting to come forward and ask what I was doing, and their coming forth became a regular occurrence. It no longer was a curious situation when another would appear at the front door. I began to realize the house, or perhaps I should say its former inhabitants, left something behind that everyone wanted to explore, perhaps some charismatic magnetism or maybe something more degenerative, but it seemed to have left everyone wanting more, or at least to know more. Somehow their lives were affected by these people, but I was sure all the interest was because of Charlotte. What was it about this woman that left people never wanting to let go of her memory?

One morning I was sitting in the kitchen looking at wall paper samples when Vito came in to tell me a gentleman was at the door and wished to speak to me. I went out to the entrance hall and met with him. He was an elderly, sort of quiet and understated looking man. When he saw me approach, he removed his hat and twisted it nervously in his hands.

"Good Morning, Madam. My name is Frederick Von Barren," he said with a German accent. Please forgive the intrusion. I am trying to find something out about the former tenants of this home. I know the house sat vacant for many years and now that I've seen people here, I wonder if you or anyone here knows anything about the people that lived here many years ago. I'm talking about after the war. I realize it was a very long time ago, but do you know anything about them?"

"Well, in fact I do know a little because a former housekeeper came by and told me about the people that once lived here that employed her," I answered.

"Well anything you can tell me, I would appreciate hearing. My brother-in-law spent time here briefly after the war, and then he disappeared. I've always tried to find out what happened to him."

"I'd be happy to tell you the little I do know. I'm renovating the home and it's quite a mess now, but please, come in. I've also been trying to find out about the former tenants, so maybe you know something I don't know." I invited him in for a cup of tea. By now I realized that not everyone appreciated my American coffee, but rather their Italian Café or Austrian coffee, which I was not quite used to yet, so tea became the safest offering.

I realized again that this person was one more person with a link to the former tenants and maybe able to shed a little light on the secrets within this house and I could not pass up the opportunity of hearing what he had to say. I led the way to the kitchen all the while pointing out things about the house and what we were doing to it. He was very interested in the details and commented about what a wonderful house this must have been at one time. It further seemed to set his curiosity afire as to what his brother-in-law was doing here, in such a grand house. Finally we sat down at the table in the breakfast nook. I put the cups on the table and the fresh pot of tea I had just made. He had a reserved and quiet nature and I could see it was hard for him to feel comfortable in telling me of his interest in the house.

"So, Mr. Von Barren, tell me about your brother-in-law."

"Well, my wife Caroline, now deceased, had once received a letter with a return address of this house, from her brother. It was many years ago, right after the war. It was the last time she heard anything from him and always wanted to find out why her brother had written her a letter with a return address of this house. He said he was staying here briefly with friends and was headed for Rome. She was not to contract him at this address because he was not returning. He said he was just staying for a few days with friends here before departing for Rome and he would contact her later to give her an address where she could write to him. Then she received a letter from a friend of his, a Dr. Van Hoaf saying that her brother had died in an automobile accident while on his way to Rome. She never heard any more and didn't know where he was buried or what happened to him. She wrote a letter one time, addressed to 'the occupants' but never received a reply. Any trace of him was just wiped off the face of the earth—very strange. She mourned him for a very long time and it was distressing for her not to know what happened to him. She even talked about it on her death bed and said I had to try to find out what happened to her brother and she wanted to be sure he got a proper burial. Do you have any knowledge of the people that lived here, Ms. Marshall?"

I had no idea how I could help Mr. Von Barren, but I was sympathetic to him and wished I could help in some way. He began to tell me more about his wife's brother, Carl.

"He was a very bright, but also an alarmingly intense person. He was always very serious and seemed to be intellectually superior, or at least gave that impression that he thought he was. Perhaps he really was, I don't know. I never got to know him, but when I think about it, you never can get to know people like that because they seem to always have their guard up and a wall around them. He made me uncomfortable and I didn't really care for him, but he was my wife's brother and I had to accept him and be gracious to him whenever we were with him, which wasn't that often. He had a busy life.

"He and my sister went down much different paths in their life and became estranged. Long periods of time would pass before she would hear from him, but she always feared for his safety. We were certain he had died sometime during the war because we heard nothing of him. But then one day, came the letter saying he was on the way to Rome and would contact her later. By then the war had ended and it was late in 1945. Then not long after that, out of the blue came a letter from his friend about the automobile accident. He had stayed here at this house for a while when the war ended, hiding out, we assumed. You see, he was an SS officer in the war and we believed he was trying to escape being arrested. We don't know what he did in the war, and he was very secretive about his life. I think we didn't want to know, but we could only assume he was on the run. Then, well then, he died. We never heard any more. We didn't know what happened to his body, if he was buried somewhere, or who took responsibility for his remains. It just ended and my wife to her dying day could not get over the mysterious end of her brother's life. She always thought about what life would have been like for her family had he chosen a different life and had stayed in touch with them. Her parents went to their grave in utter sadness always wondering where their son was. It was as if he was too good for us and for his parents and had turned his back on them, and on my wife.

"This is why I am here now. My wife and I came once before when people were renting this home about twelve years ago. It was the only connection we had to him. They said they hadn't been in the house long and didn't intend to stay and knew nothing of the house history. When I heard that this house was finally being renovated after sitting here for so many years, unoccupied, I had to know if there was anything here, any trace of Carl to explain what really happened to him, and why he would have come here. Of course, we know the SS were hunted after the war and had to try to hide or blend in somewhere and escape the wrath of the Allies. But why here and who were these people that took him in and sheltered him and why did they do so? I will probably never know. I am sorry to lay all this on you. You are here doing your work and this is not your business, but all I was hoping for is some little crumb, some little speck of information to try to put my mind at rest. I promised my wife I would try to find out what really happened to Carl."

"Oh please, Mr. Von Barren, you are not bothering me at all; in fact quite the opposite. All I know is a Mr. Contrelli owned the

*The House on Lake Maggiore*

home and built it for his first wife. After she died, he met another woman while in Germany during the war and brought her here to live. In fact, just the other day, the former housekeeper came by. She was also curious about what was happening to the house. I can't imagine what the Contrellis were like, but for some reason, they made a lasting impression on a few people that this many years later, they are not forgotten and it's as if I have awaken some sort of sleeping ghost inside the house and aroused the curiosity of many people that had probably been put in the back of their minds years ago. I really think you should meet her—the former housekeeper. Maybe she remembers something and can help you. How long will you be in town? Maybe I can arrange a meeting with the two of you, here at the house. Why don't we have a nice dinner here, all together and talk about it?"

"Oh, I couldn't expect you to do that. I wouldn't want you to put yourself out. I don't mean to cause any trouble and I know you are busy with your work here. But I would like to talk to her. Maybe she remembers people that visited here and maybe she can recall Carl. I think I have photographs of him I can show her."

"It will be interesting to have you two meet and talk. She told me quite a lot when she stopped by the other day and really made me very curious to hear more. I think I know where she lives. I'll see if she can come tomorrow night. Would that work for you? I'll make dinner right here and we can have all evening to talk. Would that be all right?"

"Oh yes, that would be so nice of you. Thank you so much."

Before he left, Mr. Von Barren wrote the phone number of his hotel down for me. I said I would call him at his hotel if Ingrid could make it and confirm the time. I was very curious myself to see if she would have any recollection of the visitors that came through this house, but it was so many years ago, I couldn't really expect her to remember those details. I hadn't mentioned the photos I found, but I would be sure to bring them out to see if they could identify some of the people in the photos and who knows, maybe he will recognize his brother-in-law Carl in one of them. After all, Adam saw there were SS officers in the photos.

Luckily, I was able to get in touch with Ingrid and she was available to come for dinner that next evening. I tried to call Felix, but I couldn't get hold of him. Seeing as he knew Gerheardt Strausner, I thought it would be interesting to have him meet Ingrid also and exchange information. It would have made the group complete.

I planned the dinner in the kitchen at my little nook office. It was a simple chicken and pasta dish with a salad and cake for dessert. The old fashioned cooker was nothing like I had ever used before, but I was able to forge ahead through the process and got a pretty satisfactory dinner prepared. I saved myself the grief of trying to figure out how to get the oven working and just bought the cake at the local bakery. I had to have the linens I found in the pantry laundered and was surprised when I picked them up that they hadn't fallen apart, given the age. I knew that whenever they were purchased they were of the best quality. I used them on the table in the kitchen to camouflage the worn wood. I used the old vintage tableware and china I found in the pantry, polished the candlestick holders, put some white candles in them and made a centerpiece from flowers from the yard of pink roses, camellias and lots of greenery. Actually, when it became dark outside and the sterility of the rest of the kitchen became lost in the shadows, the setting within the kitchen nook of the bayed windows was quite elegant and comfortable. Frederick brought a lovely bottle of Swiss white wine, which went well with the meal.

Ingrid and Frederick arrived within moments of one another and after I introduced them, they immediately began talking about their individual reasons for dropping by the house. Immediately Frederick was interested to know if Ingrid recalled any visitors named Carl. She said she could not recall anyone by that name. He brought a photo with him and we all looked at it carefully with the magnifying glass. Still Ingrid could not recognize the photo as anyone she recalled visiting the house. I

*The House on Lake Maggiore*

brought out the small collection of photos I found in the pantry and showed them to Ingrid and Frederick. I showed him one photo that surprisingly, if we made out the handwriting well enough, it might have had the name Carl on the reverse side. He looked closely at the photo and thought it might be Carl, but couldn't be certain. Ingrid didn't recognize anyone in any of the photos except for Gerheardt Strausner, and then she wasn't certain it was him, but she thought the small face in the photo resembled Charlotte's third husband, Gerheardt. She believed the photo with the name of Carl written on the reverse side was taken in Germany before either Charlotte or Gerheardt came to the house, seeing as the soldiers still had on German uniforms. It was an interesting possibility to think then, that this stash of photos may have belonged to Gerheardt Strausner and not Charlotte. Seeing as he did live in the house, after a while as her third husband, it was possible that he put things in that pantry. I also showed them the revolver I found and pointed out the initials on the butt of the handle were clearly "CD." Frederick thought it might have belonged to Carl; his full name was Carl Drummond so the initials "CD" would have been right. Then that begged the question of why was his gun in the pantry and if that was Carl in the photo, indeed Gerheardt and Carl did know one another during the war. We speculated then about how they became acquainted with Charlotte. We all talked about the relationships and wondered about what they may have meant to one another.

While eating dinner, Frederick began to tell us about Carl. "When he was young he left the family and became a Hitler Youth. Even at a very early age, he was quite fired up about the Reich and enamored with Hitler. That became the beginning of his life further apart from Caroline and the rest of the family. Caroline was younger than Carl, but she had memories of him before that time, when he was still living at home and she always admired him. She had very early memories of them and how much they enjoyed Christmas. Carl always wanted to decorate the tree and make the house festive. She believed the Christmas holidays were always more fun when they were children. But after he left, he never came back home for Christmas or any other holidays. As time went on and he became older he became an SS officer, which was the natural migration from the Hitler Youth, as long as a person met the specific criteria. People like that were superior, of course, in the eyes of the old Germany.

"There were many restrictions on his life and that is why we saw so little of him. I don't know if you know much about this, but it was part of the horrors of that war, I'm afraid. The SS was a unit of German men of Nordic type, selected according to particular characteristics. SS men who planned to marry had to obtain an authorization of matrimony. Selective breeding was strongly emphasized to maintain 'good blood.'" As Mr. Von Barren continued to talk, we were fascinated by what he was saying. He kept asking if he was boring us or if we didn't want to know all this. I wasn't sure how Ingrid felt about it, seeing as she too was German, but she encouraged him to continue.

"He got quite caught up in all that at an early age and was devoted to the country and to Hitler and all that Germanization stuff. You know, in the middle and late thirties, Germany was a different place." He paused for a moment and said, "Who knew, right? Well, he had all the credentials to be an SS officer and it was his dream to be accepted as that. He believed he was wholly Aryan, true and true and of course he had to validate that fact. That meant he had to account for his lineage for many decades, which the family was able to do. They were very proud of his achievements and helped him get all his information together. Once he got his status, he had little to do with us because his work took him away. Where? I cannot tell you because we just didn't know. My wife barely heard from him, but she was always concerned, especially when the war began to escalate. Well, over the years, we heard less and less from him." He stopped for a moment and picked up his cup and took a sip of tea. "I'm sure you know about this, Ingrid, but do you know much about these people, Ms. Marshall, I mean the Nazis and the SS?"

"No, I don't know, and I really know very little about the specifics of the hierarchy of the German military during the war. All I know is what I heard: that the SS were . . . well, the worst of the lot, so to speak." I answered. I trod carefully with what I was saying because I was at that point out of my element and speaking with a man and woman of German descent. I didn't know where they stood in their feelings about the war and it was a delicate subject.

He continued. "Yes, well it was a horribly shameful time in history and we are not proud to speak about it, but it was what it was. We cannot change history now. The SS were very special, of course in Hitler's eyes, but on the most part, were the most evil part of the war. They were branded, as the perfect Aryan. Did you know they were tattooed under their left armpit with their blood group, to mark them as being 'that special?' Anyway, so much time had passed and the war intensified and he just became lost to his family. My wife's parents died in Dresden when that city was totally set ablaze. When the war was finally over, my wife thought he might come home, but of course, he didn't. She never heard from him again, until his short letter, and then she received the letter reporting his death."

We discussed this for quite some time and then Ingrid and Frederick began talking about their own lives and soon the conversation began to take a nice turn, becoming more about present day events. All the while we kept pouring the wine and we all got a bit giddy and silly and I thought I could see a bit of a connection between Frederick and Ingrid. When the evening ended, Frederick offered to walk Ingrid home and they left together. I think they got along quite well and in my mind believed that maybe there were two people that might need one another and who knows, maybe a lasting friendship ensued. I wanted to think that was so.

After they left, I looked again at the photo of Carl with the magnifying glass. It was apparent by his uniform that he was an SS officer. If indeed this was Carl, the brother-in-law to Frederick, I too began to wonder what his connection was to the house. The letter Frederick's wife received informing her of Carl's death, was written either at the end of 1945 or the beginning of 1946. So, apparently, for some reason or another, the Contrellis entertained Nazis.

Among the photos in my little collection was one with handwriting on the back that read "Monte Carlo, 1955." This was not the same handwriting as was on the photo of Carl's, but it could have been Gerheardt's handwriting, or for that matter, Vincinzo's, the race car driver and husband number two. Ingrid identified a picture that was dated June 10, 1955, with what she thought may have been Charlotte and Viincinzo Brusta and for sure, Gerheardt. The photo was taken from a distance and it was difficult to see the faces, but she thought for sure one of them was Gerheardt. I studied that photo through the magnifying glass for a quite some time, just trying to see their faces, but they were too distant and the old photographs were too grainy.

There were also many pictures of several children in a group shot and one in particular, a young boy with blond hair. I couldn't wait to see Adam's childhood photos he was bringing on his next visit to see if we could identify him in any of the photos I had.

I sat for a while looking at the photos after they left and I suddenly realized that the silence and darkness of the house was a bit too eerie. I hadn't spent time in the house after dark before. There I was looking at photos of people, long dead and I began to hear noises, and my imagination began to play tricks on me. I knew it was probably the shrubbery and bushes outside brushing up against windows, or tree limbs resting on an outside wall. I thought about the various deaths that happened in the house and it was a bit too unnerving to be there. A chill ran through me and I decided I had to leave immediately. I hadn't thought about how I would feel being alone in the house after dark and should have left with Ingrid and Frederick. The kitchen wasn't cleaned and the table hadn't been cleared, but I decided to leave the cleaning up for morning and head back to the hotel as quickly as I could. The house was just a bit too frightening at night and even when I closed the big door behind me and locked the foreboding darkness inside, it was still a bit creepy walking through the yard. It was such a dark night with no moon and with every quiver of the bushes from the night breeze, I became agitated and didn't feel safe until I reached the sidewalk and stood beneath the streetlight. While I was under the safeness of the illuminated walkway, I turned and looked at the house, sitting there, dark and wretched, looking like some gigantic imposing monster that lives nocturnally. I picked up my pace and hurried back to the hotel and even when I got into my room, I still felt upset and wished I was not alone.

# CHAPTER 8

The matter of the dilapidated coach house beyond the yard had to be taken care of. Bjorn wanted to be a part of that project and for some reason had taken interest in that structure. He said he would collaborate with Vito about what to do with it. I was afraid to go near it, knowing full well it was probably infested with rats and it was far from being a safe structure. As I said before, the roof had caved in and it appeared that may have been the state of the building for well over a decade. After Bjorn arrived he and Vito went to the back of the yard to the building with the workmen to try and figure out how to handle the job of tearing it down and rebuilding it and determining a design for the structure that would sit in its place. Our plans intended to make it into a garage, which is what it was used for many years ago. They carefully handpicked their way through some of the rubble for quite some time and were out there the greater part of a day. At the end of the afternoon they decided to schedule the demolition to begin soon and Vito was to come up with a design and drawings for the new structure.

The day the demolition began, Bjorn kept it moving rather slowly because he wanted to have a careful look at the interior before it was completely bulldozed into a pile of rubble. He came back into the kitchen and told me that he believed there may have been an apartment in the loft of the building and it appeared there were some remnants left as evidence that at one time, someone lived there. We guessed it may have been intended for one of the house staff, such as a butler who worked for Mr. Contrelli, and then perhaps in later years when the house was abandoned, it became home to a vagrant. I found it interesting because Ingrid would have known if any of the servants lived there, but she didn't mention anything about anyone of the staff living on the premises. There were the smaller bedrooms upstairs in the house that I thought were maid's quarters and maybe in the early days of the house, the first Mrs. Contrelli had staff living in the house, like a nanny to take care of the small child, but that was not the case when Charlotte lived in the house. Ingrid clearly stated that Charlotte did not want staff near her and directed them to not be in the same room as she or her husband. I don't think she would have been comfortable having any of them live under her roof, with the possible exception of the carriage house. I made a note to ask Ingrid more about this. However, for now, the work began to bulldoze the building and rebuild it into a garage.

One morning I was sitting in the kitchen at the table reviewing my "things to do" list, and heard a noise in the pantry. I looked up and Vito and one of his workmen entered the kitchen through the pantry with very big smiles on their faces. I am sure I looked bewildered because I didn't see them enter the pantry. Vito said, "Ms. Diana, you won't believe this. Come with me." So I got up and followed him and the workman stepped aside to allow me to follow Vito. He led me back into the pantry and stopped at the corner wall adjacent to the tall cupboard and reached up and pulled on a small brass peg in the wall. The wall swung slowly forward and opened into the library. I couldn't believe this incredible bit of magic. I entered the library and turned to look at the opening. Vito closed the small door, and showed me where a small part of an entablature molding of the bookcase could be pulled and would release a latch on the side of the bookshelf springing forth the lower portion of the bookshelf making it a small hidden door about five feet high. When it was completely closed, the opening with its shelves attached, blended completely with the entire panel of built-in paneled shelving that reached up to the carved moldings at the ceiling. In fact, it was a secret passageway into the pantry and from the pantry side, the hinges were hidden behind the side overhang of the cupboard next to the opening. It didn't occur to us that there would be any more surprises about this pantry and it may not have been discovered until of course work began, as was the case, in the library, or in the pantry. The only work that was planned for the pantry was to install a sink and refinish the cupboards, replace and stain the wood floor, add the door leading to the gallery, add new hardware onto the doors and drawers and paint the entire room. Perhaps once that work began, the opening may have been discovered from the pantry side. The workman had begun to refinish the woodwork in the library, including all the bookshelves and moldings and discovered this small piece of molding that moved when he touched it. So when fiddling with it, he pulled the little knob and was amazed to see this small portion of the shelving panel begin to move forward and then swing open. He ran to tell Vito immediately because he didn't speak English and would have a difficult time explaining it to me.

    This discovery added to the mounting mysteries of the house and made us wonder how the people lived in this house and why such secret passageways were necessary. We began searching the entire house for other passageways, perhaps small openings leading to other hidden rooms or openings to the cellar or attic. We found nothing more so it seemed the pantry became the nucleus of the house's mysteries. The next time Bjorn came, I showed him this new discovery and he was fascinated. All these little secrets seemed to add another interesting touch to the house. We would definitely leave this clandestine passageway intact and he believed that if we sold the house to a family with children, secret passageways would add to the appeal.

# CHAPTER 9

Maria, the realtor, called me on my cell phone one day to tell me she had become aware of another villa on the other side of the lake being renovated to turn it into an Inn and the owners needed to store their furniture. She thought the timing might work perfectly because by the time they were ready to empty the home of its contents to begin their work, our work would be coming to completion and we could use the furniture to stage our finished home. It was a perfect solution and would help make the house show better and save us the expense of purchasing or renting furnishings that the perspective buyer might not want. Bjorn was very pleased because it saved us money for the final staging to make the house presentable when we finally put it up for sale. She called the owners and set up a date for us to meet. On the day of the meeting, Vito, Bjorn and I went by boat over to the landing near that home and walked up the stone stairs leading from a dock to the home.

The home was slightly larger than ours and had wonderful furnishings. The owners as well as Bjorn and I were all very happy that this solution could benefit each of us. They bought the home furnished and were going to do a major renovation, knocking down walls, raising ceilings, putting all new heated floors down so wanted to completely empty the home. Some of the furnishings were quite worn and we agreed that if we decided not to use any particular pieces, we would store them in the cellar until they were ready to retrieve the entire lot. There were also wonderful pieces that would work very well in our house and the moment I laid my eyes on certain items, I knew pretty much where I would place them. We were certain that even some of the window furnishings would work. This was all at no cost to us and they would even pay to move the contents to our house. We set an estimated date and now Bjorn and I had a date to work towards, when our home had to be complete enough to be able to accept the furnishings. I was happy to have set this firm date and now believed the work just would not go on forever.

I took a good look at some of the art pieces and although, mostly reproductions and not of great value, they would work well, and I could work with a color pallet now for each room. We looked at everything and the owners made an inventory list with every item that would be coming our way. I could work with the list and by the time everything arrived, I would have a good idea where to put it all. The home also had some wonderful frescos that needed repair, and the owners had already contacted an artist to do the work and gave me her name. They would not be ready for their work before us, so that timing would work out well also.

When I returned to my hotel that afternoon, I contacted the artist and set a date for her to meet me at the house later that week. The fresco artist, Dorthea Donherri, came when Bjorn was at the house and the three of us walked to the rooms where there were frescos that needed to be repaired. She also had some ideas about other places where some type of frescos would dress things up a bit and add color, such as the ceiling in the breakfast nook in the kitchen and a couple of the bathrooms, which were very plain. I was becoming ecstatic with her suggestions so we agreed she and her team of three other people would begin work immediately. Since we were saving on the cost to rent furniture to stage the house, we could afford to do this work. The artist would follow the workmen who were repairing plaster and once that work was complete, it led the way for the artists to begin. She brought a portfolio with photos of some of the murals and frescos she had done in other estate homes, as well as churches. She was extremely skilled and her work would add some wonderful drama and panache to the house. From her ideas as well as the loaned furniture pieces, I could further define colors or themes for that particular place, such as a hallway, or a room. I was also pleased that some of our damaged frescoes could be repaired and salvaged. I began putting together a sketch book with drawings of all the rooms and how I would complete them.

Bjorn heard about a landscape architect and scheduled a meeting at the house at about ten o'clock one morning. The landscape architect's name was Vittorio Gramaldi. He showed up before Bjorn so I brought him out to the yard to look at the property while we waited for Bjorn. It appeared Vittorio loved a good challenge and commented on how overgrown the yard was and also the house, covered with vines. There was a lot of clean up to do before planting a new garden.

"We have a lot to do, but we have a lot to work with. Some of these plants are very old and have grown wild. We will keep some, but perhaps move them to different areas. I can't believe you have so many wonderful Lily plants. They are absolutely wonderful. I will take inventory of what I can identify here and be certain that we do the best we can to preserve as much as possible." It began to drizzle so I suggested we go into the kitchen and have some tea while waiting for Bjorn to arrive. We sat at the table where I had many drawings, fabric swatches, and papers strewn about. We had tea while making small talk at first about some of the sketches and my plans for the house. Mr. Gramaldi seemed to know a lot about carpentry as well as landscaping and he was interested in what architectural details were being attended to. I suppose it was important to him to understand the interior of a home in order to have an idea of what the exterior should be like, seeing as so many of the windows looked out at the property and would welcome a nice view of the gardens, as if it were a landscape drawing as part of the aesthetics of each room. I brought him into the library to see the carved moldings, which he found very interesting and believed that the originality of that alone added quite a value to the home. He also thought they were fascinating and an extraordinary work of art. I found Vittorio to be a very interesting and intelligent man and we hit it off quiet well.

I felt like I had made some very good friends and acquaintances with the people I met who were to work on the house, as well as those that had some diverse connection. Each person, in their own area of expertise, educated me and I began to see more depth and magnificence in the house than meets the uneducated eye. The richness of the experience working with the house seemed to increase every day and I began thinking about the articles, or book I would write and was certain that it was the people, the many talented and diverse people and artists that I became involved with that richened the entire experience and were becoming so important to me. If for no other reason, the renovation was such an education that I knew I would be more in tune with my appreciation of art and my career as a decorator was enhanced.

Finally Bjorn showed up and we took our umbrellas and all went out into the yard and talked about the work that needed to be done. Vittorio was sketching on a pad and had some good ideas for types of plants, arrangements for small sitting areas, possible water features or fountains and also plans for trees that needed to be removed. He suggested that the three of us take a trip over to Isola Madre, one of the Borremeo islands, to look at the gardens and fountains and he would point out the type of plants he thought we should have in the gardens. He said he was going to go and do some thinking and sketching ideas and would come back in a few days and we could go visit the gardens at Isola Madre. This worked well for Bjorn also since he was going to be in Milan, just a fifty mile train ride away for a few days for some investment meetings. I figured I would be seeing him periodically during these few days as he liked to keep a close watch on what was happening at the house. I didn't mind and thought that sometimes I needed him to help shake things up a bit seeing as some work with the contractors was moving a bit slow. I, of course, was impatient and being a results-oriented person, couldn't wait to see progress, but seemed to lack a voice of authority and sometimes needed him and his persuasive ways to get things done. Once the wiring, walls and plaster, plumbing and fixtures were replaced and repaired, the fun part for me would begin with the decorating.

The next day Bjorn stopped in again to see how things were progressing. I was a little caught off guard, but luckily I was busy and there was other important work going on at the house. I wanted him to see the progress. The plasterers were on the second floor repairing the damaged walls in many areas that had collected water, or were cracked. Bjorn was becoming attached to the house and to this project and obviously found it hard to stay away, even though I knew he had business elsewhere, perhaps other renovations. I was happy that he was so interested, but of course, always a little nervous that he might find something wrong, or a decision I made not to his liking.

In a few days after his initial visit, Vittorio showed up bright and early with some sketches for the front and back yard so we sat down at the kitchen table to review and hear his plans. Bjorn came about an hour later and we all left to take a launch across the lake to Isola Madre to visit the gardens.

Vittorio led the way as we walked the entire length of the island passing along the way a special bird sanctuary and several small secluded private gardens that would have been easy to miss, if it weren't for the experienced eye of Vittorio. Some were only entered through a small space between two trees or a break in a wall of sculptured shrubs. Upon stepping into these private gardens, we discovered small benches or pergolas where we could sit and enjoy the privacy.

Isola Madre is the largest of the islands on Lake Maggiore, out of view of Isola Bella and Isola die Pescatori. The island has beautiful botanical gardens lush with grapevines, orange, lemon, walnut, fig, apple, olive, cherry and quince trees. Pellegrina Tibaldi was a prominent architect to the Borromeo family and in 1583 he began the work designing the gardens and buildings that still stands on the island. All of Lake Maggiore and its islands and structures are full of history and romance. The mansion, a beautiful terracotta structure, has an adjacent chapel separated by a chapel square adorned with a centered fountain. The entrance to the mansion is through a loggia on the ground floor and is now a museum and opened to the public. There used to be a theater with an extensive display of puppets and dolls, which they used to perform plays and puppet shows for the children. We also toured the home that day, as well as the gardens. While on the second floor, there are expansive views of the surrounding gardens and the lake.

There were lily ponds and flowering plants of every variety, especially hundreds of varieties of hibiscus. Vittorio had a note pad and we all sat down on a bench while he added to the sketches of his ideas for the design of the yard for our house. He wanted to include a fountain and a lily pond that fed into the fountain, as well as shrubs and tall trees and flowering vines that would cover the pergola. He pointed out the espalier surrounding some of the gardens, which is a trellis of lattice work that supports and trains the climbing trees and the ornamental shrub or fruit trees to grow flat at the back so they are flush against a wall or fence. He said we could have these against the rear of the yard, to block the wall that surrounded the yard and the rear of the new garage that was being built.

I remembered what Irene said about our house once having a pool and it was buried over, or torn out. Vittorio thought that was interesting and surmised that there may remain some underground plumbing, which he noted on his sketchbook.

While we walked along, I updated Bjorn on the progress and said that I thought we were on schedule and there didn't seem to be any barriers. I also told him about the most recent visitors that came to the house. He was quite interested and said when we returned to the house, he wanted to sit down and hear more about them and their stories.

When we returned to the house, Felix Van Streiner had just dropped by, so I introduced him to Bjorn and Vittorio. I told

Bjorn that Felix was one of the visitors that had dropped by a couple weeks before inquiring about Mr. Strausner, who he knew during the war. Bjorn became very alert and repeated the name. "Did you say Strausner? Did you know a Mr. Strausner?" he asked, to which Felix answered yes he had known a man by that name during the war. Bjorn asked if I would be kind enough to put the tea kettle on for them while he took Felix into the yard to show him what Vittorio was suggesting for the garden design. Then he excused himself to me and the three of them went off by themselves while I went into the kitchen to prepare tea. I looked out the window from the kitchen into the yard and saw Bjorn, Vittorio and Felix attentively listening to Vittorio as he pointed out certain trees and parts of the yard, obviously discussing his plans.

Several moments later, Vittorio came back into the house saying he had to leave, but wanted to say good bye to me. After he left, I looked out again and saw Bjorn and Felix standing in the middle of the yard talking. Bjorn's arms were folded while one hand rested his chin and he appeared to be intensely listening to Felix. I assumed Felix was telling Bjorn about his visit with me and his inquiries, which had perked Bjorn's interest and curiosity when I said he was inquiring about a man named Strausner. I thought it was nice that Bjorn and Felix appeared to be hitting it off quite well. Soon they came back into the house and we all sat down for some tea and cookies. Bjorn said he told Felix a little about what I found in the pantry and asked me to get the photos that I found and show them to Felix.

Felix studied the photos carefully and after a moment commented that he thought possibly he could recognize someone resembling Gerheardt Strausner, the man he inquired about that he traced to this house. He took a closer look with the magnifying glass and said he was certain that he recognized Gerheardt Strausner and I said that Ingrid, the housekeeper, had verified that it was him. I told him that I tried to contact him because I had a small dinner party I wanted him to attend, so he could meet Ingrid, the housekeeper I told him about before, but

I was unable to reach him. Felix looked at me with a smile on his face and a raised eyebrow and said he was so sorry he didn't get the call because he would have loved to have met her and talk to her about Strausner.

"I didn't know you met this woman. How interesting. You had a dinner party here?" asked Bjorn.

"Yes. Nothing too elegant—just a small dinner in the kitchen, but we had a very interesting evening. Of course I would have invited you, but you weren't in town," I said. I was a bit surprised because I wouldn't have thought Bjorn would have been interested in such a gossipy little gathering and would have been much too busy.

"I would have loved to have been at that dinner party. What all did she say?" asked Bjorn. I gave him the highlights, telling him that Strausner was the third husband of Charlotte and that Ingrid had been the head housekeeper for many years, and knew him. All through the years, even when Charlotte was still married to Mr. Contrelli, this Mr. Strausner was always around.

"Well, I'd like to hear about that and for sure, Felix here needs to meet her. Why don't we do this dinner again? Would you mind, Diana?" he asked.

"No, I think it would a great idea, and as I said, I was sorry I couldn't get a hold of you, Felix. Also, you know I met a woman named Irene that once had a villa near by and knew both the first and second wives of Mr. Contrelli. Maybe I'll invite her as well as Adam," I suggested.

"Absolutely! Imagine, getting all these people together in one room that knew someone that lived here! It would be great fun, don't you think, Felix?" asked Bjorn.

"Yes, of course. I'd love to hear what these people have to say," answered Felix.

"Well, it's settled then, Diana. When can we do this?" I suggested we do it on his next visit to town and that would give me time to be sure everyone would be available and also it would allow me time to prepare.

Felix began to come by the house often to see what progress we were making. I was beginning to look forward to his visits and enjoyed his company, and in spite of our age difference, we seemed to always have many things to talk about. I guessed he was a very young man during the war when he was a soldier, so I thought he was in his early eighties, but he seemed quite young at heart. He had a good sense of humor and it was refreshing to be with someone and share a good conversation and a few laughs.

One day as Felix visited, we walked through the house and he commented on the latest work, some complementary as well as pointing out suggestions for how to fix some other things, like the creaking floor boards and then suggested we walk into town for lunch. I was eager to get out of the house for a change, so took him up on his offer. As it was, other than visits from Felix and Adam, I was spending a lot of time alone and always welcomed their visits and company. It was a beautiful sunny day with a nice cool breeze coming off the lake. We walked to the village and took a table outside at one of my favorite cafes.

"So my dear, it looks as if you are making good progress with the house. Everyone is buzzing about it you know. People in town can't wait to see the finished product, and even more so, they can't wait to see who buys this house," he said.

"I'm happy with the progress and also looking forward to seeing it finished. But to tell you the truth, with all the talking we've been doing about the people that lived here, I've been obsessing so much about them all—Charlotte, Gerheardt Strausner, and the others and trying to imagine what this house looked like then. I would love to maintain some of the influence from that period. I realized I was thinking more about that than who would live in it after this."

"Well, you can't fix a house up for dead people, you know," said Felix. "You should have some idea in mind about who you are fixing this house for now."

"I know you are absolutely right, and I'm certain that whoever purchases the house will have to be very wealthy.

They will have to be in order to buy it in the first place and then afford the taxes. I'm not sure how people like that live. They will probably be British because I see this is a favorite place for many British to visit and have holidays here. I envision a large family with lots of children to fill up the bedrooms. Can you imagine being a child and living in a house like this? But there are so many things about the former owners that I'd like to know, like how they lived, how they used the various rooms and lived in this house and how it was decorated, the paintings they hung on the walls—you know, that sort of thing. It is important to retain some of the authentic period of the home. You can't put Mies van der Rohe in a house like this, of course. It must be extremely stately, just as I imagine it was when Charlotte lived here. Listen to me talk about her. It's almost as if I am living with her ghost. Tell me Felix, I saw a look on your face when you looked at the photos and recognized Gerheardt Strausner. How well did you know him?"

"I knew him from the war, but as I said, not personally," Felix answered, in a way that seemed as though he wanted to stifle the subject.

"But Felix, you sought him out when you came to this house. Tell me, just what is it that brings people here to this house and wakes up such strong memories? You didn't know him well, but you knew of him and something about him made you come to this house. Why do all these people come around, and I might add, they are a lot more curious than I am. Maybe it's contagious. What was it about the former tenants that even after all these years people gravitate to this house, just looking for one more morsel of information about them? And Felix, you are just as curious. What was it about these people?" I asked.

"Well, Gerheardt was an interesting person, even though, as I said, I didn't know him intimately, but still knew I didn't like him very much. He was extremely arrogant and loved to order people around, including me. He was a pretty cruel man. I was very young and just an army lieutenant and he had me doing personal things for him, like having his boots polished, and being his driver. Many things were outside my responsibility, but he didn't seem to care and I just acquiesced and did what he ordered me to do, but I didn't like it and resented him. He was a physician, you know, and quite impressed with his position."

"No, I didn't know. Ingrid never mentioned that," I said.

"I was assigned to his hospital for a while. He was pretentious and superior and quite full of himself, just strutting around letting everyone know how important he was. I suppose when you go through life, certain people impact your life either in a good or a bad way. Because I felt he was rather vile, I did often wonder what happened to him and how life turned out for him, not that I really cared, but sometimes you might hope that people get what they deserve from life, and you want to believe that justice prevails. Deep down I suppose I wished that he had some difficult times and got what he deserved."

"Well he died rather tragically by falling over the balcony railing in the front room," I said.

"If it were possible for him to die a thousand times, tragically, it still may not have been justice. He was a very bad man in the war. I can't go into any detail, because I'm not positive about what he did, but I heard rumors and I had no reason to disbelieve them. You know what went on—the entire world knows. I just believe he should have been arrested, but he somehow slipped away. When I read a small newspaper article so many years after the war with his name, I was shocked that he had never been apprehended and that he was free. I became curious and wanted to know what happened to him. I couldn't believe that he didn't change his name. Now I wonder how in the world he ended up here! But then also, this woman of the house, Charlotte, that the housekeeper told you about seemed like a larger than life character. I think she was interesting because people wondered how Mr. Contrelli found her, and what was he doing in Germany during the end of the war? And why would he have married a German woman and then bring her here? Surely there had to be some wagging tongues about that because Germans were not all that popular in Italy after Mussolini was kicked out of power and the Badoglio government surrendered to the allies. So what was he doing in Germany during the war? There seems to be a lot of reasons for people's curiosity."

"Well, from what Ingrid said, he went to Germany seeking out a doctor for his cancer. Maybe Gerheardt was that doctor," I said.

"The boundaries between Poland, Germany and Italy were a bit blurred early on in the war and Gerheardt was free to travel between Poland and Germany, wherever he needed to be. Italy and Germany were allies until 1943 and Germany occupied Poland. At that time an Italian could very easily go to Germany, but as the war intensified, it would have been much more difficult to cross those borders," said Felix.

I pointed out that the interest is not just Charlotte and Gerheardt. "They were fascinating enough, but then this man named Carl appears on the scene. Just when I thought I knew the names of all the people that lived here, the name Carl enters into the picture."

"Carl? What about this man named Carl? Where did you hear that name?" asked Felix

"Well, the other man that came to visit, Frederick Von Barren, was inquiring about his wife's brother, Carl. He was an SS officer. Frederick was the other person I had at the little dinner party I wanted you to attend. He had quite a lot to say about Carl at the dinner. Well, you have to talk to him too. He said that many years ago, after the war his wife received a letter with this return address from her brother Carl, but he instructed her not to write to him here. That night we looked at some of the old photos and he was sure he saw Carl in the photo, wearing an SS uniform, and the reverse side of the picture named the people in the photo. One of the names was Carl," I explained. "The fact that he was an SS officer makes it curious to me, why he would have been at this house."

"That's interesting. I'll have to see that photo. You know, after the war, people scattered everywhere they could hide, for fear of being arrested for war crimes, especially the SS. Maybe somehow the Contrellis gave them a safe haven for a while, but I wonder why they would do that," said Felix.

"Frederick said his wife's brother, this Carl person, sent a letter to her after the war with a return address of this house, saying he was on his way to Rome. Then they received another letter from some doctor, telling them that Carl died in an automobile accident on his way to Rome. They tried for years to find out what happened to him and what happened to his remains. She wanted to give him a proper burial, but never heard anything again about him. So, Felix, does the name Carl Drummond seem familiar?"

"Perhaps. I may have come across him at one time or another, but who knows. There were probably lots of Carls, I'm sure. But I think there was a man named Carl who was an SS officer who was an associate of Strausner. I don't remember his last name though. It's probably a coincident and I'm sure it's not the same man. But isn't it interesting that the man I knew that lived here, Gerheardt, also knew a Carl during the war and this name pops up now? It may have been the same Carl. I vaguely recall him," he said.

"Ingrid has no recollection of a man named Carl being here. He must have just passed through, as he said in his letter. Maybe he was friends with Charlotte or Gerheardt, because they were both German, and they may have helped him, or hid him." I suggested that he should look closer and see if he recognize anyone else in the photos and if the Carl in the photo is the one he knew.

"Yes, I'll have to take another look at those photos. Could be the same man, if I can remember what he looked like. It was so long ago and I have a vague recollection of him. Yes, Mrs. Contrelli may have known him from Germany, but if she did hide him here after the war, what was she up to? Makes you wonder, doesn't it? How did she know people like that?" asked Felix.

"Yes, and maybe Carl was a friend of Gerheardt and these photos could have just belonged to him," I added. "Ingrid said that at one time Charlotte told her she worked in a hospital during the war and when Mr. Contrelli became very ill, she was able to take care of him. So, if she worked in a hospital during the war, maybe as a nurse, she may have known a lot of people who passed through. Now we know that Gerheardt was a doctor, so that's how she probably knew him. From what Ingrid said, that's how she met Mr. Contrelli. He may have fallen in love with her, married her and brought her home. After she was ensconced in the house, she may have brought some of her friends here. I think she may have been a bit lonely because I don't think she was embraced by the people here so maybe she had to import her friends."

"I would imagine life was awkward for her being in Italy after the war, and being German. Mr. Contrelli may have been protective of her," Felix speculated.

"Strausner was her third husband, but he was always around, Ingrid said. Even during the entire eight years she was married to Mr. Contrelli before he died. She thought they were good friends. So if Carl passed through here immediately after the war, he could have been either Charlotte's or Gerheardt's friend, since they were both here," I added.

Felix thought for a moment before replying. "Strausner was a doctor and the man named Carl that I remember, worked in the same hospital, so I think there is a possibility this ironically enough may be the same Carl."

"Well Frederick was pretty sure he identified Carl in one of those photos I found. I hope he can come to the dinner. He lives in Germany and he may have already left for home. If he can come, he said he has other pictures of Carl. Maybe you will recognize him. If this is the same Carl, I'm sure he would appreciate knowing anything you can remember about him."

"I'm looking forward to that. Well, after the war, it may have not been too difficult to cross the Italian border and maintain a lifestyle unquestioned." He motioned to the lake. "As you see, Switzerland is just over there. Switzerland was neutral so Germans could cross the border there quite easily and from there, a hop, skip and a jump and here they were in Northern

*The House on Lake Maggiore*

Italy. This would have been a good place to immediately blend in and take refuge. Most SS officers had good reason to hide."

"I know. Frederick gave me quite an education on the SS and what they were about, although he didn't know what Carl's particular job was during the war," I added. "He said Carl was first a Hitler Youth and then an SS officer and as such, had to prove a definite lineage of Aryan heritage. I recall reading stories about what happened to many of them after the war and where they hid, and also how they were found, even many years later."

"They were never really safe, and I imagine had to live their life looking over their shoulders. I was a soldier in the German army also, but I was a good person, Diana. I had no reason to hide and I certainly had no duties of any prestige. I want you to know that. I despised the SS myself and then after the war when more things were learned about what went on, I was horrified myself," he said. I could hear his sincerity and understood why he wanted to clarify the curiosity I might have about his role during the war.

Felix continued. "When the war ended, I just went home to my family and stepped into my father's farm and worked with him and eventually, after he died, I inherited the farm and it was my life until it became too much for me, and then I handed it off to my own son. It was a good transition for me and for my son."

We returned to the house after lunch and I showed Felix the photos again and the one especially with the name Carl on the reverse side. He walked to the light of the window and held the magnifying glass directly over the photo. It was a very small photo of a group of men, taken at a distance, but it was possible, he believed, that could have been the same Carl that he remembered who was a friend of Gerheardt. The name we thought said Carl, but vaguely written, was also on the back of the photo, along with other names, but he didn't recognize any of the other names or faces in the photo.

The more we talked about the house and the former inhabitants and made assumptions about all these old lost souls that passed through the door of the house, the more curious we became and believed that if we could piece all the disjointed facts together, it might be very interesting. The photos of SS officers, the names that seemed to rise up out of all the little stories and remembrances became fodder to our curiosity and the more determined we became to figure it all out and try to understand what their life was about during those years immediately following the war, and what their particular role was in the war for them to have even connected to one another.

# CHAPTER 10

After meeting so many interesting people, each gravitating to the house for their individual reasons, I was left wondering more and more about the source of their curiosity and their personal connection to the former owners of the house. I knew Bjorn was right and we needed to have another dinner party and bring them all together. I believed the stories each person had would feed off the other and perhaps unveil a greater understanding of the overall larger stories of lives so long ago that may have been connected and remained stagnant and smothered as if in a closed book. It was as if the cover of the book had lifted ever so slowly and each character stepped off the page. With each visitor and each bit of information shared with me, I became more titillated to hear more and learn what life was once like in this house and how people lived in those old days. From what I already knew about them, they were certainly interesting people. I invited Irene, Jean, Frederick, Ingrid, Adam, and of course, Felix and Bjorn. I was most happy to find that Frederick was still in Italy and could return for the occasion. I set eight place settings onto a lovely large table set up in the living room. The kitchen nook was too small so I decided we would eat in the front room by the fireplace. The chandelier in the dining room and living room were unwrapped and cleaned, but still not rewired and working, so we would need the light from the fireplace and candles for an evening dinner party.

I used saw horses I borrowed from the workmen and an old door to create a table and covered it with one of the vintage linen table clothes. I used all the odd chairs I could find in the cellar, as well as those I had already brought to the kitchen. I set the table with the old china and silver I found in the pantry as well as candlesticks I used for the first dinner, which I found in the pantry and placed the candles around the flowers in the center. I brought in a large bouquet of Casablanca lilies and lush greens from the yard and had them in jars for the centerpiece. After the sun set, the entire setting of the table in the living room, lit with candles and the glow from the fireplace, looked quite elegant. The shadows from the twinkling candles sent light up to the prisms of the chandelier and a spray of shadows reflected off the walls. Vito helped me get the oven working and so being able to cook in the oven gave me more possibilities about what to prepare. I found a recipe in a magazine for Tuscan leg of lamb slathered in a paste made of lemon juice, crushed garlic, olive oil, Italian Parsley and Parmesan cheese, which gave the lamb a nice crisp crust and kept the juices of the meat intact. I roasted it with root vegetables, sliced potatoes and tomatoes in the same pan. I also baked bread and made a small salad of tomatoes, basil and mozzarella cheese and served a good Chianti wine and again a purchased cake for dessert. It was a good hearty Tuscan dinner.

After my preparation in setting the table with all the lovely things and planning the meal, it took on the essence of quite a stylish affair. The table setting in the beautiful living room, with the fireplace alit as well as the candles, set the stage for a very elegant evening. As it was, our guests all seemed to feel it was a special event and all seemed to dress up for the occasion. They were, after all, coming to dinner at the very special house on Lago Maggiore.

Jean and Irene arrived a little early and I could see this was an important event for Irene and probably set her mind into reliving those visits to the house so many decades ago with her husband at her side. When Irene first stepped into the entrance hall, she stood for a while looking up at the ceiling and on through the gallery, and it seemed as though her memories that were long silent in her mind had overtaken the moment. She appeared to want to just enjoy the moment reflecting on years past, probably entering the house on the arm of her husband. This was to be a special evening for her. She looked beautiful and maybe in her mind was reenacting those earlier events because she dressed for the occasion. She was stunning and wore a lovely plain black dress, with a black coat with a fox collar over her shoulders and black leather gloves. The elegance of her clothes accented her beautiful face and white hair against her olive skin. She wore her pearls and a beautiful diamond bracelet and ring, all what I believed were representative of the wealth she once enjoyed and perhaps still maintained, camouflaged by her much more sedate life in the little apartment. Jean confirmed later that evening when we were working together in the kitchen that Irene was still quite wealthy with what her husband left her and the good fortune on the sale of her home, but preferred to live a simpler life style now. She had given Jean many of her most esteemed possessions including some jewelry pieces, seeing as she had no children of her own. She felt very close to Jean and it was my guess that Jean would have a nice inheritance from her aunt one day. They were obviously very fond of one another and Jean said that her mother had passed away many years ago and she looked to this aunt as a sort of mother figure. Irene was most charming when Bjorn offered to take her coat for her and they became engrossed in conversation immediately. I am quite sure I was not mistaken in seeing a little flirtation on her part. He led her off to fetch a cocktail, arm in arm, while Jean offered to help me in the kitchen.

As each person arrived, Adam greeted them at the front door and brought them into the kitchen by the table where he had set up a little bar and served them drinks. All the introductions and excursions through the house gave Jean and I extra time to work in the kitchen.

I knew there was no end to topics that could be discussed, but most were strangers and breaking the ice was a bit of a challenge so the evening began a bit slowly. Then I began to think, perhaps it was the influence of the house and the history it represented that seemed intimidating and shed some trepidation over the discussions. Each person had their own story with special memories that may have been overly nostalgic and emotional for them. Maybe they felt a presence in the house, as I often seemed to. Their own connection and those special memories or interests seemed to grasp hold of each person.

They began to gather around the kitchen table, cocktails in hand, chatting away, and asking the others about their connection to the house. I was busy working on the meal and just listening with one ear. I loved the dynamics of the assembly of such dissimilar people and knew we were in for quite an interesting evening. The diverse personalities would complement one another and coming together in such a strange way at the same dinner table would undoubtedly generate interesting conversations.

When Frederick entered, I introduced him immediately to Felix and the two of them took a cocktail and went off to a corner to talk alone, comparing notes on the now infamous curious man named Carl. The two were similar in age and were young men at the onset of the war and well into their eighties or early nineties. Ingrid and Adam also engaged in a conversation by themselves. I took Jean on a tour of the house. When we got to the Library, Irene was already standing in that room with Bjorn, telling him of her memories.

Jean said, "You know, Diana, this is really a pretty extraordinary evening. All I can think about is the theatre we are watching with these people, and this house. Well, my friends in Chicago just won't believe this when I tell them."

"I know. Look at these people! Look at this house—this old run down house screaming with memories to all of these people. I think it represents their youth. Maybe that's what the real attraction is. They were all young when they knew this house, or they knew people that once were here. They are sure getting off on this. God only knows what's in store for us this evening. I've already heard a little from the old housekeeper, Ingrid. Wait until she gets going; you just won't believe it." Jean was as titillated as me and I was so happy to have her there; at last a person I could relate to. Being two people with a similar cultural background somehow became amusing because we seemed to roll our eyes or raise an eyebrow simultaneously. As the evening wore on, we purposely avoided eye contact in order to hide our mutual amusement with the characters around the dinner table. Once we were alone in the kitchen, we compared notes and had a good laugh about certain parts of the evening.

I was especially attentive to Ingrid and felt that this would be the first time ever that she was a guest in the house and not expected to serve others. I wanted her to feel special and deserving. As it were, she was probably the most important guest because she knew more about the ghosts of the house than anyone. I took her aside and showed her the passageway we discovered in the library. She was incredulous with this discovery and had to try it herself from both sides of the entry, first the library and then from the pantry. She thought it was extraordinary that all the years in the house and she didn't know it existed, nor had an explanation about why there was such a passageway and never had a clue that such an entry existed.

Seeing that Irene was in good hands, Jean left her with Bjorn and helped me with the food preparation and took the serving dishes to the table while Adam poured the wine. Everyone approached their seat at the table amongst endless chatter. Bjorn began by toasting the welcomed guests and also me, for the lovely dinner. Everyone exchanged pleasantries, discussed the progress of the house, how delicious the food was, how beautiful the table looked and how I did such a nice job making it so elegant with all the fascinating old things I found. Ingrid remembered the china very well, having handled it for years and being in charge of the pantry.

Adam and Bjorn both took hold as a host and made sure everyone had a drink or a glass of wine. While eating, the chatter began to cease and I wasn't sure if the intent of the gathering would really come to fruition. It may have become awkward because most of these people were strangers, but Adam broke the ice and talked about the Christmas parties, describing what the very room we were in looked like as he remembered it when he was a child, with the large Christmas tree and holly ropes going up the stairway. Irene added to that memory also and talked about how she and her husband also attended those parties. Their comments were like the flood gates opening and soon everyone was joining in and they had so much to talk about that we were all spellbound thinking about it and about that very room where we now sat, how festive it must have been and with so many people.

"There was a piano in that corner," Irene recollected as she pointed across the table with her long slender diamond appointed hand. "They paid a musician to come and play the piano and he played Christmas songs and we would all sing at the end of the evening. It was really so lovely. I also remember the library. Mrs. Contrelli also had a small Christmas tree in that room. It was such a nice cozy room, of course so much smaller than this room and so inviting. She and I had a nice glass of champagne there together one time, discussing the moldings around the room. I was telling Diana about that. The former Mrs. Contrelli had the moldings made for her daughter who died in the swimming pool. They depict literary tales that she read to her daughter. I remember how the second Mrs. Contrelli spoke about fashion and style and literature. She was quite charming, but then again, it was only at those Christmas parties that I talked with her."

Adam spoke up. "She always invited the neighbors and their children and I came along with my parents. How odd that she didn't show those moldings to the children. I never saw the library when I was in the house. She had some attraction to children and had the neighbors bring them for the Christmas and Easter parties she had. Do you recall seeing a lot of children attending her parties, Ingrid?"

"Oh yes. She seemed to like children. She always wanted her neighbors to bring their children, especially at Christmas and Easter. I think the parties were really intended for the children. She decorated the house so beautifully and had small gifts, like toys and candy for them. And at Easter, she had egg hunts in the yard and always gave away lots of candy. She was such a kind woman in that regard. Of course the children liked her because she always had gifts for them. She believed that Christmas was a magical time for children and she said she had many wonderful memories of her childhood and Christmas."

"Well, I was a young boy with very blond hair. My parents lived close by in Baveno and she always invited us. I recall those events quite well. Do you have any recollection to a child of that description, Ingrid?" asked Adam.

Ingrid turned to Adam and said, "I was always very busy serving people at those parties and I wouldn't recall anyone in particular. She had all the staff working very hard. We were always glad when it was over. But isn't it interesting that we may have been in the same room at the same time? And here we meet again."

Adam smiled and nodded his head in agreement and said, "Yes, it is quite inconceivable, I think."

Bjorn seemed quite enchanted with Irene. "Irene, tell me about when you met her. What was she like when you met with her that evening in the library? What did she look like? You know, your general impression of her." He waved his hand into the air to emphasize his thought, and said "I'm just trying to get a vision of her in my mind."

"Yes, I can see now why you would all want to know about her and as I see now, maybe she was more important to the history of this house than I realized. After all, it seems that now, after all these years you may all be here because of your curiosity about her or someone connected to her. I'm sure Ingrid knew her best. I may have known her as she wanted to be presented to people, with her persona intact and rather superficial I felt that she was, well, artificial and pretentious. I don't want to taint her memory to any of you and hope I'm not offending anyone, but I must be honest," said Irene.

"Oh please, don't worry about me. I quite agree with you," said Ingrid.

"I never felt that she was truthful, or the kind of person I would want for a friend. Don't get me wrong; she was charming to her guests and very lovely and gracious, but I didn't see a sincerity to her. I felt her character was unnatural and affected, a bit icy and guarded, if you know what I mean. Did you see that also, Ingrid?" asked Irene.

"Yes. She was icy, just not a very warm person at all. In all the years I knew her, she just couldn't be real or normal, it seemed," said Ingrid. "I think she showed affection to the children, but still maintained her guard and really didn't touch them or hug them."

Irene continued with her personal view of Charlotte. "Underneath it all, I felt she was invented and her new wealth by marrying Mr. Contrelli brought her into a lifestyle strange and different to her. I'm sure she was still in awe of herself, maybe couldn't believe it herself that she was now living in a higher style. Her pathetic accent, her posing, and even her laugh seemed artificial. She was like a caricature; nothing about her seemed real. I thought it sad that the first Mrs. Contrelli died so suddenly and felt even sorrier for Mr. Contrelli, that he must have been so lonely to have married this woman, this strange looking and acting woman. I really felt so sorry for him being stuck with her, and yet, he acted very proud of her and was good to her. So then he died, and she inherited this house and everything. Very sad ending, I think. She didn't deserve to have this home and she didn't fit in here in Stresa."

"She didn't seem real to me either," said Ingrid. "Never did I think she was genuine and real—all those years and I never felt I knew or saw the real person. I was telling Ms. Diana that in the first years of her marriage to Mr. Contrelli, how I used to be walking down the hall upstairs past her bedroom and through the crack in the door I could see her sitting in front of her mirror at the dressing table, just admiring herself, putting on makeup, changing her hair style and trying on her jewelry. She loved to primp in front of that mirror. It was really quite funny, how she seemed to dote on herself."

"Narcissistic," said Bjorn. "Sounds like she had quite an ego. I wonder why and if it was real, or just an image she was portraying to people, because maybe she was really just a simple German girl and in awe of herself, as Irene said, having gotten this man to marry her and give her all of this," said Bjorn as he motioned with one wine glass cradled hand circling the air. "Maybe she was insecure within herself, but most likely it was as you said, Irene. She was posing, acting maybe. She wasn't sure how a person that had lived with wealth all their life would act. This was all new to her and she may have surprised herself that she could be deserving of this new wealth and lifestyle."

"Well, we don't really know that. I mean, we assume, but we don't really know what her life was like before she married him. She may have come from a very wealthy family in Germany. I suppose anything is possible," I interjected. I was a little surprised at the negative comments about Charlotte and somehow, because I had built her up in my mind, felt like I had to defend her, like she was some old friend because I was living in her house all day, feeling her presence and maybe her spirit.

"That is possible, I'm sure and she didn't seem all that awkward when she was alone with the staff," said Ingrid. "She never seemed to feel bad yelling at them and she had no problem spending Mr. Contrellis money, all those trips to Switzerland and coming home with boxes and boxes of new clothes!"

Adam added to the comments. "Of course, I thought she was strange too. I thought about it for many years. She would break away from her party and her guests and take me into that pantry, just her and I, and sit me down and talk to me, questioning me about my friends, what I liked about school, how I was doing with my studies in school and what sports I liked to play. Why was that her business? That's what I didn't understand about her. She turned on the light and closed the door. She would light a cigarette and lean against the cupboards and just stare at me and ask me questions almost as if she were interrogating me," said Adam.

"I wonder why she did that," said Bjorn. "Seems strange that she would leave her party and guests and take a young boy into the pantry for a conversation. Maybe she was trying to get in touch with some sort of 'real life.'"

"I never could figure it out. She would go to my parents and ask if they minded if she took me with her for a few moments. She led me to the pantry, closed the door and sat me down on the stool," said Adam.

As I began to clear the dishes and prepare the coffee, Bjorn relayed the story of how I found the pantry. He made it very amusing and everyone laughed, including me. He also said that he believed the carriage house had a small apartment in the loft and how he had gone through the rubble and discovered a mattress and other things that indicated signs of life long ago. He talked about how he and I imagined the house to be back in those days and tried to guess what life was like then, when the house lived. "Miss Zinger, tell us about those old days while you were here. We are so curious about the history of this old house. I understand you were here for many years working for Mrs. Contrelli. What was it like, all those years working in this house? What was she like?" he asked.

Ingrid was a bit shy. Because she knew the history of the house better than anyone, everyone's eyes and ears were focused on her. Once she got going, it seemed easier for her to open up and she overcame her shyness. "Please, Mr. Turner, call me Ingrid. She was an interesting woman, for as much as I could tell that early on. Mr. Contrelli was a wonderful man—very kind and sweet. He was much older than she and we all suspected, you know, the other staff and myself, um . . . . well, that she married him for his money. He had plenty of it, I'm sure and the house was quite opulent then. He built the home in the twenties for his first wife as a holiday home. They had another permanent residence in Milan. I think after the first wife died, he was very lonely and he was very proud to have such a young and lovely wife to bring to the house, and to show off to people. He sold off the house in Milan and spent all his time in this house then. He gave her anything she wanted and she tried very hard to become accepted in the social life here. People were somewhat hesitant about accepting her, um . . . being German and all, but everyone loved Mr. Contrelli, so it was his friends that came to call. She loved to entertain and have parties. But people came with the written invitation to the parties; no one ever really just dropped by to visit. I don't think she had friends like that—you know, that close," said Ingrid.

"Do you remember if any of the staff lived on the premises, either in the small bedrooms upstairs or in the garage apartment?" asked Bjorn.

"No, never. I didn't even stay here, ever. Those rooms in the house may have been used by staff when the first Mrs. Contrelli ran the house, but not while I was here. I thought maybe one of the larger bedrooms was for the little girl and then a smaller room for her nanny or other servants. And I never knew of any apartment in the carriage house. No one ever went into that building except just to park the cars that I recall. Even Mr. Contrelli's butler didn't live on the premises. I don't recall that I had ever been in that building myself," said Ingrid.

"Did her marriage to Mr. Contrelli seem like a good marriage?" asked Bjorn.

"I think so. She was nice to him, but I could see it was not a loving marriage. Oh, I think he cared for her, or at least liked having her around, seeing as he was a recent widower and probably lonely and I imagine he couldn't keep that house going himself. He may have needed to be married. She was young and maybe it made him feel young and kept him entertained. I think with his illness, he may have been depressed and with her around, he might have felt he had a new chance with life. They seemed to get along well. She was very respectful and kind to him and I don't think she really loved him, but I think she liked him very much. Well, the poor man's cancer reoccurred after a while and he was very ill for a long time. She was very faithful to him and took good care of him, I must say. I commented to her about how well she was taking care of him and she told me she had a nursing background during the war. But it wasn't long after his death that she remarried. She didn't waste much time. Maybe she found it difficult to be alone. But then, after just two years, her second husband Vincinzo died in a boating accident on the lake. She and her second husband lived very well, probably from the money she inherited, but I think it was a strain keeping the house up and of course their life style. After he died, she then remarried again, to Mr. Strausner. By this time the house was becoming a bit forlorn and in need of repairs. It became obvious that her money wasn't holding out. Her clothes weren't quite as stylish and new and she stopped wearing her jewels. I think she was selling things off to make ends meet. She began to let the staff go and she had me just working for her part time. As time went by, she became sadder and less self-involved and some days, she didn't even put on makeup or fix her hair. It just hung to her shoulders or she would tie it back, but she didn't seem to care what she looked like anymore."

"In those early days, when you first came here to this house, what do you remember about her the most?" I asked.

"When she interviewed me for the housekeeping job, I found her interesting to look at, striking I would say. She wasn't really a beautiful woman, but strikingly attractive because she had an interesting bone structure in her face and she was very tall and had excellent posture, as if she were a ballet dancer. Um . . . always very erect and sat very straight and crossed her legs just so. Always a lady and almost posing, as Irene said. When she walked through the room, she seemed to almost float because she had long legs and she moved so gracefully. As I said, she was very well dressed and put together, always with her hair and makeup done perfectly. I never saw her without her makeup or her hair done up just perfectly in the early days. But as the years passed, she changed. With Mr. Contrelli, she was happiest I think, because he took good care of her. She was more good natured. She would leave though for short trips to

Switzerland, shopping she said. She loved to go to Switzerland to shop. Sometimes she would be gone for days and then come home with boxes of new clothes and things. She knew how to spend Mr. Contrelli's money. With the second husband, I think she loved him very much, but as I said the relationship was not mutual. He was gone so much."

Ingrid recalled that one day Charlotte was miserable because her second husband was neglecting her. Ingrid overheard Charlotte begging him to talk to her and tell her why he was acting so distant. "He was a playboy, a race car driver she met in Monte Carlo. It was obvious that she was much more interested in him than he was in her. He married her, but the relationship soured quickly. She moped around the house when he was gone. And um . . . . when he came back, she had every one hopping to wait on him and make him wonderful dinners and she fawned over him like he was a child. He would easily push her aside and wasn't impressed at all. I remember her saying, 'Vincinzo, what happened? Don't you find me appealing anymore? What has changed? I missed you. Your little Charlotte sat here waiting for you, so anxious for you to come back, and all you do is ignore me!' It was really pathetic, the way she begged him to pay attention to her. She tried to act like a little girl, sort of coquettish, but she made herself look ridiculous. He brushed her aside as if he were shooing a cat off his lap. He was obnoxious, I thought, and rude to the staff. He acted just like a spoiled child. He would never talk to us other than to order us to do something or get something for him. Now, I think she truly did love him. She acted like she worshiped him and did everything possible to get his attention, but Vincinzo seemed to ignore her, which made the staff think he probably married her for her money because he was so inattentive to her during their marriage and he would go off for long periods of time without her. Everyone assumed he was off racing his cars, in Monte Carlo and other places and there were snippets in the newspapers with pictures of him with other woman. We would all chatter about it in the back service room while we were doing our work. He was somewhat of a celebrity and a well-known playboy and womanizer. It infuriated Charlotte and she confronted him each time, but he just shrugged her off. She would spend hours in her room alone or sitting in the garden looking so sad. Um . . . I really felt sorry for her. It was pathetic. When he was there she followed him around and tried to occupy his time and wanted to be with him, but he would soon go away again and then she was left alone. Seldom did she go with him. It was apparent he wanted his freedom, but he also liked the life style she provided him so he eventually returned here to this house. He had a pretty good thing going. You see, no one took care of her after Mr. Contrelli died. She ended up taking care of the next two husbands who did little for her. After Vincinzo died, she was depressed for a while, but she got over it quite quickly." Ingrid paused for a moment to take a sip of water. Everyone just sat waiting for her to continue. Bjorn prodded her along.

"What about Mr. Strausner? When did he enter the picture?" asked Bjorn.

"Well, her friend Mr. Strausner was always around, from the day she moved into this house after marrying Mr. Contrelli, I recall seeing Mr. Strausner, either in the kitchen visiting with her, or at the parties. He would just pop up and be here. He was included in their social functions and even later when she was married to Vincinzo, and after he was gone, Mr. Strausner was always here visiting. So maybe it was natural that after her second husband died, that she should marry Mr. Strausner, but it still surprised me because I thought they were just very good friends. Like I said, he was always around. Sometimes I would find him in the kitchen reading the newspaper, over coffee all alone and smoking his pipe. Many times I smelled the tobacco from his pipe and figured he was around but didn't always see him. At times I wondered how he got into the house or the kitchen when I thought I had locked the door, and Charlotte was elsewhere in the house but then I assumed she had given him a key. I asked him if he was waiting to see Mrs. Contrelli and he said he was, but she knew he was there and would be with him shortly and she asked him to wait there in the kitchen for her. He said I should run along with my business and not concern myself. He talked to me like I was a child, um . . . like he had some right to be so arrogant with me."

"Well, that sure sounds like the Dr. Gerheardt Strausner I knew. He was always arrogant and full of himself," said Felix.

"As preposterous as this might seem, suppose for just a moment that he was the person living in the carriage house," said Bjorn. "Would it be possible that he would come into the kitchen from the yard? If he was a friend of Mrs. Contrellis, maybe she let him stay in that loft apartment over the carriage house."

"That never occurred to me, but I suppose it could be possible because he was here a lot and I never saw him with a car parked outside. I assumed he lived nearby and walked to the house," said Ingrid. "But I was busy and had a lot to do, so I may not have been paying any attention to that. Also, I turned the other cheek many times, because I just wanted to avoid him."

Bjorn added "Also, we recently discovered a secret passageway from the library into the pantry. Maybe he was always in the house and just wandered between the kitchen and the library though that pantry passageway. Maybe Mrs. Contrelli had that installed for him so he could move freely about the house, or disappear quickly if someone was entering the library from the hallway. Maybe he did just that for all the years through her first two marriages."

"Well, another possibility might be that the passageway was always there for Mr. Contrelli's convenience so he could pass through to the kitchen from the library for a late night snack, when he was working in the library," suggested Ingrid. Everyone was interested in that new passageway and after dinner Bjorn had to demonstrate to them how both that door and the door from the kitchen worked. Bjorn was all too happy to lead the way and demonstrate how the latch worked to open the little door in the library. The entire concept of secret passageways led to a multitude of ideas and suggestions about the purpose and that discussion took the greater part of an hour.

It seemed as if the darkness of the house and the long shadows from the candles and the fireplace created a mysterious ambiance that may have contributed to the drama of our suppositions about these long gone people. There were no working lights in the gallery and library and most of the fixtures were on the service porch being polished. There they were, all my dinner guests, walking in a line following one another through the dark gallery, led by Bjorn carrying a huge candelabra to light the way, into the library where he showed them the latch and opened the secret passageway. How often in one's life do you sit in front of a fireplace in an empty cavernous room, in an abandoned mansion, eating dinner with perfect strangers and talk about secret passageways, dead people, and superimposed fables from sixty odd years ago? It almost made me want to say, Colonel Mustard did it, with a rope in the library, but then I had to remember my dinner guests were not American and probably had no idea of the game of Clue. I sometimes had to work very hard to suppress my Americana and reprogram my brain to adjust to this other, foreign culture that was always so serious. Of course the subject of the conversation was serious, but it was almost too conjured and it at times exhausted me. The evening was especially esoteric. There was a Polish man, an Italian woman, one Swiss man, three German people, one of which was a onetime German soldier, and of course Jean and I, the only Americans. I stayed behind while they were on their excursion through the gallery to the library to witness the magic of the secret latch that opened into the mysterious world of the, by now, infamous pantry. They were all a bit tipsy from so much wine and thought it was great fun and I heard them giggling as they followed Bjorn and then when he released the latch, they all exclaimed loudly "AHHHH!!" I had to chuckle but I think for them it was the highlight of the evening. They snaked through the dark pantry exiting through the other secret door into the kitchen.

Finally everyone came back to the living room and we sat down at the table again and I served dessert and coffee. The conversation hadn't missed a beat and they just took up where they left off. The adventure itself may have given new life to their imagination. When we began dessert, Bjorn continued. "So Ingrid, getting back to your memories, how did Gerheardt and Mr. Contrelli get along? Did they have any interaction that you can recall?" asked Bjorn.

"Oh yes, every now and then the three of them had dinner together. The two men got along fine, it seemed, but Mr. Contrelli was still involved in his work, some sort of finances I think, and he would go off alone and work in the library in the evenings and leave Mrs. Contrelli and Mr. Strausner alone. I don't think he ever thought they were anything other than friends or he wouldn't have left them alone. Well then of course, after a while Mr. Contrelli got sick again and was up in his room, he was sort of out of the picture. She and Mr. Contrelli had separate bedrooms. Their relationship was not sexual, I was pretty certain of that, even though Mrs. Contrelli tried to act otherwise, but we knew better. We all knew, um . . . . me and the other house staff and we whispered about it. They did the laundry and changed the bedding. Never a trace of a woman in Mr. Contrelli's bed, or of any type of, well you know, rowdy goings on in his bed. I thought that maybe the cancer surgery he had in Germany left him impotent—it was prostate cancer that he had, and he was also so much older than Charlotte. But Mr. Strausner seemed like a very good friend to Mrs. Contrelli, um . . . you know, supportive and sympathetic and there at her side, maybe even like a brother. I believe that's how Mr. Contrelli saw their relationship."

"Yes, it appears so," added Bjorn. Ingrid shrugged her shoulders and shook her head as if she was now trying to remember more.

Adam asked, "How did the marriage with Charlotte and Gerheardt seem to be?"

"Well, they had problems right from the beginning. Maybe she was sad about the two husbands dying, but she seemed to change and had a meaner disposition. She was cross often and yelled at me for not folding the laundry correctly or something like that, you know small things—unimportant things that she never worried about before but just to find fault and take out her rage on me. I didn't like her very much then. She was a perfectionist, almost obsessive. Every towel had to be folded and stacked perfectly in the linen closet. Things had to be even, squared perfectly and lined up. The silver could not have spots on it or she would fly into a rampage. I was constantly polishing the silver, standing in that pantry!"

Ingrid picked up a spoon and played with it for a moment. "My God, I wonder how many times I held this very spoon. Well she was obsessive about things like that. Maybe she was stressed, or something, but she snapped at me more than she ever did before. She was as sweet and charming as she could be when others were within hearing range, but when she was alone dealing with the staff, she could be quite brutal."

She paused a moment and took a sip of her coffee and then continued. It was as if she had become emotional with the unleashing of suppressed feelings. "She and Mr. Strausner fought like cats and dogs. They tried to keep it behind closed doors, but when she tore into him, she was oblivious to anyone within hearing range inside the house.

"She had a terribly short and hot temper then that I didn't see quite so much before. They said horrible things to one another. I remember him exploding at her one day. It appeared he had just had enough and she was trying his nerves. He told her to remember where she came from and if it wasn't for him, she wouldn't be where she was now. I was curious about that statement. It seemed to me, um . . . she was much better off before she married him, so I didn't understand what he meant. I don't know what benefit he provided for her when they married. It seemed quite ridiculous for him to make that statement. Where she was at that point and where she was when her first husband was still alive, were not the same things, of course. She had more money and lived a better life during her first marriage. It was very obvious her money was running out and the house was beginning to be rundown and she had already let the gardener go as well as most of the staff. It wasn't as if he was making life any easier for her or providing for her. The way I saw it, he was living off of her. By then she only had me there and it was all I could do to keep things up, what with the size of the house and all. How could I, just being one person, keep this house clean! All those bedrooms and bathrooms! Just dusting the stairs and sweeping the carpet was an all day job. I did the best I could but she had also cut me down to just part time work. But of course by then, she was only living in part of the house. She had closed off several rooms so she didn't have to heat them in the winter, like most of the bedrooms upstairs, the solarium and this room. She spent most of her time in the library with a fire going in that room or in her bedroom. But she lived very well during the first two marriages, and she also spent a lot of money on herself and entertaining. All those parties! She loved to have parties and loved to have lots of people around. But as I said before, I noticed her clothes weren't quite as in style or fashionable as they were before and she stopped going on her trips to Switzerland shopping. And she stopped wearing her jewels, which I think were long gone by then. I think all of this made her very angry and she was always tense. Mr. Strausner didn't do much that I could see to bring in any money. I really don't know what he did as a profession."

Felix found that interesting, but of course his interest in all these people was Strausner. "That's interesting because, as I said, Gerheardt Strausner was a doctor during the war. I think it is very interesting that a man who was trained as a physician could be idle and do nothing, and especially because he was still a relatively young man, and when I knew him, he was extraordinarily hubris."

Bjorn straightened in his chair and leaned toward Felix to speak directly to him. "That is very interesting. What was his specialty as a physician, do you know?"

"No, I did not know his specialty, but he performed surgeries," answered Felix.

"Even though he no longer practiced medicine, it seemed he maintained his hauteur and felt superior," said Bjorn.

Ingrid continued. "He was at the house all the time. Never gone off on a regular basis, um . . . . like to a job or something. I thought he was a bum so it surprises me to hear he was a doctor. He probably helped spend their way through what little fortune she had left after the death of the two husbands. I think her poorer lifestyle embarrassed her, you know, for me to see. I don't think she wanted me to know and tried to hide it, but it was so obvious. I knew what was going on. I even noticed some artwork disappear. I think she was selling off some of the furnishings. I mean, for years there was a huge painting hanging in the gallery and then one day it was gone. What could have happened to it? I never mentioned it to her that I noticed it was gone, but I knew that she was struggling. Maybe that is why she and Mr. Strausner argued so much. He didn't do much to take care of her or to keep up the house, but he sat around smoking his pipe and drinking brandy. I do recall the last argument I heard. It was brutal and there was a lot of shouting. She said, 'Oh shut up, Gerheardt.' And then she said something to the effect of him not being able to take all the credit, and 'God knows where he would be without her.'

"Now, I'm trying to think of the words she used and she kept saying them over and over again. Oh yes, something like, Verewigen (Perpetuate), Aushalten (Endure) and Bleiben (Abide). She kept saying, 'oh for God's sake, Gerheardt listen to your own words as you invented them. Live the plan!' She just screamed at him. It actually scared me. I had to say, I had my ear pretty close to the door one time, but stepped back immediately when I heard her scream at him," she said with a sort of giggle. We all laughed and thought it was comical, just visualizing her standing on the other side of a closed door, with her ear pressed to the door, and jumping back with freight. She joined us in a shy giggle.

By now it was obvious that a couple glasses of wine made Ingrid more comfortable and she was like an open book. She continued, "She kept asking what should she have done and did he realize how difficult it was of her and what was she to do? It was their own special code. I just couldn't make sense out of it. He asked her if she realized how difficult it was for him to wait, so from that I gathered that he loved her all along, and maybe she didn't know it. He would say, 'Do you realize how difficult it was for me to wait, all these years?' I listened to this same argument over and over again. They never stopped yelling and this same subject came up time and time again. I did not know what they were talking about. I thought maybe it had something to do with their wedding vows or they were talking in code! That might have been the intent. They didn't want me to know what they were talking about. They didn't care if I heard them arguing, but they didn't want me to understand what they were saying. They argued very well in German! I think she forgot I spoke German because we conversed in English most of the time, but she also spoke Italian quite well and could converse with Mr. Contrelli and also Mr. Brusta and the staff in Italian."

Bjorn spoke up. "I'm very curious about these words, Ingrid. You seem to recall this very clearly." He asked her again and wrote them down in a little notebook he took from his jacket pocket.

"Yes, because the arguments always were repeated. They never seemed to resolve anything while arguing. Normally, I think if people argue about something, they come to a resolution and they shouldn't have to argue about the same thing again. They seemed to always repeat the same arguments, as if they were each trying to give their own interpretation of these words, but they couldn't seem to agree," said Ingrid.

"Tell me more about how Mr. Strausner died. I understand you told Diana that he fell over the balcony upstairs, is that right?" Bjorn asked.

"Yes. It was just horrible. In fact, I hate to say this, but his body landed just where this table is now." We all looked up at the balcony over the living room from the upstairs landing at the top of the stair case. A chill ran down my spine, as I'm sure it did everyone else's. We all had a look of mortification on our faces and gasped a bit.

"That was quite a fall," said Bjorn. "About thirty feet or so, I'd say. No one could live after a fall like that."

"Well, no and of course there was a large glass coffee table here in front of the fire. It just shattered with the thrust of the fall from such a height," Ingrid added. Bjorn asked if she thought they were arguing all that day, the day he died.

"I don't know, but I can imagine they were. I was there briefly that afternoon and they were arguing in the library. They had the door closed but I could still hear. I left about three o'clock that day and they must have continued their arguing and obviously finally left the library, maybe realizing I had left the house and no one was in ear range, so they could argue throughout the entire house. They were always fighting. Supposedly he lost his balance while leaning over the railing and he fell and died immediately. She said it was an accidental fall and he broke his neck, as well as his back, so he had multiple injuries, but he died right away. I wasn't here and after I heard about it, I stayed away for two days, and then when I came, she was very relieved to see me and was grieving very badly. She took to her bed and cried for days. I don't think she left her room for quite some time after his death. I felt so bad for her, the poor thing. I tried to comfort her and surprisingly enough, she actually let me. I actually sat down next to her and embraced her and she let me. She put her head on my shoulder and wept for a moment. I think she needed someone to be with her for a while. It was so unlike her to let her guard down like that, but she was so pathetic. Then it was like she realized what she was doing and checked herself and straightened up and composed herself. She told me she was fine and thanked me for coming and she would be all right and I was free to go. I was one moment consoling her and the next, I was dismissed. She wanted to be alone, but on my way out of the room she asked if I could get some tea and toast for her before I left. She hadn't eaten anything for a while, I was quite sure. I kept my distance but watched over her and she just stayed in her room for days at a time. I brought food up to her but I couldn't convince her to get out and go into the yard to get some air. She was very depressed but she did at times go out to the terrace off her bedroom and sit there smoking cigarettes and staring at the lake for long periods of time. She would get all wrapped up in a blanket and just sit there in her lounge chair looking at the lake. It was so sad to see her like that. She told me that I need not come by for a while and that she would be all right and that she would call me if she needed me. She was quite emphatic about that. Well, I stayed away but looked in on her every other day or so, but she was still in her bed and didn't realize I had come. I was worried about her. I thought she might call me but she didn't and I recall I struggled in my mind about whether to go look in on her or not but after several days, I decided not to go anymore and thought if she needed me she would call, as she said."

"It seemed she got over the deaths of her first two husbands quite quickly. Seeing as she and Gerheardt argued so much, I wonder why she was so broken up about him dying," said Bjorn.

"Maybe she didn't have anyone else to be with, or take care of her, and after all, she and Gerheardt had been in one another's lives for many years, even before they married," suggested Felix.

Ingrid continued, "Well, I was a bit surprised also that she took it so hard. As I said, after a while I stayed away, but she owed me money, which I needed very badly. I hated to bother her at that time about money, but I needed to be paid. So I waited over a week before I went back and then, well . . ." Ingrid paused to compose herself. I could see this was very difficult for her to talk about and of course, I knew from my first meeting with Ingrid, what was about to be revealed.

"I'll never forget that day. It was raining and a very dark overcast day. A heavy fog hovered low over the lake, and it was quite damp and chilly. When I got to the house, the front door was ajar, which I thought was strange, seeing as it was cold and raining outside. Leaves and the spray of the rain had blown into the entrance hall making quite a mess and the house was quite cold. I assumed the door was left ajar and forgotten and the wind had blown it open. I came in and called for her, but got no answer. I got busy cleaning the entrance hall. I had to get all those wet leaves and debris up that had blown in and mop up the floor. Then after a while it occurred to me that the house was unusually quiet and I had called out to her but got no answer. I thought she might be asleep and was certain she was in her room, probably still depressed and crying about Mr. Strausner's death. Her car was in the drive and it wasn't a nice enough day to be out for a walk. I found it strange that I couldn't smell the fireplace, which was normal during that time because like I said, she was living mostly either in her room or the library and always had a fire going in the fireplaces. Especially on rainy days, she always had a fire going to take the dampness out of the air.

"I looked in the living room first, of course. The carpet had been pulled up because, you know, his fall left quite a bad blood stain. I think she had someone come in and take it up and get rid of it. Then I looked all over the house, first checking the library, the kitchen, then her bedroom but the bed was empty and the bedding was all knotted up, um . . . as if it hadn't been made up in a long time. I went back down stairs and checked all the rooms on the first floor, the cellar, and then back upstairs and looked in all the other bedrooms but they had all been closed off for a long time. And then as I walked to the back of the upstairs landing to the servant's stairway, I saw a light on in the attic at the top of that stairway. I first called to her, but got no answer, so I went up the small staircase leading to the attic and there she was, hanging from the rafters. I almost fainted. It was horrible." She stopped for a moment and took a sip of water.

Irene cried out in a startling burst of emotion, slamming her hand down on the table to emphasize her shock. "Oh my dear God! You've got to be kidding! Who would have known that was how her life would end! It's just incredible!" It seemed a few glasses of wine really put her into a much more animated character than I had witnessed up until that point. Even Jean looked at her in disbelief. Irene was having the time of her life and loving every morbid detail. Everyone else began to squirm in their chairs and mumbled words of shock and long sighs.

When everyone began to settle down, Ingrid continued. "I can see it in my mind as if I just laid eyes on her now. She had on a pair of tan trousers and a black sweater and her feet were bare. Usually her hair was piled up on her head, but it just hung down to her shoulders and across her face. Motionless! She must have been hanging there for quite some time. I never did find out how long she had been like that. A chair was beneath her, turned over on its side. She must have kicked it out from under her. Beyond her was the window of the dormer that looked down at the front yard and the lake. I think the lake was the last thing she saw. I was horrified and began to back up and almost fell down the stairs. I scraped my hand on a nail reaching for the railing and it began to bleed. I still have a scar from that cut. Every time I look at it, it is a reminder of that very instant. All these years I have thought about it and wondered what possessed her to do that. I imagined she was running out of money and was despondent after losing a third husband, but she was still so young. Such a shame! Every time I walk by this house, I look up at that little attic window on the third floor, and I cross myself and say a little prayer for her and just think about her for a moment. You know, it was really a cruel thing for her to do, to let me find her like that. She knew it would be me that found her. No one else came around the house. She may have intentionally left the front door ajar for me. It has haunted me all these years."

Bjorn, in a very sympathetic voice, said "It was extremely cruel to do that to you, but she seemed like the kind of person that could easily dismiss concern about other people. What did you do after you found her?"

"I ran down the stairs and out of the house and up the street to the antique shop and told the gentleman inside to call the police for me because something horrible happened at the house. I just wanted to get out of the house quickly. I could have called from the telephone in the library, but I just couldn't stay in that house alone. The man at the shop gave me a towel to wrap my hand in because it was bleeding and sat me down in a chair and tried to compose me. After a few moments I went back to the house, but just to the yard and when the police came, I told them what I had found in the attic. By then I wasn't feeling good at all. I think I was in shock and my hand was bleeding quite badly. I thought I was going to faint. The policeman got me a stool to sit on and a glass of water. Then they drove me to the hospital to have my hand tended to. I never went inside the house again until that first day I met you, Diana. You see, I still have a scar," she said as she held up her hand pointing to the scar.

Everyone expressed their sorrow for Ingrid and how difficult that must have been for her. She was quite emotional when telling the details of that day and we could see it still affected her quite badly. "You poor dear. Let me see that scar," said Irene as she reached across the table to look at Ingrid's extended hand. "How horrible that must have been for you. It was indeed a very cruel thing to do to you. Just plain bitchy, I think. She should have burned in hell for doing that to you," she said as she crossed herself.

I refilled their coffee cups and Bjorn offered everyone more dessert and cognac. Irene skipped the dessert and went right to the cognac. Ingrid continued answering the questions everyone had for her concerning Charlotte. She told them how pretentious and snobby and sometimes rude she was to her help, but then at times would make up for it by doing something nice or giving them a small gift.

During this evening, each had a little story to tell. All of these little stories unveiled a little more of Charlotte's secrets and her life was becoming a vast open book with flowing continuity and the histrionics of that era slowly unfolded. Still, there were many missing pieces. Each story laid out a little morsel of information that begged for more, or created a barrier that made me realize that just when I thought I was beginning to understand her, I felt I was all wrong and she was not the kind of person I assumed. More information generated more questions. No part of Charlotte's life seemed normal and it made us wonder, how

*The House on Lake Maggiore*

a nice young girl from Germany ended up living in this house with so much pain and sorrow and how was she connected to Dr. Strausner, a Nazi doctor? She was still a young woman but it was all too overpowering for her, obviously and she took her own life because of it. Or, was there more to it? What fed our curiosity was the mix of people she seemed to associate with that visited her at this house that seemed to be extremely diverse.

I brought out the photographs for us all to look at again and Felix and Frederick pointed out the man they thought was Carl and they both also looked at the pistol and said it was a German Lugar and that the initials on the gun, "CD," was probably for Carl Drummond, who was the extremely inexplicable and vague houseguest and mysterious brother to Frederick's wife's. Irene stepped up and wanted to hold the gun. Everyone just sort of backed away and watched her. She fumbled with it, and said, "I've never held a revolver before. Imagine, this thing could kill someone." She aimed it at the fireplace and said, "It's a bit heavy, don't you think?" Bjorn smiled at her and took the gun from her delicate hand. I knew it was time to try to get more coffee into Irene.

Ingrid tried to remember Carl but could not recall seeing anyone like that at the house. She thought she would have remembered anyone that was German coming to visit. She remembered other men, but they were mostly Italian and friends or business associates of Mr. Contrelli. Mrs. Contrelli had no friends of her own, other than Gerheardt of course. She said that perhaps Bjorn's idea of the loft might be right. Maybe Carl spent time staying in the loft in the carriage house, but she could not recall any activity there or other strange people visiting. Carl died in late 1945 or early 1946 according to the letter so it was not long after Charlotte came to the scene, early on at the inception of our knowledge of her arrival at the house.

Ingrid recalled when she first noticed that the house was beginning to deteriorate. Things that needed fixing were left untouched. Leaks in the pipes left water marks on the ceiling, light fixtures no longer worked, door hinges needed to be oiled or repaired. It appeared there was no money to keep the house up and that was when Charlotte discharged Ingrid. At times, she would ask her to come back to help, but couldn't offer her steady work. Ingrid knew that hard times had hit the house on Lago Maggiore.

She recalled a serious leak in one of the upstairs bathrooms, and in fact, that was one area that I had the plasterers repairing as well as taking care of the mold behind the walls and rotten floorboards that resulted from so many years of the leak not being repaired. Ingrid remembered another time very early on in her employment with Charlotte, when she found a small leak and the carpet in the dining room was wet. It might have come from the laundry room, which in the early days, was in the pantry, through the wall. She went into some detail about that leak and how upset Charlotte became because it happened on an evening when she was expecting guests. Charlotte lost her temper and went into a rampage. She was briefly interrupted when Mr. Contrelli entered the room and she immediately changed her tone. This was indicative of Charlotte's character; she was a complex woman of many moods it seemed. After Mr. Contrelli left the room, Ingrid said she watched in disbelief as Charlotte took matters into her own hands and moved a liquor cabinet, fully loaded, by herself to cover the spot on the carpet and she was astonished that Charlotte seemed to have extraordinary strength.

The conversation continued well into the late hours of the evening. I have to admit, it was all very interesting and I was to fault for digging up all this mystery and connecting all the proverbial dots from the information dropped on me from all my visitors.

Jean and I were in the kitchen straightening things up when Irene sort of staggered her tiny frame into the room. "*Bshorn* is going to drive us home, Jean, but I wanted to *shay* good night to you, Diana." She grabbed both my hands in hers and looked up at me, with eyes a bit glazed over. "This was a most extraordinary evening and your dinner was *delicioush*—you *musht* give me that recipe. Honestly, I don't think I've had this *mush* excitement in one evening since my dear husband dropped dead on the kitchen floor, twenty-three years ago. Now, you really did open up a little Pandora's Box with this house renovation, didn't you, dear? Pure genius on your part, I *musht* say, the way you *schook* things up here. I mean, good Lord, who were *theesh* people anyway that lived here? *Sush* goings on. What I wouldn't give for one more evening in the *shame* room with Charlotte, that little strumpet! And to think all *thish* was going on just a few doors away from my *housh*! I'm truly surprised but *ichs sho fashunating*! Thank You *sho mush* for inviting me. I wouldn't have *mished* this for the world." She leaned up so I could kiss her on the cheek and then took Jean by the hand in an attempt to lead her out of the kitchen, but I think she really needed Jean's support because her step was wavering after her obvious appreciation of our wine selection. "Come dear, *Bshorn* is waiting for *ush*. *Heesh* got my coat." Jean looked back over her shoulder at me and smiled. Irene was truly one of the bigger surprises of the evening. Charlotte hanging from the rafters took second place.

The dinner party was a success, albeit a bit exhausting and emotional. Everyone made an interesting contribution to the conversation and all the information exchanged opened up a clearer perspective of what life in this house was like, and as it turned out, it certainly was not as glorious as we had once suspected.

Soon after that dinner party, I realized that working in the house, sitting in my little kitchen office wasn't as exciting as it had been up to that point and I was losing my motivation, but I did not lose my focus. I would find my mind wandering and thinking about Charlotte, about Strausner and their truculent relationship, about his death and what might have led to that horrible fall over the railing, and then of course Charlotte and her ultimate suicide in the attic. I would get a chill up my spine thinking about any remaining spirits in the house and suddenly wish I wasn't alone and would seek out the company of one of the workers for a chat, or of Vito, and of course, I so looked forward to Adam's visits and our dinners in the village. I was still driven to complete the house and make it spectacular. I dove into catalogs of paint chips, fabric swatches, furniture designs, and bathroom fixtures; anything I could do to divert my attention and stop thinking about the resident ghosts. When Adam did come to visit and we had our usual dinner, there was nothing else to talk about but the historic daemons and why this happened or why that happened or what was that person to the other. It was a redundant discourse of never-ending queries and speculations. We were all addicted. All our conversations centered on Charlotte and her associates. Sometimes I tired of it, but then I realized I was just as obsessed with these ghosts as everyone else and the theories we all had about them. I tried to stretch my imagination to the future inhabitants and how they would bring new life to the house and all that old history would be gone, painted over and polished, but it saddened me to think I would never be there to see that. I would be left with my memories of what the house was like while I was there, and how entrenched I was in that history and it was no longer just a house. It was almost a tomb, encapsulating the ghosts—Charlotte, poor Pietro, Vincinzo, and of course that horrible man, Gerheardt. Their spirits were all there milling around encased in a nebulous cloud hovering overhead, trapped in that house. I would lay my head on the pillow at night in my hotel room and awaken abruptly with the vision of Charlotte hanging from the rafters. I could not get that image out of my mind and felt compassion for her, being young and yet so hopeless. I relived Ingrid's description of that day, how she came and found the front door opened and the foyer floor scattered with the leaves that had blown in, and her kneeling down to clean it and then wondering where Charlotte was. Then I envisioned her roaming the house looking for her and then a scream in the attic when she ascended those stairs and found her. Sometimes it broke my heart thinking about it.

# CHAPTER 11

All the sleepless nights and nightmares began to take a toll on me and I became exhausted from the work as well as the emotions that accompanied the histrionics of the house. I realized I needed a break. At that time the remodeling in the kitchen was about to begin. The demolition would take some time to remove the old appliances and fixtures and move plumbing and walls. Also, Vittorio came back to let me know work was about to begin in the yard and I could expect to hear a lot of noise as they began to pull out all the overgrowth, cut down some trees, pull the vines off the façade and then begin sandblasting the exterior of the house. It was going to be a noisy couple of weeks. I decided it would be a good time to take a break and remove myself from the madness for a while, so I decided I needed to go home for about a week.

My business in Los Angeles was in good hands and I was delighted to see my associates were busy keeping things going for me and keeping my clients happy. It was wonderful being back in the comfort of my home and surroundings and the culture I knew so well. I took a couple days and visited my little mountain cabin and found everything as I left it. However, all the time I was home, I couldn't get the thoughts of the house in Italy out of my mind and was anxious to get back to work and finish it all. After being in Italy those few months, my life at home looked more appealing and I realized how much I missed the comforts of having a real home, instead of a hotel room and with familiar things and places. Even just going to the supermarket and the local drug store was a treat for me. I was happy to be home where everything was familiar, but was anxious to return and conclude the work, see the finished home and return home again for good. A favorite quote by Thomas Jefferson explains why we are always most happy and comfortable in our own homes: "That which we elect to surround ourselves with becomes the museum of our soul and the archive of our experiences." The relics of our own life become our history and I was happy again being in a place that had some of my own history and residue of my own life and experiences. Of course it was short lived and I had to return to Italy to finish the work.

The best part of the trip home was a good visit with my daughter in New York on my way back to Italy. For two days, she took care of me and cooked for me and we had great conversations. She wanted to hear all about the house and everything that happened, and we talked nonstop. It was very nice to be taken care of for a change and I relished in it and hated to say goodbye to her.

I located a photographer and arranged for him to come to Italy and take loads of photos to use for the book and articles I was planning to write. I had also gotten a call from Bjorn that an Italian decorator magazine wanted to come to the house and interview me and do a "before and after" article. I had been taking lots of pictures along the way, so I could furnish the "before" photos.

When I returned to Italy, I was happy to see the pace of the work in the house progressing more rapidly. The roof had been repaired and the missing tiles were all replaced. The kitchen was one of the biggest efforts. Everything in the kitchen was torn out and brought down to the bare bones of the interior walls and the remodeling was coming along well. The kitchen was being done in an old world Tuscan look with limestone floors, beautiful maple cabinetry and a huge island in the center with heavily carved moldings and a white Carrera marble top, making it more

*The House on Lake Maggiore*

a piece of grand furniture than a service island. The rest of the kitchen counters were dark granite. All the marble and granite came from local mountain areas, as the Carrara Mountains are close by. We installed the top of the line appliances in the latest Italian design and technology. The old industrial cooker was an incredible appliance, but cumbersome to use compared to current technology and luckily we found a restaurant that gladly gave it a good home. The stove we installed was extremely expensive, but for the type of kitchen we were building, we decided not to skimp on anything. Any gourmet cook would have paid a high price to have such a fabulous kitchen and it was my hope that the potential buyer would fully appreciate all the thought that went into making this a state-of-the-art kitchen.

    I shopped in Milan for the lighting and we brought in a chandelier to be hung over the island and another smaller one to hang over the table in the nook by the bay windows, as well as task lighting under the cabinets. While in Milan I also bought light fixtures for other places in the house where fixtures were either missing or inadequately impressive.

    A new laundry room was rebuilt at the back of the service room behind the kitchen and that cleared up the rest of the hallway leading to the side entrance to the house and out to a side garden. The service stairway coming down from the second floor was repaired and refinished and now with the new laundry room out of the way, the area was larger and could serve other purposes besides a good entrance from the yard, such as a mud room, perhaps a workroom or a place to store gardening supplies and tools.

    While the work was taking place in the kitchen, I moved into the Library where the desk I found in the cellar had been refinished and placed, along with two of the reupholstered chairs and a small divan all reupholstered in rich dark teal velvet. I had the wood floors in the library refinished and brought in a new area rug of beautiful terracotta and teal colors. The beams of the coffered ceiling were also refinished and I found the perfect chandelier for the library while shopping in Milan: a black iron three tier fixture with small gold silk shades, which added a rich finish to the room, as well as a perfect ambiance. French doors replaced the small window and opened onto the new loggia on the back of the house, which also let more natural light into the room and provided a view of the new gardens. The bookshelves and paneling had all been refinished. The library was just about complete. I resolved the mystery of the moldings when I fortunately found several books in the attic. These helped me decipher the moldings with the discovery of intricately illustrated children's books. After studying the allegoric carvings on the moldings, I realized they each represented different stories and some of the illustrations were almost identical to the moldings. The authors of the fairytales were Grimes, Dickens, Perrault, and Anderson and were mostly well know stories, of Puss in Boots, Tom Thumb, Bluebeard, Sleeping Beauty and Little Red Riding Hood. More importantly I believed the artist used the various illustrations from many stories, all done by Gustave Doré, a very famous illustrator of children's stories, bibles and also such famous works, including Cervantes, Shakespeare and most impressive, Dante's "Inferno." The moldings were so closely related to the illustrations, I believed the artist followed these interpretations from these books very closely when doing the carvings.

The only thing left to do in the library was hang one of the tapestries that was coming with the borrowed furnishings from the other villa, where two sconces had been wired into the wall that would be on either side of the tapestry, and the books had to be brought in to be placed on the shelves. It turned out to be as I first envisioned the room—a very comfortable room in which to work and I now had a good view of the garden and yard through the French doors.

With the close proximity to the kitchen, the noise from all the work going on in there was sometimes too much, even with the doors to the gallery closed. Finally when the demolition of the kitchen was complete and the cabinets and flooring were put in, the noise subsided a bit. Fall had set in and there were quite a few rainy days. The new boilers were doing a good job and the

*The House on Lake Maggiore*

house was comfortably warm, although a bit drafty in places, which would be expected in a house of that size. On some rainy days, I made a fire in the fireplace next to the desk in the library and loved the cozy atmosphere of that room. I thought about Charlotte in the last part of her life, almost living entirely in the library and the dark dreariness of the room as it was before, would not have done much to lift her out of her depression. Now the room had a bright warm feeling and I imagined the new owners, whoever they were, finding this one of the most comfortable rooms in the house and one would want to curl up and read forever in front of that fireplace.

The bathrooms were all completely gutted and replaced and I had wallpaper hangers working in each of them, as well as the muralist and her team moving from one room to the next, either painting new murals, or fixing the ceiling details, or a bit of Trompe L'Oeil, which added some dimensional details around doorways. They did beautiful work that added special interest and detail to the decor of the house. In the kitchen, once all the walls were painted and the sawdust had subsided, the muralist began doing a little ceiling detail in the breakfast nook, with vines and flowers and the seamstress made some small roman shades in blue and white toile fabric for the tops of the tall windows. The old table was replaced with a lovely round table and chairs, which I found at an antique store and had refinished with new cushions made to match the fabric of the shades. The frosted glass door from the kitchen to the pantry was now in place. The pantry was kept as it was, except for fresh paint and a small sink put in to make it more of a service pantry and we added a good sized wine cooler and a small refrigerator with ice maker. A new door of beautiful rich wood with beveled glass panes was installed leading from the gallery into the pantry, so the little room could now be entered from either the kitchen or the gallery and became a very functional butler's pantry where drinks could be prepared.

The marble floors with their marquetry inlays in the gallery were cleaned and polished and the wood floor in the entrance hall was refinished and graced with an antique Savonnerie area rug. The sconces and chandeliers in the gallery were also installed and a lovely silk fabric in a pale gold tone with a Chinoiserie brocade design graced the wall while the chair rails and paneling below were refinished in a lighter wood tone to make the room brighter. The furniture borrowed from the other estate was finally delivered and put in place and had many wonderful pieces. There was a very stately Bombay chest with a marble top that was perfect for the gallery and a huge painting of a fox hunt with horses and dogs hung over the chest with the sconces on either side, as well as buffet lamps. I had four antique chairs, which I found in the cellar, refinished and the seats reupholstered with rich teal silk brocade and placed in the gallery against the walls. We brought in tall potted palms and put them on the pillar plinths. It was a very elegant gallery that led to all the other beautiful rooms.

The old front door was refinished and put back in place, where it had been for what we estimated the age of the house to be, about ninety years, but it no longer moaned and groaned but now opened on new hinges and was adorned with new hardware. The stairway had been refinished and a new carpet runner put in place. The railings, balusters and ironwork was all refinished and polished.

The columns leading to the living room were painted and the capitals repaired. One of the elaborate Corinthian capitals had broken away but was now fixed. The workman created a mold from a section of the other pillar capital and used it to make a plaster reproduction and once put in place, it was impossible to know it had been repaired. The marble around the fireplace had been cleaned and polished. The brass andirons were also polished and gleaming. It was nice on these cool days to have a fire in the fireplace in that large room. Once some of the furniture pieces were refinished they were brought back into the house along with the furnishings from the other villa, one by one and soon, the furnishings were coming together and filling up large empty spaces. The lot of burrowed furniture from the other house included a lovely grand piano that fit beautifully in one corner of the living room and took up a substantial amount of empty space. This worked very well for the final look, and would be a nice feature for the party to celebrate the open house. I brought in some sofas, tables and lamps and spread everything out because the room was so large and I didn't want gaping spaces. The borrowed furniture was a blessing and helped me fill up a lot of empty space without having to make big purchases. This would help to stage the house and make it more appealing to potential buyers. The chandelier over the living room was working and cleaned, and the lamps on various tables scattered throughout the room created a lovely ambiance and brought comfortable warmth into the room.

The main bedroom, which I knew from stories Ingrid told was Charlotte's private chamber, was decorated very elegantly. The new paint and refreshed frescos on the domed ceiling made the room quite regal looking, with Chinoiserie again on a Chinese lacquered armoire, polished light fixtures, crystal chandeliers, paintings, pilaster moldings around the French doors leading to the terrace, and elaborate Baroque moldings on the closet doors and walls. The bathroom was finished with marble counters and nickel faucets, new cabinets, a beautiful large tub and shower. The marble surround of the small fireplace in the sitting room was polished and a floral painting hung above the mantel. It was a perfect palace bedroom fit for royalty. I had a dressing table refinished and mounted an antique mirror above it and hung new drapes by the French doors leading to the terrace, which was also refinished and we placed some patio furniture from the other estate.

The solarium became brighter as soon as the overgrown bushes outside the window were cleared. The windows covering the three walls now let in more light and the wood floors were refinished. I had some bright areas rugs from the borrowed lot that were perfect for the room. I also bought new light fixtures and the room had a Palm Garden motif that was quite cheerful. It was becoming late fall and the room was chilly, so I brought in some space heaters and hid them around the room for the night of the opening party, to make the room warm enough for people to spend time there, perhaps sipping their cocktails. We also brought in a lot of plants and palms to emphasize the motif. It would be easy to imagine what a wonderful room that would be in the summer, with the glorious view of the lake across the street.

The gardens were finished with the concept of small rooms, with fountains, and the loggia outside the kitchen area ran along the back of the house. We put in new French doors leading to the loggia from the kitchen, as well as from the library. This provided a wonderful outside living space with a fireplace and seating area. There were lovely trellises, pergolas, and potted plants on the patio beyond the loggia, as well as patio furniture from the other house. Vittorio even made a pathway with pavers winding through the yard to the new carriage house, which was now a four car garage. The new building would be functional and well connected by the walkway to the back of house. The pathway was covered by a pergola that would eventually be grown over with Wisteria.

I began to plan the open house and the celebration party. I arranged for a pianist as well as a string quartet. We would set up a bar in the gallery for the evening's celebration so I also had to arrange for a bartender for that night. All the details planning for that big event kept me very busy but I looked forward to this because it meant all the restoration and remodeling work was finished and soon the house would be on the market and even more important, I could go home.

# CHAPTER 12

As the renovation became complete and the work in the house was winding down, I was beginning to have mixed feelings about leaving. I looked forward to going home, but I had gotten so attached to the house that it would be a difficult departure. It was painful for me to imagine walking out that front door and closing it behind me, never to look back. I spent so many hours imagining what this house should look like and then seeing it come together so nicely with the furnishings in place, my vision and expectations were truly fulfilled. I also spent too many hours thinking about the old history and people and that was what was going to be so hard to leave behind. I would not have the closeness I felt to them and many of my questions may never be answered and would have to remain here furtively forgotten.

There were many last minute details to tie up loose ends, such as to finish hanging paintings and tapestries, putting plants in place, getting throw pillows placed just so, wiping finger prints off mirrors and tables; all these little things needed to be done to make the house look complete. Then I had to prepare for the open house celebration. I scheduled caterers to bring hors d'oeuvres and desserts and servers to serve them, and ordered liquor and wine scheduled for delivery the day before the party. Bjorn had taken care of inviting people, running advertisements in just the right media to attract the most prestigious people who would be perspective buyers. I ordered fresh flower arrangements for most of the downstairs rooms, as well as a huge floral centerpiece for the dining room table, which I set with some lovely china that was part of the other estate, just for effect. The frescoes on the walls in the dining room were retouched and brightened as well as the ceiling fresco, the chandelier refurbished, the dining table and chairs from the other villa fit perfectly, making it a very elegant room. All the fireplaces would be lit and I believe we achieved our intent to make the home look warm and inviting for the sake of any prospective buyers who may be attending. The work on the house was complete and we were ready to put it on the market.

My first deadline to have everything complete was in regard to the photographer who was scheduled to take photos of the entire house the day before the opening. I was overwhelmed with last minute details to make everything look camera ready. Bjorn called me very early that morning and said he wanted to come and have an inspection and also talk to me. As much as I hated to take the time, he insisted it was important. He knew I was busy but only needed about an hour of my time. I knew he wanted to do one last walk-through of the house before we opened it up to strangers and potential buyers but I couldn't imagine what he wanted to talk about that would take an hour. I was pretty sure I couldn't afford to take the time but it sounded like saying no was not an option.

Bjorn arrived that afternoon and after we did a complete walk through and inspected the house together, he said he wanted to talk in private so I brought tea into the library and we sat down in front of the fireplace. I will never forget that day and how our happiness and joy with the culmination of our work turned to such intensity when he closed the door to the library so we could talk in private, away from photographers and the floral arrangers working in the various rooms. He began by complementing me and telling me what a great job I did and he couldn't have been happier with the end result. But he had more to tell me and he became very serious. A sinking feeling began to settle into my mind and I felt I was going to hear some disconcerting news about something I did wrong, or he was out of money and I wasn't going to get paid. I was totally clueless as to what this was about.

"Diana, this renovation was more to me than an opportunity to make money. I think it is time I was honest with you. It has been much more. My entire adult life has been consumed with a sort of quest. Not just to make money, but the money was just to finance this quest. This house—this house was always more than it seemed to me. I knew a couple of years ago that my quest led to this house and perhaps what I would find out about what happened in this house, would let me find answers I was looking for most of my life. It was the people, Diana. The people you found that finally ended my quest.

"You helped me more than you will ever know. This renovation was an excellent idea and I'm sure we will find a buyer and it is truly an extraordinary home, thanks to you and your hard work. But I must confess, in a way I used you as, well, sort of bate—someone to be there when people came from out of nowhere, people with curious natures that would come to you as if they were crawling out from the woodwork seeking information and perhaps, providing information. I knew people would be curious and would also, in their minds, be looking for answers or some sort of closure for their memories. Well, you see what happened. They did come and I knew they would. All these discussions we had and all these people, each bringing little stories with them. When the owners of this house died, they took some very important secrets with them. Only those secrets would help me end my life long search for answers. I needed someone here to sort of sift through the minutia that went with this renovation, to perhaps be the force to forge through it all, to uncover what I was looking for. You did that for me and I am ever so grateful. You helped me find my answers and I know you are a bit confused, but I need to tell you why this was so important to me."

"Bjorn," I interrupted him. "Do you mean to tell me that before we even began, you knew things about this house, even before people started to come and tell us? I don't understand."

I recall that afternoon so well, sitting in front of that fireplace. It was raining and I could hear the rain drops hitting the large leaves of the fig plant beyond the loggia. The fire in the fireplace crackled and spit embers from wood a bit too green but still gave off a sweet fragrance. The moodiness of the room made it the sort of day I would love to have nothing else to do but sit there reading a good book enjoying the ambiance. Of course, I could see from the look on Bjorn's face, he had an alternate agenda. He looked very somber and rather sad. I had no idea what was on his mind but I could see that he was about to tell me something serious; a knot was beginning to form in my stomach.

Bjorn began to unveil the tragic history of his childhood. He told me how he continually kept coming by the house during the renovation, not just to see how things were progressing, but to see if I had found anything, any trace of the history of the people that lived in the house. He had known things about the house and he believed it contained information that would provide answers and therefore it became necessary to peel away the layers of grime and dirt on the house to uncover any trace that could lead him to those answers. His story began to unfold that grey rainy day with just the two of us sitting in that library.

"I engineered this entire fiasco in order to find answers for the search that led me here. I needed to find a way to see the inside and I wanted the truth to come out about who lived here. It was not just my curiosity; it was more of a driving vindication. It's difficult to understand I know, but my entire life I have been searching for people, who I believe lived here or spent time here. I followed a path for decades and one day a few years ago, I happened upon this poor shamble of a house. I did some digging and found out a little about its history. A name surfaced—a name I had in my mind almost my entire life: Gerheardt Strausner. I knew many things about him and my investments were my way of financing my search for him. Diana, when I was a child in

Poland, I lost my family in Auschwitz." He stood up and rolled up his shirt sleeve and showed me a tattoo on his left forearm. I was astounded and had no idea.

"I somehow survived my time at Auschwitz, however my brother and my parents did not. I have hunted for people responsible for killing my family, as well as the families of many others, most of my life. It was not just for me that I hunted Nazis. It was for other people who suffered the same loss. Through the years I found them. I sought them out from behind doors many years closed, places far away; many times I found they had died, but I at least would find them and could put that one lead to rest and close the loop. Many times it was a ghost-hunt and especially now, so many years after the war, if any of them are still alive, they would be very old, but I still needed to close the loop. I found them for other people and for other people's stories, but this particular path that had gone cold decades ago, was a personal search. This search involved my life and the life of my family. I had many leads but they often came to nothing at the end of a very long path. I needed to resolve this last long search so I could stop and live the rest of my life in peace. Dead or alive, I had to know what happened to those I searched for who killed my family. Time was running out. Anyone with answers was of course aging. Time would not stand still for me. That path led to this house." He paused and looked at me for a moment, giving me an opportunity to speak.

When I tried to speak my mouth was so dry, the words were barely audible and more like a whisper. "You knew about Gerheardt before? He was who you were searching for? You traced him to this house and then you found he had died. Is that why your search is over?"

"There was more to it, but yes, I found that everyone I was looking for had died so now, my search has ended, but I had to know for sure and now I know," he said.

"Why Gerheardt? I realize he was not such a good person but how was he connected to you?" I asked.

"That's what I want to tell you. After our dinner party and all the things that came out about how Strausner lived here and how he was sort of hiding behind—dear Charlotte, the fire inside me was lit again and I needed to be sure of what their connection was and how she fit into his life. Why was he here? I had to put it all together in my mind. He was a Nazi doctor in the Third Reich—that much we know, but he wasn't just any doctor. He was a physician who performed experimental surgeries and Carl, the infamous Carl whose name keeps popping up was more than a lab technician, as Felix well suspected and as I have discovered. This Carl was a very powerful person and he and Gerheardt worked together, thus their war crimes. We found out a lot about Carl. Many of the things I needed to know, I found out from Felix. God bless Felix. Thank God for the day that this man walked up to the doorway here and introduced himself to you and inquired about Gerheardt Strausner. Felix and I became very well acquainted over the last few months and he helped me enormously. We were on similar quests and he had information I needed and was willing to help me. The two of us worked together to dig deep into the long lost history to find what I, we were both looking for."

I sat in disbelief and shock and was not quite sure how I should feel or react. Maybe I felt betrayed because Bjorn didn't confide in me, but rather he manipulated me and kept so much from me when I thought we were becoming good friends. "Well Bjorn, there was always the chance I could have refused to talk to the people that came here. That would have thwarted your plan, wouldn't it?"

"Well, I hadn't thought about that. Thank heaven that wasn't a problem." I settled back in my chair and listened while he continued.

"Felix remembered Gerheardt and he remembered Carl. He remembered a lot and he was very discrete. He wasn't sure how much he should tell you or Frederick because he didn't want to upset either of you. It was believed by many in the German army, not just by Felix, that Gerheardt and Carl were homosexually involved with one another. It was strictly taboo to engage in that sort of relationship and was in fact punishable by death. They had to be very cautious and discrete. However, it was clear that they were notoriously obsessed with sexuality; it became their work and involved the type of experimental surgeries Gerheardt performed. I thought at first, really hoped, that Gerheardt might still be alive. When these visitors came to this house and poured their hearts out, I had small bits of information to work with. Ingrid was so helpful with everything she knew. I found out that Gerheardt had died, but what about this Carl? I was unsure about Carl and what happened to him. Carl became important to me and it was through Felix that I could put some pieces together and figure out their connection to one another.

"Then one day, just as if God were still looking down on this house, he led Frederick to our door. Pure happenstance, but just as I hoped it would be. There he was, someone that knew Carl. So here we were all these weeks asking ourselves, who was Carl? He appeared to be just some infrequent visitor who passed through this house, maybe staying for a day or so. That was about all we knew about Carl, but Carl became an important character in our little drama here and as we learned more, there was no doubt that he should have been captured and put on trial with other criminals of the war. He had reason to run and knew his future was bleak. We found out that he held awards, had high visibility, and was recognized as an influential SS officer, and of course the perfect Aryan.

"I have to give you a little background, so you understand what I am going to tell you, so please bear with me for a while. In war time in Germany it was the role of the SS to contribute as best as they could to the Eugenics program and Germanization. This program belonged to Himmler and he created a program called Lebensborn. At first it was just a place a woman could go to give birth, as opposed to having an abortion. Part of Germanization was to raise the birth rate of not just German people, but Aryan looking German people. Procreation was the purpose of Lebensborn. You see, Diana, on the other end of the spectrum, they were exterminating Jews, and on this end they were working on baby farms to repopulate Germany. We don't hear as much about this part of the Germanization programs, but it was just as evil. So many men were killed in World War I that the German population was already significantly decreased. This was why Eugenics was so important. How could Germany be a powerful nation without people? But not just any people and it was what Hitler's book 'Mein Kaempf' was all about. This program of Germanization and Eugenics tore families apart. It created a mass of children with no loving parents, and many orphans. Himmler was totally in charge of this. As time went on during the war, woman were selected or volunteered to give birth to children that would be given to German families and incorporated into their family to raise as their own. The women in this program many times came from Norway because they had to be Aryan, blond and blue eyed. They were baby machines. That was their job and they were paid for it. It was like a farm, if you will. They were impregnated by the perfect SS who were expected to father at least four children. If they weren't married, then they were expected to go to Lebensborn and impregnate one of those women. The program never involved having the father or the mother remain a part of the child's life. They were only to propagate.

"The other part of this program was the kidnapping of Polish children that were taken from their homes, given new identities and adopted by German families and their birth records were destroyed. After the war, it was impossible to return these children to their Polish families, and it was agreed that after so much time had passed by, it would be cruel to remove these children from the only family they remembered. It was a mess to try to straighten all this out after the war. The children were too young to remember their birth families and if they were reunited, if it were possible at all, they would suffer another tragic psychological blow to their young life by being taken from the parent they knew when they were first put into strange homes. The theory of these kidnappings of Nordic looking children was to immobilize other nations and deter their further population, and strengthen that of Germany by producing more Germanic looking children. You see, less children in Poland, and more in Germany.

"As the war continued, Himmler intensified his efforts to produce more children and SS men were even encouraged to have multiple wives, if necessary and continue to procreate. So we see why homosexuality was punishable by death. It went against everything Eugenics was about.

"Now, here is the personal part. My twin brother and I were taken from our parents in Poland. We were twins and there was a special appeal about twins. Experiments were made that related to enhancing racial excellence. They separated their prey for these experiments from the others interned in the concentration camps. Young boys were operated on as part of a study on sex organs and reproduction. They would perform surgeries on one twin and then make comparisons with the two. I'll get to more of that in a minute.

"After the camps were started, vast genetic experiments were undertaken. The range of the testing was broad and specialized. The two major groups of experiments were first to refine the master race and second to determine the cause of defects. Dr. Josef Mengele's research on twins and Gypsies was to further his genetic studies. He of course became famous after the war for the horrendous things he did and he was called the 'Angel of Death.' When the trains arrived at Auschwitz and after the victims were unloaded off the trains and stripped naked and divided into separate groups of men, women, and children, he would sort through the thousands of people and decide their fate. Most went straight to the gas chambers and others to hard labor in the camps. The twins, dwarfs, and anyone with unique physical ailments were selected to be assigned to the experimentations. Those that died in the gas chambers were better off, believe me, than those selected for his experiments.

"The other SS who helped unload the transports had been given special instructions to find twins, dwarfs, giants, or anyone else with a unique hereditary trait like a club foot or two different colored eyes. They were led away to be processed and taken to the showers and then tattooed. They were treated special, but in the end after the experiments, it was no different than others and most of the time, after the experiments were complete, most people weren't needed anymore and ultimately were killed. Those specially selected were meant to undergo various medical experiments and every day they would wonder what was in store for them that day. If they were called, they were taken to one of several laboratories. They put my brother through a series of tests, which were horrendously painful. They drew blood from us, sometimes every day and sometimes blood tests included mass transfusions of blood from one twin to another. After the war, I read a lot about what happened and why twins were so important to him. It was horrifying. Sometimes in an attempt to fabricate blue eyes, drops or injections of chemicals would be put in the eyes, which besides being painful, many times resulted in blindness, if not death. They would inject diseases like hepatitis and typhoid fever into one twin and not the other. When one died, the other was often killed to examine the corpse and compare the effects of the disease. Luckily, it was very near the end of the war and many of these experiments were not performed on us, but what happened was bad enough.

"Well one day they took my brother away. I cannot tell you how I felt. We were only seven years old and had never been separated and we had already been taken from our parents. I was left all alone. It was weeks before I saw him again. I was all alone—no parents, no brother; just me being held in a block with strangers. When they finally brought my brother back to me, he was very weak and thin. I almost didn't recognize him. He could barely walk or speak and worst of all, he could no longer cry. Finally when we were alone, he pulled down his pants and showed me that they had removed his genitals. It was the most horrific moment of my life to see my poor brother like this. Soon after he was returned to me he became very ill, probably from infections and died. I was alone again. It was a miracle that they didn't kill me because that was part of the process. I think I was spared because the war was almost over and I was left over as some sort of residue; however, I was almost dead from starvation. Before he died, my brother described what happened to him, as far as he could remember. He said he recalled people talking and he heard the name. Dr. Strausner and then someone called another person by name and said, 'Carl.' He did not remember any faces, just words.

"So Diana, I needed to tell you this. There is more to this and I found out a lot about our dear Charlotte and the roll she played in what I discovered. Let me just say, she was indeed the synthesis of a very long and complicated story. Our Gerheardt was then what we might think of as the thesis, and I suppose we could say, Carl was the antithesis. I am also afraid to tell you that some of what I found out has to do with Adam. What I found will end his wondering about Charlotte's interest in him. I'm sure it will not please him, but he is a big part of this story and I think he needs to know. I'm hoping I'm right about that. Tomorrow night, after the open house celebration, Felix and I would like to sit down with you, Adam, Ingrid and Frederick and talk to you all. I think they especially all need to know who these people were that we have all been jabbering about all these months and I owe them all an explanation. Those people all need to know and deserve to know. I wanted to just give you a little special warning, and a heads up, if you will. I hope this didn't upset you too much and I don't want to distract you from your work and certainly hope I didn't ruin your day, but I wanted to prepare you. I think I need to be honest with everyone, as brutal as the truth may be. Also, Diana, we have been working together so closely, I think we need to know one another better. So, there you have it, all my secrets are out of the bag."

I recall how speechless I was after all he told me. I felt so horrible for Bjorn having such a sad life. My heart just broke for him, but needless to say, he left me in a state of confusion and I knew there was more to the story. I would be patient and wait for him to tell us the next night.

# CHAPTER 13

It is impossible to put into words what I was feeling on the night of the open house celebration. This was a day of jubilation mixed with trepidation. We were going to show off this beautiful house in grand style, but after talking with Bjorn and hearing his story the day before, I had major anxiety about what this day would have in store for me and also for Adam. My mind became consumed with worry, which distracted me from the last minute items I needed to take care of. I had to remind myself to stay focused. I knew it was not Bjorn's intent to ruin the event, but for him, his mission was more meaningful than it was for me; it was a personal celebration and culmination, perhaps a lifelong sought after achievement. He didn't finish his story and said that he would lay it all out tonight after everyone left except us few and what he found out involved Adam. This was my biggest apprehension. In no way did I want him to be the victim or the subject of whatever it was that Bjorn discovered.

The house was finished. Every piece of furniture, every painting, every tapestry, every rug was artistically and aesthetically put in place. It was again a palace and both Bjorn and I were very pleased with the results of our long effort. I spent a lot of time planning the evening, but there were many last minute details to finish. The caterer was coming to work in the kitchen to prepare hors d'ouvres and desserts as well as a bartender who would serve drinks at the bar we set up in the gallery. The fresh flower arrangements were all in place in all the downstairs rooms and of course the master suite upstairs.

A photographer came that morning for a tour and to take pictures for an Italian decorator magazine. I was also busy with the photographer sent from an American publication who took a video of the house, as well as photos that I would use in an article I was planning to write. I had a long list of things to do and there were people coming and going all morning and afternoon to prepare for the evening celebration event.

I had a new dress I bought in Milan on one of my house shopping days and dressed early in the afternoon because I was to be in many of the photographs and would be interviewed and of course we needed to photograph the yard and garden in daylight. I had to describe the details of the renovation and walk the photographers through the house, describing all the important architectural details of the home that I felt needed to be pointed out. We were indeed very proud of the results of our efforts.

I was again feeling unsure and anxious about this project coming to an end. I would be able to return home in a few days, but I would have to say good bye to my new friends. I wasn't quite sure how I would feel about that. With all the work and so much of my heart that I poured into the house, to have to turn it over to someone and close the door behind me and walk away would be difficult. This was always the objective, but I didn't realize in the beginning what an emotional experience this would be or the feeling I would have at the conclusion.

The evening began on schedule with a parade of cars pulling up into the drive and a constant procession of people entering the house. Bjorn stayed near the front door to greet people and wait for his special invited guests, who were the investors and potential buyers. Upon their arrival he personally took them on a tour of the house. I also greeted people, made sure they had a drink or glass of wine, introduced them to others, and sent them on their way to browse the house. Vito, the architect and Vittorio were also there and talked to guests about the particulars of the work that was done on the house and gardens. The pianist was at the grand piano in the living room with the string quartette playing beautiful soft music that streamed through the house. I believe at one time there were over a hundred people in the house milling around. I imagined myself playing the part of Charlotte as she hosted her glorious holiday parties.

Adam took people into the library and the dining room and also showed them the passageways through the pantry, while Irene volunteered to be stationed in the library to point out the wonderful frieze moldings. I showed her the Gustave Doré illustrations in the books I found and she thought it was quite fascinating and that it was an important detail to point out and explain to interested people that came into the library. We left the books with the illustrations open on the desk in the library, which she referenced when discussing the literary details of the allegoric panels. Ingrid and Felix also helped guide people through the rooms, pointing out details. It seemed like a very nice party, but in my mind I knew the culmination of the evening, after everyone left except our very few special friends, would end on a questionable note. I kept watching Adam, who was enjoying himself so much, talking to people, greeting guests, and making sure they had drinks and guiding them through the house. I was afraid for what Bjorn would be telling him later and hoped it would all end well.

# CHAPTER 14

The evening was winding down at nearly eleven o'clock and the house was beginning to empty. It was a long tiring day, but I knew there was much more left to the evening. I was becoming more nervous about Bjorn's after party plans. Bjorn was happy with the evening and he felt everything went off well. The guests were extremely positive in their comments about the house and he felt confident that an offer would be presented soon. He had invited our select group to stay after and when everyone else had left, Felix and Bjorn took us all to the couches in front of the fireplace in the living room. Bjorn brought out the old bottle of Cognac I discovered in the pantry and had small juice glasses for everyone and poured a little in each glass for each of us. As he said, he and Felix worked together to make sense out of all our discussions and now it was time to let us know just what they found out and lay to rest all of our speculations. Frederick, Felix, Ingrid, Adam and I sat and listened as Bjorn began to speak to us. He began by toasting me for the fine job I did with the house and in doing so, was setting the stage to present his story to all of us.

"Diana, the house is beautiful. You have done a magnificent job in this renovation. I am quite certain we will see this was well worth the investment and we should have a serious buyer very soon. I'm glad that you have all decided to stay after this party, because we seem to have become close friends with a common interest. We all shared a personal interest in this house and soon we will have to say good bye to it, as well as to one another. I think we have made some good friendships along the way. This house has brought us together in a very mysterious way. We are all people of various walks of life and would have had no reason to ever come together, or to cross one another's paths. While you all had some attachment with this house, and shed some light on your experience with it, I was in the background, not only writing the checks to pay for the restoration, but trying to connect so many small pieces of information that each of you provided and find what it was we were looking for.

"The first time we opened the doors of this house to begin our work, people began navigating towards it as if the proverbial moths to a flame. I think we all agree, there proved to be something magnetic about this house, some mystic nucleus that must have surreptitiously screamed out to us to gather around and peel away at its surface and dig into the bones and to find the answers to the secrets we kept unveiling. At certain points, I believe finding the hidden story of the previous tenants may have become a higher priority than actually making the house livable and lovable again. For me anyway, I have to confess, that was the case. Don't get me wrong. With everything I do, I expect to make a profit, but that was not my only reason.

"I for one had another very secret ambition that is not as obvious as my main interest of turning a profit. My other reason, as it will surprise you I am sure, was my main reason, which was my life's work. You see, other than being a man with very deep pockets and a judicious investor, I have been searching for something my entire adult life. Things happened in my childhood that set me on this course. You see, my family lived in Poland. My parents were both university professors and were active resistors of the Nazi occupation. At the onset of the war, the SS began rounding up people that were resisters, people they felt unfit due to mental or physical problems, and of course Jews, and sending them to concentration camps. They were also driving Polish people from their homes and making those homes available to Germans living in Poland. I was not so young that I didn't understand what was happening, but nevertheless, I was a young boy and my dear brother and I were robbed of our youth. The first years of the war were difficult and of course it got worse as the years wore on. Then it all changed in late 1944. Let me first say, among you are Germans, but you are people I have come to care about over these last few months. I have no animosity to German people for what happened to me. It was those that ruled over Germany and those very few that made the history of that time so atrocious. I do not want anyone here to be uncomfortable or think I have blame on all German people because in reality, the German people were powerless and were treated just as poorly as so many thousands of others.

"When we were taken by the SS, it was the end of our childhood and we were thrust into a existence we were not prepared for. We were never to be allowed to enjoy our youth again, but instead be part of the madness of another world. We were separated from our parents and I believe they were killed soon after. My brother and I were at least kept together for the time being and sent to the Lodz Ghetto in Poland. Now, mind you, this becomes an arduous story, but I guarantee you all that your questions will be answered, and you will hear some things that may be unpleasant, but I think you need to know." Bjorn stopped for a moment and looked at each of us as we sat totally enraptured by him. I assumed he was reading our faces for approval, or disapproval. I interjected and asked him to please continue.

"There were many elements of the war, but the most appalling and deadly was of course the Holocaust. Enough will never be written about it and what barbaric scars are left on that century because of that war. The issues relating to Eugenics and the Germanization programs touched my life personally as a child and the life of my family. The City of Lodz was selected by the Reich to be Germanized and the Polish people and Jews were to be replaced by the Reich Germans and ultimately sent to the ghetto. In the Lodz Ghetto, hundreds of thousands of people died from starvation or disease, and if they lived long enough, they were then sent to an extermination camp. My brother and I were twins, which put us into another category and we were plucked out of Lodz and sent to Auschwitz, for other reasons, which I will explain in a moment.

The Nazis created a farm, metaphorically if you will; a breeding ground to create the perfect Aryan. This was established in several ways. One was to steal other people's children that looked perfectly Aryan. The children were taken from their families and put in German foster homes and after the war, most could not be reunited to their families because either they didn't know where their families were, or were too young to remember they had other families, or they were dead, or they had grown accustomed to their new German homes. My brother and I were perfect towheads, very blond, and we were more importantly twins. The Nazis experimented on people, and especially liked twins. I went into great detail with Diana about this yesterday. I won't give you that much detail tonight but I am sure you are already aware of these things that happened during the war.

"Let me just say, I survived the war. My brother did not. My parents disappeared and as I said, I assume were killed immediately because of their vocal resistance and if not that soon, then they died in one of the camps, but I never heard. I remember the night the door to our home burst open and two officers came in and took my brother and me. I can still hear my parents screaming and trying to stop them. One of them hit my mother in the face with the butt of his rifle and she fell against the wall. My father ran to her side and just sat consoling her and watched as my brother and I were taken out of the house. I looked over my shoulder and that was the last I ever saw of them. Every night for the rest of my life I relived that moment and can still hear in my mind my mother screaming for us and I can see her laying there on the floor with my father cradling her head in his lap. I have many memories, but the most unexpected memory I have had was the faces of the two SS officers that took us away. I remember

*The House on Lake Maggiore*

what they looked like and I remember how they laughed as they shoved us into a truck in front of my family's home and drove off with us. I tried desperately to sit high enough to look out the rear window and watch my home disappear from sight. We were seven years old and frightened. We had never been away from our parents before. My brother and I clung to one another. When the two officers were pushing us into the truck, they laughed and then one said, 'take his feet and pull him into the truck, while I hold the other.' We put up a fight, my brother and I. We struggled, but to little avail. They drove us off and then we were sent to a small building where there were other people congregating that were also taken from their homes that night. Then after a couple hours, they took us by truck to a train and then we were loaded onto the train and taken away to Lodz and held there temporarily as prisoners for a long time.

"Well, that is what happened to me and all these years, I have searched for the people connected to crimes such as these, not just for my brother's sake, but for all the other children that were victims of the war. I helped many people with stories such as mine, find the people that did this to them, that tore their families apart. I have found many. During my search, I learned many things about what happened during the war that I was not aware of. All of these things changed the focus of my efforts and in many ways, I was successful in finding people that believed they were well hidden and especially with the length of time passing, their histories became more lost, but they were always hunted. Someone was always looking for them and their connection to the crimes committed during those horrible times. I, as indiscrete as I could be, never gave up my quest, even though I hid this quest by my work of investments, such as renovating this house and many others. Underneath all my efforts, was always the search." Bjorn paused for a moment and looked at each of us. We all sat in silence, and that silence was an affirmation for him to continue.

"I am leading up to the history of the people that lived in this house, as I am sure you already realize. What I am going to tell you is unpleasant, but it is true. I guarantee you that with what I tell you, your love affair with the past history, or your affinity to this house, will be dissolved. It is not a pretty story."

Bjorn paused for a moment, perhaps to give us a chance to digest what he talked about and to create the proper distance to the continuation, as if it were the adequate white space following a paragraph, homologous to the breath of the author. He sipped his cognac and continued.

"Have you heard of Lebensborn? Some of the people that lived here, or passed through here were connected to Lebensborn." Bjorn told me about Lebensborn the day before in our conversation in the library. The rest of them answered that they may have heard of it, but were not certain what it was. By this time each of us were hanging on every word Bjorn was saying, but I'm sure each of us, in our own mind, wondered where this very lengthy story was headed.

"Let me tell you about Lebensborn. It was a program devised by Himmler. Women who looked Aryan or Nordic were impregnated and produced children. They were paid for it, so they volunteered. There was no love involved. It was a process. Now in order to be an SS officer, they had to be one hundred percent Aryan, and their family was traced for several generations to validate this. They were expected to procreate and required to have at least four children. If they were not married, then they would impregnate a Lebensborn woman. It was a baby factory. The children were then taken away immediately after birth and given to German families. This was the breeding ground of Germanization. It was truly analogous to an animal farm. Well, let me get back to this later, and I will continue with my brother and me. As much as we tried desperately to stay together all the weeks since we were first taken, that day they took my brother away. As I said, they experimented on twins. It was Dr. Mengele's special program. Many horrific experiments were performed on twins, which usually ended in the death of both. After the war I did a lot of research on this and found out that it was rare that they would leave one twin alive if the other died. It was just my good fortune that the war was about to end, and I was spared. A few more days and I would not be sitting here now.

"My brother was the unfortunate chosen one. They took him away and I didn't see him for several weeks, then one day, they brought him back and put us in a room together. He was very thin and weak and could barely speak. While he was away, they removed his genitals. He told me the surgeon that did this was Dr. Strausner. This of course I believe to be Gerheardt Strausner, Charlotte's third husband. He was a Nazi doctor. My brother was quite definite when he heard someone say his name; they called him Dr. Strausner and at the same time he heard someone address another person as Carl," said Bjorn.

Everyone gasped when he said this. Ingrid especially appeared to be almost in shock and covered her mouth with her hand, perhaps in order to stifle her shock. Bjorn had already touched on his recollection of a man named Carl. Frederick sat silently, waiting to hear more. Bjorn continued.

"Now the test to be performed on my brother and I would be how he might be different from me. While he and I sat and talked, he lowered his trousers to show me what happened to him. He was very ashamed, of course, but as I said, he had no more tears to shed and was terribly depressed and ill. We were kept at the concentration camp in Auschwitz. In his weakened condition, he died soon after, probably from pneumonia or typhoid fever or infections. They didn't care about sanitary conditions. That did not matter to them. The war was ending and they had to dispel all signs of the activities quickly, which in many cases that meant mass killing. I almost starved to death and was very ill, but I hid and escaped that final solution for me. After the war and when everyone in the camp was liberated, I was put in a foster home and when I was old enough, I tried to find my family, but to no avail. Their public opposition to the Reich was reason enough for them to be picked up, I am sure. They were taken away and that was the end of them.

"When I became an adult, I began my war. I spent all my free time trying to find these war criminals and the rest of my time I became an investor, trying to make enough money to support my quest. I was successful with my business and invested heavily in real estate, so I knew a lot about restoring homes and making them palaces again. But always as busy as I was at my work, I never forgot my real work: that of finding the perpetrators of those horrible crimes committed during the war. One lead would send me on a chase, sometimes all over the world and many times I solved other people's problems and hunted down old, tired Nazis. But never the ones I was looking for, but I knew Gerheardt Strausner was traced to this house because of his own recklessness in never changing his name. There was an old, ever so small newspaper article I found on microfilm about some social event that took place many years ago that listed many in attendance at this house and his name was listed. So when I saw this home abandoned, this was the magnet, if you will, that I needed to try to pull people out of the woodwork, to find what I was looking for. It was just a shot in the dark because that event happened decades ago, but it was something and I was looking for any detail I could find, no matter how infinitesimal it seemed. Carl was the name of the officer that pulled my brother and I from our house. The other man called him by name and said: 'Carl, hold his feet.' There appeared to be no leads to the man named Carl. But I remembered his voice and that day in that room with my brother when I heard him speaking in the hallway, I looked through a crack in the door and I recognized him. I believe it is possible that there may have been a plot against my parents because they were high profile university professors and spoke out against the occupation. We being twins and their children may have been the way the Nazi dealt with them, by taking us. We may have been intentionally signaled out as a punishment to my parent's protests against the Nazis. Why else would such high level Nazis humble themselves to get their hands dirty with this sort of thing? I believed it was the same Carl, but then Carl just seemed to drop off the face of the earth, or so I thought, until you came to the door, Frederick, looking for a man named Carl.

"Sure enough, one after another showed up at Diana's door step here and shared a story or two over a cup of tea in the kitchen. Diana, the good sport that you were, told me about these visitors. Then I knew I was on the right track and this was more than the mere shot in the dark I thought it was. That small old microfilmed article was the beginning of this quest, and it paid off. It was only a matter of time before I could find my answers. Of course, it was all too late, as my prey are long dead, but at least now I know and my quest is over. I have to say, all my life I so wanted revenge, but that was not to be."

Finally a pause in his story allowed us to ask questions. Adam spoke first. "Why in the world would Strausner never have changed his name, or identity?"

Bjorn poured some cognac into his little juice glass and sat back reflecting for a moment on Adam's question. "I wondered that also. I believe Gerheardt was an incredible narcissist. I think that he really believed his work was important during the war, and also that he was safe, hiding in the shadow of this house, protected and maybe he envisioned that one day he would become a doctor again, perhaps a famous physician. From what I found out about him, he was also probably the man that castrated Mr. Contrelli, performing his cancer surgery. It's possible that didn't have to happen, but it fit into Gerheardt's plans better, to leave Mr. Contrelli impotent."

Ingrid asked: "Then Mr. Strausner was brought to this house by Mr. Contrelli? Perhaps he felt he owed him something for saving his life."

"Well, I have a theory about that, but first Ingrid, as you recall Mr. Strausner, do you think he could have been this man? Do you think he had the intelligence to have at one time, been a physician?" Bjorn asked.

"I am very surprised that he could have been a doctor. He had no profession, as I said before, at least while he lived here. Oh, he was no dummy and probably intelligent enough. He never went off to work, ever. He was here so much, um, I thought he was pretty much a bum. If he were hiding, it is no wonder that he stayed close to this house. It may have shielded him. I didn't know him well and I avoided him because I didn't care for him at all. I think very possibly he could have been that evil of a person. He was rude and arrogant and after she married him, he was even more arrogant and I suppose he felt he had a higher position in the house then and was more justified in giving me orders. I didn't want to be around here because the house was so unpleasant then. It was very upsetting. I shudder now to think of being in the same room with such a person. He was terrible to her, but she argued just as much with him and also just said vile things," said Ingrid.

"Yes," said Bjorn. "Charlotte is really the main character here, of course. She is the one we have all wondered about the most. She was the center of a very interesting drama at this house. I found out quite a lot about her, and as I continue, you will see just what a fascinating person she was."

He looked at all of us, again seeking approval to continue. Then he leaned back, took another sip of his cognac and began. "I need to first give you some background about the days of the German Reich and what life was like. I have studied long and hard about this. Frederick and Felix I am sure knew all of this very well, having lived through it and perhaps you too, Ingrid, as a young woman in Germany. By the way, may I ask, what brought you to Italy?"

"I had an aunt that lived in Milan and ah, when I graduated from school, my father died of a long illness and my mother and I came to live with my aunt, who was my mother's sister. My mother had no profession so my aunt took us in. We just stayed in Italy and never returned to Germany, and then the war broke out we couldn't go back, even if we wanted to, but um, my aunt provided a good life for us and was very kind," said Ingrid.

"I see. I think you were fortunate to leave when you did, before the war broke out. God only knows what your life would

*The House on Lake Maggiore*

have been like had you stayed. And how did you come to work at this house?" asked Bjorn.

"There was an advertisement in the newspaper for a German speaking housekeeper for a family in Stresa. It was when Mr. Contrelli brought Charlotte to this house, after the war, and he wanted a German speaking housekeeper to work for Mrs. Contrelli, so she could communicate easily. At first her Italian was not very good, but it did improve after a while. I was working as a seamstress at the time, but thought this was a good opportunity for me, so I came for the interview and was hired," answered Ingrid.

"So there you were, at the beginning of this drama when Charlotte first arrived. Thanks to you, your stories filled in a lot of gaps for me in trying to piece things together. In order to understand many things about people that were in this house, we need to understand the culture they came from, or evolved from. I need to say again, poor unfortunate Mr. Contrelli was a good man, from what I surmise about him. Was it his misfortune that he sought out a specialist to help him with his cancer? Maybe not because he did live for eight years beyond that, so perhaps Gerheardt was an expert surgeon. I believe that is why he went to Germany towards the end of the war. At least I think so; however, he was also a financier so he may have had his finger in some avaricious pie looking for an opportunity, but his cancer took precedence. He was very ill with prostate cancer and if Gerheardt really saved his life, than it may have been Mr. Contrelli's way of repaying him, by bringing him here to hide. The price he paid for getting eight more years of his life was high because he then became a pawn and most likely died not knowing the truth himself or how he was deceived. He was not the problem with this history. He was a very smart man and knew finances and knew how to make money. Mr. Contrelli was sixty six years old when he had his surgery and he married his second wife, Charlotte soon after that. She was only twenty three. Perhaps Charlotte gave him a new lease on life, when he may have been facing his own mortality because of his cancer.

I am going to tell you about her, but first there are other things I need to tell you to get out of the way before we get to her and what she was about. I asked each of you to stay because what Felix and I found out affects all of you in one way or another, if only to set straight your hypothesis about the past history of this house.

"So, we need to back up and think about what life was like in those times. We need to think about what Germany was like then, even before the end of the war because Pietro was there. Charlotte came from Germany and it's important to the story to know that culture in order to put everything in perspective. The war years. What was going on in Germany in those times? Eugenics, which was increasing the population of the German Aryan, because so many lives, especially men who were soldiers, were lost. This became top priority. The Nazis gave an incentive for marriage. Two stipulations: The woman could not work outside of the home and both partners had to be Jew free for two generations. The reward was one fifth of an average worker's annual salary. To fund this, unmarried people paid a bachelor tax of about five percent of an average salary. Marriages created jobs for men because it forced women out of the workforce.

"The SS was a unit of German men of Nordic type, selected according to particular characteristics. SS men who planned to marry had to obtain an authorization of matrimony from the Reichsfuherer because they had to marry someone equally as Aryan as they. Selective breeding was the only way to maintain 'good blood.' After a while Himmler wanted SS men to divorce if, after five years, their marriage produced no offspring. He wanted to practice human stock breeding and, as he declared again and again in his speeches to officers: 'I have set myself the practical task of raising a new Germanic stock. I shall eradicate the weak and unfit through selection by physical appearance, through constant exertion and through selectivity, applied brutally and without human sentimentality.' Falling in love, romance, trying to be happy and sentiment had no place in his thinking. It was all science and it was all to improve the race.

*The House on Lake Maggiore*

"Hitler and Himmler together planned and organized this campaign, established the Race and Settlement Office, with which three other organizations worked in a program of kidnapping and the Germanization of children. These were:

1) Festung des Deutschtim, which carried out the Germanization process.
2) NSV—Nationalsazistlistssche Wolkmefort, which operated a network of children's homes to which the youngsters were brought. It was mostly Gestapo who did the actual kidnapping.
3) Lebensborn, meaning the well of life, which placed the children for adoption by German families.

"The plan was to reduce the populations of other countries in order to weaken them and to strengthen Germany. Hitler created the Strengthening of Germanism and appointed Himmler as its Reichkommissor. Racially acceptable children was what they wanted and the inferior children were marked for destruction.

"When my brother and I sat alone in that room that horrible day when he was finally returned to me, I heard those voices outside the door and I recognized the voice of the man called Carl. There was no link to Carl ever again, but then I met you, Frederick, who had a link to a former SS officer named Carl, to this house. As you have told us, Frederick, your wife was Carl's sister and she received a letter from her brother from this house. Supposedly he only stayed here on his way to Rome, and of course, we have heard that it was reported that he was killed in an automobile accident on the way to Rome, and was never heard from again. When I learned that Dr. Strausner lived here, it made the possibility of the man I was searching for more realistic. Would it be too much of a coincidence that Gerheardt Strausner and Carl both spent time here? They obviously knew one another and both appeared close to one another in the block where my brother and I were detained. Could there be such irony? I had nothing else to dissuade me so I followed my instinct, as weak as it might have appeared.

"Now, Carl enters out story. Who was Carl? You, Frederick, know about him and you came here trying to trace Carl's infamous journey to and from this house. Carl became a footnote to this little house history. We know he was an SS officer and he briefly stayed at this house and Felix knew of him. Well as part of his duties as a good SS officer, he was busy impregnating German women in the Lebensborn program. Our friend Felix here knew about this. He knew Gerheardt and he knew a man named Carl, even though just vaguely. It was a certainty that Carl never was emotionally or romantically attached to any of the women. It was his duty and perhaps he had such an ego that he may have believed he alone might be able to stock the herd, as it were. Yes, Carl—that name. It just came from out of nowhere. It was a bit foreign to me at first and then too uncanny to believe it may have been the Carl I saw as a seven year old boy. He was at first a non-entity, but he became the important detail in this story I am about to tell you. Carl was a very important man. He had ambition, perhaps wanted to be another Himmler. He was really more important than Dr. Strausner and it is possible Dr. Strausner reported to Carl. Now our friend Felix here, well he was in the German army and for a time was appointed to the degrading and subservient duty equal to 'licking the boots of the arrogant doctor,' and waiting on him hand and foot. As Felix recalled, during the war, people that knew Strausner and Carl speculated about their relationship. Homosexuality was punishable by death and if they were homosexual, they had to desperately cover it up, but there were others that were curious about their relationship. Carl, having sired his requirement of children, most likely may have been bisexual. He quite frankly might have been happy either way. It didn't matter because it was a nonsexual experience and was all business." He paused again and asked if anyone wanted a refill on the cognac. We all brought our glasses forward and Felix filled each one. We then settled back into our chairs and Felix asked Bjorn to continue.

Bjorn sat down and continued. "I found out more about the gentleman named Carl, even though I thought the trail had ended long ago with this person of that name. But then Frederick told us that Carl had died in an automobile accident while on the way to Rome. We had a photo of Carl that Diana found in the pantry and Felix and Frederick identified him in the small photo. I began to think about timing. He was supposed to have died soon after the war. Well, that may have been so, but who did he know here that he made a stop at this house in the first place? Maybe he didn't die. Maybe he just lived on in a disguise. There were other possibilities." He took another sip of his cognac and continued.

"When the war was about to end, Carl and Gerheardt had to cover up their activities and feared for their lives. It became apparent to all of them that they had to figure out an escape, a way to try to blend into society somewhere, to drift into some obscure woodwork somewhere because they would surely be arrested as war criminals for what they were doing. An opportunity presented itself that may have had benefits for both Carl and Gerheardt, the Nazi doctor."

"According to Frederick and Felix, Carl was a very handsome SS officer, as we may see from the small photograph of him. He was a very good SS officer. He was required, as a perfect Aryan, which was the criteria of being an SS officer, to sire at least four children. He fulfilled his duty. He was active in the program of Lebensborn." Bjorn paused and looked at Adam. "Adam, I am going to tell you how you were connected to these people. You often wondered why Mrs. Contrelli, ah . . . Charlotte, was so attracted to you, am I right? How she would take you into the pantry and fawn over you and ask about your life and give you gifts. Did you ever ask your adopted parents who your real parents were, or what happened to them?"

Adam sat up stiffly and answered emphatically. "Yes, of course I asked. They said my parents died early in the war and they were friends of theirs and they became my foster parents and then they adopted me. I'm not sure I understand where you are going with this."

Bjorn continued. "Well, let me continue. It will all fall into place, I assure you, although you may not like it. Maybe you should decide if you really want to know the truth. You've had a very nice life, as I understand it. I am sorry that your wife passed on, but you are fortunate to have children and grandchildren. Sometimes it is best to leave well enough alone." Bjorn again looked to Adam for a go or no go signal.

"Well, Bjorn, this is a fine time to ask me this question. What do you expect me to say? That I don't care and don't want to hear and maybe we should change the subject and discuss the weather? It's a bit late for that, I think. Continue. You've gone this far. I may not like it, or I may not believe what it is you are going to tell us, but I have to hear it. Please, continue," said Adam.

"Yes, of course. I am sorry, but Adam, be certain, please. I don't mean to be cruel. It was just that the things I discovered involved you. I didn't know that would be the result. It is mere fact that it involved you. Perhaps I should have talked to you in private. If you would prefer we can talk privately."

"Bjorn, whatever you have to say, can be said in front of all of us. I hear what you are saying about Lebensborn and I'm trying to put the pieces together in my head and what I've come up with, which I can't say I believe, but are you saying that these men were friends of Charlotte or she was part of Lebensborn and part of this baby factory in Germany, and from there she knew this Carl? You are certainly not implying that Charlotte was my mother, are you?"

"No Adam, it isn't that simple. Hold on for another moment," said Bjorn. "Please hear me out. This gets complicated and I want to be sure I am speaking very clearly, but I have done my research and I am not fabricating anything. I will tell you about my facts and how I found things out. You don't have to believe any of this if you prefer not to. I have struggled with all this and debated whether I should keep it to myself or not, but believe you are all intelligent people, thus your endless probing and I decided, you all deserve to know.

"There was more to Carl than what we have heard, or what we know about up until this point. When Carl was a young man he joined the Hitler Youth and from there became an SS officer. Think about this. He had a rather unusual life, not what normal young men may have had. He lived with men the greater part of his life and may have had homosexual tendencies. I believe homosexuality in those circumstances was quite common, but because it was punishable by death, people had to be extremely discrete. Carl, as I believe now, was probably happy in either sexual role, that of a woman or that of a man, but his strong sexual preference was men. Even though he had the facade of a very strong man, as an SS officer, he had a secret life. Now we know Carl sired four children, but it appears he and Gerheardt had something more than a friendship going on. As the end of the war became evident, people like Carl and Gerheardt had to figure out how to survive. They had to have a plan to escape somehow. They would have been captured and tried for war crimes and they knew the war was lost. They had to devise some sort of plan. The very wealthy Italian gentleman, Mr. Contrelli, was admitted into the hospital for cancer surgery, which left him impotent, which again, in my thinking, may have not really been the necessity, but more to the convenience of Dr. Gerheardt Strausner, as I've said before. The doctor found him quite attractive, probably due mostly to his apparent wealth and between he and Carl, they decided that an opportunity existed. This gets very complicated, and I'm sure sounds unbelievable, so I'll come back to this.

"If Carl were represented as a woman, Gerheardt's relationship with Carl would be perceived as natural, and that of a man and a woman. Adam, the issue becomes incredulous I know, but I guess the time is right to answer your question. No. Charlotte was not your mother. She was your father. Do you understand?"

We all gasped again and each of us, except of course Felix and Bjorn, were utterly in shock, and disbelief. Each of us, with jaws dropped in disbelief and gaping mouths, muttered something, like: No, it couldn't be, that's ridiculous! Adam sighed deeply and sat back in his chair, his glass of cognac held limply with his two hands on his lap. He began to laugh. "This is too preposterous. Can you prove any of this, or are you just making it up?"

"I can prove it. Do you want me to continue? Because if you don't, I won't say another word?" He looked sympathetically over the rim of his glasses to Adam and waited for Adam to decide if he should continue or stop.

"Well you've gone this far. You might as well keep going. I don't want to guess the rest of the story. I'm not buying a word of this, mind you, but go ahead. You have to prove this somehow, and I can't imagine how you will do that, but continue." Adam has a sort of smirk on his face, but I felt it may have just been a cover up to what he was feeling inside, perhaps defensive, trepidation, or total disbelief and hoping Bjorn would look foolish with his speculation.

Ingrid interrupted. I was watching her and she just sat with her hand covering her mouth, opened in disbelief. She began waving her hands as if to rid the air of lingering words. "Wait a minute, if you please. I have to say something. I'm not sure I'm following you. I knew Charlotte for many years, um . . . certainly longer than anyone. Are you saying, she—was a he? I can't believe this." Then Frederick spoke up, who had been sitting very quietly up until now.

"You are saying my brother-in-law was a homosexual and dressed as a woman? No wonder he stayed away from his family. He truly had a secret life. And he became Charlotte? So that's what the letter was about. Someone just erased him by declaring him killed in an automobile accident, but in reality he masqueraded as a woman. My wife would have been mortified, if she knew this," Frederick said in total astonishment.

"Yes. This person was quite something, wasn't he? He duped you Ingrid, for a long time." Bjorn realized then that he had several people he needed to be sensitive to. "Ingrid, are you sure you want to hear more because I can stop if you would rather not hear the rest. Sometimes it might be best to keep memories as they are." He looked at Ingrid for an answer and sort of cocked his head and raised one eyebrow, waiting for her to answer.

"Are you kidding? Of course I want to hear more. Please go on," she replied.

"And you Frederick? Shall I continue?" asked Bjorn.

"Oh God, yes; I want to hear everything," said Frederick as he stood up to refill his cognac glass. Everyone was now on the edge of their chair, almost salivating for Bjorn to continue.

"All right then. To take this one step further, if Carl could pass himself off as a woman and became involved with the Italian gentleman, and perhaps married him, he would then be assured of being wealthy, as well as hidden. What better camouflage? Behind the scenes Gerheardt would tag along and continue to be Carl's secret homosexual lover, all tucked away in the carriage house apartment and Carl would somehow take care of him while Carl lived a comfortable life in this lovely house on Lake Maggiore. Since Mr. Contrelli would be left impotent, it would be a marriage of nothing more than companionship, and he would never know about Carl's original gender. Remember, Carl may have been bisexual and most certainly homosexual, so living intimately with a man was fine with him; however, Mr. Contrelli was quite a bit older and in extremely poor health. I think Carl and Gerheardt counted on him dying in the not too distant future, but he fooled them. Isn't that right, Ingrid?"

"Yes. It was eight years before he died. He seemed fine the first year or two and was in his library working or at an office, and then his illness became worse and he just worked at home and was more housebound. Then he became gravely ill and he seldom came out of his room upstairs, or out of the library. If he came down stairs from his room, it took forever for us to help get him back upstairs. Sometimes the men would put him on a chair and carry him up. He never recovered, however he lived for eight years of their marriage, and most of that time in very poor health. But when she, or he, um . . . . oh my . . . had the parties, he was always there, even if he was just propped up in a chair quietly talking to his guests," answered Ingrid.

"They most likely believed he wouldn't live very long, and I'm sure Carl counted on that and then Carl and Gerheardt could live happily ever after on his money. But Mr. Contrelli lived for eight years, and when he would eventually die, Carl would have the house and the money and then he and Gerheardt could live there forever. They may have believed that time would erase everything. There were no children for Mr. Contrelli to leave his fortune to. Living that way could have been simple, but Carl decided he liked his new transgendered life and wanted to continue as a woman and perhaps test this new womanhood. You even commented, Ingrid, on how you saw her sitting and primping in front of the mirror. Either she was enjoying her new beauty as a woman, or she was practicing to be a woman. Even Irene remarked how Charlotte seemed to be play acting and never genuine. Well evidently playing the part of a woman was pulled off quite well and he began to physically change his gender during the later years in the marriage with Pietro. All those little shopping trips to Switzerland were actually to have a series of surgeries and hormone doses. Carl, who of course became Charlotte, could continue his relationship with the Nazi doctor, Gerheardt Strausner, who would assume a new persona and blend in here in Italy, and the person Carl, would be lost forever feigning death in an automobile accident. Their scheme worked. Dr. Strausner and Dr. Johann Van Hoaf, his cohort during the war, would perform gender reassignment surgery on Carl. In the little stack of things Diana found in the pantry, there was a card for a Dr. Dresden in Switzerland. I went to that address and found many of the links to tie all of this together. Of course, Dr. Van Hoaf is long gone, but he was also a Nazi doctor that worked with Strausner, also at Auschwitz. He probably sent the letter to your wife, Frederic, about Carl having perished in an accident on the way to Rome. After the war he changed his name to Dr. Dresden."

"Wait a minute. That name Van Hoaf is familiar," said Ingrid. "I am pretty sure I remember Gerheardt telling Charlotte, during some of their arguments, that Van Hoaf would be calling him and would find a place for him. I didn't understand that conversation either, but Charlotte said something about twelve years having passed and he hadn't called yet. I remember that name Van Hoaf because that conversation repeated many times, just like their other arguments. He would say, 'you wait and see, Van Hoaf will be contacting me.'"

"Well, Dr. Van Hoaf, who became Dr. Dresden, was indeed a busy man with his practice in Switzerland. Evidently he put into practice his experiments from the war days. I would imagine it may have been very dangerous for him to have Strausner too near him. He successfully changed his identity and his name and entrenched himself into a respectable medical practice. Strausner never bothered. He may have thought he was well shielded, but it was foolish of him not to take on a new identity. Perhaps he felt protected enough hiding behind Charlotte, but try to imagine if you will, he was a surgeon and now he was just someone that wandered around this house, hiding out in the garage, skulking through passageways to and from the pantry. He was really nothing, but maybe he lived the dream that one day he would again practice medicine and be highly recognized for his progressive methods. Dr. Van Hoaf, or rather Dr. Dresden became Carl's surgeon.

"The first surgeries of Carl were minor and it was over a period of time before the surgeries were complete and he was more a woman than a man. He probably enjoyed his life of wealth and status being married to the rich Italian, and then the new persona as a beautiful young woman and social queen who had lavish parties and was envied by others. He was at home and safe living as Mrs. Contrelli in Stresa, in the beautiful house on Lake Maggiore, the home we have grown to love and must soon leave. The Italian was deceived, the poor man. Imagine what went on within these walls. It's incredible. Only you, Ingrid knew what it was like. How I would have loved to have been a fly on the wall observing the theatrics of it all." He paused again and looked at Adam who looked as if he was in shock.

Adam spoke quietly, as if he was thinking out loud. "Sometime she would give me small gifts, perhaps a toy, a watch, a small key chain, or money. I was very young and in awe of this woman and very docile. I remembered saying yes ma'am, no ma'am, and I was instructed by my parents to be respectful to Charlotte—Mrs. Contrelli, and be polite to her. I think they realized how uncomfortable I was with her. I loved the parties, but there was always that inevitable trip to the pantry to talk. My mother would tell me 'it is only a few minutes out of your time; surely you can tolerate that much time and be nice to her. She thinks you are a nice young man and she is just being curious about you.' I never suspected, perhaps because I was so young, that there was anything more to her attraction to me than that. However, I felt uncomfortable in her presence and as the years went by, after those parties stopped, I remembered those times with an uneasy feeling about it and a lot of curiosity thinking maybe there was more to her attraction in me than I thought. The way she sort of dropped out of sight made me think about it even more. Her actions made her a mysterious person. Even now at my age, I was curious enough to still wonder what her intentions were and why she had such a special interest in me, and each time I saw this house, it all came back to me again." Adam asked.

Bjorn continued. "Did she ever do or say anything inappropriate to you? Remember, she was a man at that time, early on in her marriage to Mr. Contrelli, and even always, in her psyche no matter what she looked like, underneath it all, she was a homosexual man. Do you recall if she ever touched you inappropriately?"

"No!" Adam answered emphatically, as if to push the entire idea out of his head. "She did embrace me, but it always seemed uncomfortable for her also. She never hugged me, like my adopted mother did, you know, very motherly. It seemed unnatural for her and as if she didn't know how to show affection. When we were finished talking and I stood up from the stool she had me sit on, she just sort of drew me close to her and then opened the door of the pantry and told me to run along. We never left the pantry together. She had me leave and then she would come out later. But while in the pantry, she just talked to me."

Bjorn continued. "The Italian, Mr. Contrelli, knew nothing of a child that lived with his adopted family, but stayed close to Carl, who eventually became Charlotte, so she could keep a watchful eye on your life. I imagine with her new money after the marriage, she was able to finance your family. She may have even considered bringing you into her home, and being part of her family. Maybe she wanted to be a parent to you and that may have been what all the private talks were about with you—to see if that was a possibility, that she could be a real parent. I believe, even though Carl sired four children, he took a liking to you because you were a beautiful child. He probably thought he had created a masterpiece and wanted to keep watch over you. I'm quite sure, Charlotte as it were, would have wanted to be even closer to you, as it appears with this much attention she paid to you, as well as possibly paying your foster parents to keep you nearby, she must have cared about you. Maybe not like a real mother, or father for that matter, might have, but what would this person have known about parenting? I can only imagine that she wished for more in a relationship with you, but she could not dare. Too much was at risk. First, what would Mr. Contrelli think of this and how could she explain it to him? Whether a man or a woman, something in him took pride in you as his child. There were other children Carl sired, but they were long gone; just a biological factor that came and went, who knew where. For some reason, you were different. From the pictures of you that you have, you were a fine looking boy. You were the perfect Aryan, tow head, blue eyes, and he probably looked at you as his divine creation, a work of art. How could he have really gotten to know you and think of you as a son? It just couldn't be, so to have you close by safely ensconced into the care of foster parents, who could worry about raising you, was the best he could hope for, plus the little visits in the pantry on holidays where he, she, would attempt to get to know you and find out how your life was going."

I asked Adam, "Think again, Adam, about what she looked like when she was with you. Do you recall? I know it was a long time ago, but while in that room, just the two of you looking at one another, and talking, do you ever remember that she was odd looking, or too masculine, or just strange looking?"

"No. In fact she was quite lovely. In her own way, I think she was attractive. She always wore makeup, her hair was always done very well and she was dressed extremely fashionable. She appeared to be very neat and meticulous. She wore beautiful jewelry, too, I recall; very beautiful earrings, rings and bracelets. And there was one broach I remember, when she talked to me, my eyes kept looking at that broach because it was so beautiful. I had never seen anything sparkle like that before. I just thought she must be very rich to have such a beautiful broach. It had rubies and diamonds in it and it sparkled beautifully," said Adam. His demeanor had changed and softened. I think he was letting all this sink in and maybe understanding the logic in what Bjorn was talking about.

"Yes, I remember that broach," said Ingrid. "It was stunning. She said it was a wedding present from Mr. Contrelli. I still think about her and how fastidious she was about her looks, sitting for a long time in front of her mirror, brushing her hair or putting on makeup, fussing with her jewelry. I was amused when I would walk by her room and the door was open just a crack and I could see her sitting there primping. Honestly, you would not know by looking at her that she wasn't a she. I swear. You would not know. Well, she sure had me fooled."

"Well, perhaps she was practicing being a woman, rehearsing in front of the mirror. Remember, how Irene said she always looked like she was posing. She probably always had to be conscious of trying to appear feminine. When I went to Switzerland looking up the address for Dr. Dresden, I found he had passed away and a Dr. Krantz now owned that practice. He had worked with Dr. Dresden and when he died, he took over the practice. Well, oddly enough, not long before I arrived with my questions, he had been busy cleaning out old files. Dr. Dresden passed away several years ago and at that time, Dr. Krantz just put all of Dr. Dresden's files into boxes and left them alone. Just recently he was moving to new offices and decided to sort through those old files and get rid of them. Well, when he began looking through them, he was astonished at what he found. We had several long chats. He was very honest with me because he too had questions about what went on in that office with Dr. Dresden and he could see that Dr. Dresden kept meticulous notes. When he found files, he was surprised to see the type of work Dr. Dresden was doing. Well, according to Dr. Krantz, the files he found there were many surgeries over several years. I believe by the time Charlotte got to husband number two, she was pretty much a woman. Maybe at that time, she realized that you, Adam, were better off with your foster parents. Vincinzo, her new lover and soon to be husband would probably have wanted no part in parenting or having children around. As you said, Ingrid, he was a notorious playboy and probably married Charlotte for her money. It was about that time that your foster parents adopted you. Maybe she married Vincinzo to test her womanhood. I think the plan was to marry Gerheardt, but she was in control and could do as she wished. She became powerful having inherited Pietro's money and the house; Gerheardt had nothing and was at her mercy. He was safely tucked away in the loft of the garage and wasn't going anywhere. She put Gerheardt off and married this man instead. Gerheardt had to wait his turn. She wanted to have some fun."

I remember how my mind was spinning and about to burst with so many questions. I had to know how this could have been possible. "Bjorn. How was it possible that she could have fooled Vincinzo. I am pretty naive about all this, I'm sure, but I can't even imagine how she could have fooled him entirely."

"Well, the surgeries were very progressive, but remember, these doctors performed experimental surgeries during the war and were far ahead of what would be considered normal at that time. This is what their experiments were all about. Dr. Krantz explained this to me and also showed me the files Dr. Dresden kept, which were very precise. He knew he was ahead of his time and might have wanted to publish his work, but of course, he had to keep a low profile also. He was a masquerading Nazi who did horrible things to prisoners, and he knew he would have been hunted. He never mentioned the patient's name, just a case number. 'Case Number Three,' he called it, but said she lived in Stresa on Lake Maggiore. Only God knows who Case Number One and Two were.

"One of the first surgeries was to remove a tattoo from her left armpit. All SS were tattooed under their left armpit with their blood line, as you told us, Frederick. There is no mistaking that this was Carl. Dr. Krantz was able to get her death records, which described her body. Because of the way she died, the police had to investigate the death to be certain it was not a homicide and indeed a suicide. There was an autopsy report, which indicated many scars around the genital area, as well as a scare under her left armpit. But to answer your questions, Diana, Dr. Krantz deciphered Dr. Dresden's reports for me in great detail, breaking it down into simple language. Please excuse me if I am too graphic, but we are after all adults here and I'm certain we are wondering about this.

"Among a long series of operations, one intricate surgery takes part of the tip of the penis and keeps the nerves and blood vessels intact and makes it a clitoris. The penis is removed, but the skin of the shaft is inverted making it the vagina. Of course the testicles were removed. She could very well have experienced some sexual gratification. Dr. Krantz explained this, and also let me see the files. Now today, this sort of surgery may be quite common, but remember this was in the late forties and early fifties, so it was quite progressive for that time. Also, with her new constructive surgery, intercourse was quite possible and perhaps her male companion would never have known. It's complicated, and a bit crude for this conversation, but evidently his surgeries were successful. After completing this series of operations and hormone treatments, she could perform sexually as a woman. Of course, Dr. Krantz didn't think she could experience a real organism, but believed all the cosmetics and mechanics, if you will, were in place to fool a man during sexual intercourse. We have to realize, Charlotte was a fake. She was busy getting all of her façade in place, and play acting as a woman. Of course she had hormones and she looked the part and may have begun to feel more like a woman, but she went into this as an actress would. She could probably fake her way through an organism quite easily, if it didn't happen naturally," he said.

"Yes, I'm sure," said Ingrid without thinking. She put her hands to her mouth in embarrassment and she even laughed at herself. We snickered a little, but Adam was solemn faced and wasn't finding any of this amusing and actually looked at Ingrid with a raised eyebrow. I was becoming concerned about Adam. Not once during this, did he make eye contact with me or anyone, except Bjorn and he watched him with a look of contempt.

"This was something very new for her and she probably wanted to explore this new part of her anatomy; thus, her affair and eventual marriage with Vincinzo. Remember, in her psyche she was a man and as a likely homosexual, and had a strong sexual appetite for men. Vincinzo was very appealing to her, no doubt. Evidently he couldn't tell anything was different and went ahead and married her. Charlotte must have been very happy with herself, but imagine how Gerheardt felt," said Bjorn.

"This is just so incredible, it's hard to believe," said Frederick who all this time had been quite solemn taking it all in. After all we were talking about his wife's brother. "Now, what if Vincinzo hadn't died? You said, Ingrid, that he died in a boating accident on the lake. What if that accident didn't happen and he and Charlotte stayed together. Gerheardt would have had to stay in that garage forever. What do you think happened to Vincinzo?" he asked.

"Who knows if it was an accident? As you said, Ingrid, he was a womanizer and cheated on Charlotte. Maybe Charlotte had enough of him and reached a breaking point, or maybe she was worried that he might be on to her, or think something wasn't quite right. She may have always lived with that fear that he would find out, or guess. She couldn't chance being disclosed. Nor could she risk the visibility of being with him and having her picture in the newspapers. She had to keep a low profile to protect her identity. He of course didn't know this and didn't want her with him anyway because it cramped his style. I'm sure he enjoyed his celebrity and having female fans falling all over him. Maybe she resented this so much that she became spiteful and hateful, but it was suspected because of conversations Ingrid overheard, that their marriage had a lot of problems. She felt he wasn't sexually interested in her anymore and she wondered if maybe he had some suspicions that she wasn't quite right and this frightened her. She had to get rid of him to protect herself and feared that he might have disclosed her or made his suspicions known to someone else. Her entire life would be tormented with wondering if people were on to her, or suspected her secret. She was allowed no peace of mind, after her first husband died. She was safely protected in that marriage and ensconced in that home on Lake Maggiore as Mrs. Contrelli. After he died, there were no guarantees that she was safe. What do you think, Ingrid?" asked Bjorn.

"I told you, I also thought something was very suspicious about Vincinzo's death," said Ingrid. "He didn't treat her very well and he was gone often. She was so depressed waiting for him to return and then when he did, she wanted his attention, but he ignored her and they argued about that. I think she loved him. Um, well, from what I could see, he could make her very unhappy. The day after he went missing, I noticed her boots in the back service hallway had mud on them. It had rained the day before and I couldn't imagine why she had gone out in the rain, or where she might have been to get mud on her boots. I just let it go, um, but I did wonder. Then his body washed up onto the shore a couple days after he was missing. Well she was upset for a day or so, and then she was over it quickly. She didn't mourn him for very long. She was ready to move on. Then soon after his death, maybe a couple months, she married Mr. Strausner. Then as I said, that marriage was made in hell with all the bickering they did."

"So," said Bjorn, "Charlotte probably left Gerheardt waiting in the wings too long and by the time it was his turn, they may have hated one another. Maybe he didn't like Carl as a woman and preferred him as a man. He probably didn't know what to do with all this new female paraphernalia. The thrill may have been gone for him and he may have been full of resentment. Remember, they more than likely had a homosexual relationship. Imagine, now he had a man in a woman's body and he didn't know what to do with all that. There may have been no way their marriage could have worked.

"Also, before their marriage, the police had their eye on Charlotte after Vincinzo's death, which may have caused some problems for Charlotte, and also for Gerheardt after their marriage. It looked like a boating accident, but when they recovered the body, there were injuries to his body and head that appeared to happen before he entered the water and they believed he may have died first and then was thrown into the water because there was no water in his lungs. When Charlotte didn't appear to mourn for very long before marrying Gerheardt, it seemed she wasn't too broken up about it, which made her look suspicious."

"I had my suspicions also," said Ingrid. "But I pushed them back into my mind whenever I began to wonder about Vincinzo's death. I just didn't want to believe she was capable of such a thing, and yet now after hearing all this, I think she was capable of almost anything. I just didn't know this person at all. I shiver thinking about it. I may have worked for a murderer," said Ingrid.

"Well, yes of course, she was a murderer, if not then, she certainly was during the war. I would say she was responsible for hundreds of deaths. Remember, she took me and my brother from our home, as well as many other children that eventually died horrible deaths. As I said before, she, as Carl, was an over achiever all her life and became an important SS officer. She—He followed Himmler's thinking and probably wanted to be another Himmler. Gerheardt probably worked for Carl. Just because this neutered person threw away his manhood did not mean he could dispense with the person he really was as if he were a snake shedding his skin. This androgynous person was still Carl and Carl was a murderer," said Bjorn. "The revolver Diana found with the initials of CD may have ended the life of many of Carl's victims."

"And then after she married Mr. Strausner," said Ingrid. "All those horrible arguments and him falling over the balcony. Maybe she did push him."

"I have no doubt that she killed Gerheardt also," said Bjorn. "He was not useful to her and caused her grief, and probably threatened to disclose her. He would always be likely to hold that over her head, as if it was his insurance."

"Yes, they acted as if they hated one another. I told you about those words they used and how their conversations were so strange. They spoke as if in code. I never knew what their arguments were about," said Ingrid.

"Yes, those words. Let me tell you about those words. When I got into the debris of the coach house, as I said before, I found a few things that made me suspect that someone lived there at one time. Old shreds of bath towels, a mattress and a metal bed frame, tins that held cigarettes and pipe tobacco, coffee cups. Things like that as I mentioned before, but also there were two pieces of paper. They were in pretty bad condition, but I was able to get something from them. One was a page that looked like it had been torn out of a journal or diary of some sort, and another handwritten, as if it were a letter. It is all handwritten in German by two different people. I had to take it to a German man who is a handwriting expert and works for the police to have them translated and deciphered because I couldn't read them. The first was written in an old European Script, and a bit elaborate, but they were both written by a man, he was sure.

"The words you recalled before mentioned in their arguments, were on this paper. I believe those words were labels they put on their plan and when they spoke and used those words, they held deep meaning for both of them and only they and possibly Dr. Van Hoaf knew what they represented. The letter begins with a sort of instruction paragraph and ends with the initials: 'GS,' for Gerheardt Strausner. There are no names or an intended recipient of this letter. I think it was used as a guideline and referred to over the years to remind them all of that plan and keep the course. When I say, them all, I mean Gerheardt, Carl and Dr. Van Hoaf. I think they were all part of this plan, from the inception. It relates to a process. I'll read to you now." Bjorn pushed his glasses up further on his nose and then took the paper out of his jacket pocket and unfolded it.

"It begins like this: 'You must fully understand and grasp the following. Think about each segment of this. If you feel that any part is not attainable, you cannot go forward. You cannot even begin if you do not believe you can fulfill each phase. You cannot have one without the other. Only with all these phases completely understood and accepted can the ultimate plan work. You must hypothesize each word and feel its meaning and know that it is within your power to enter and leave each phase completely putting your entire self into the full meaning, or you will not move forward to the next phase. Understand completely what these words mean.'

"So I believe what he's saying here, Gerheardt that is, is that with each phase, meaning possibly the phases of the plan to make Carl play the part of a woman and then eventually become a woman. The message is that 'you cannot undo that and you have to keep going forward.' If he was to dress as a woman and play that part, and marry Mr. Contrelli, there was no way she could undo that. They were inventing a person here. He had to continue with that part and always dress and act like a woman. One would have to assure they were committed to move forward and keep going. There would be no looking back, ever. Think about that, especially after the gender transformation began. How could Carl begin and then decide he didn't want to complete the process? What kind of freak would he become? He couldn't be physically half man and half woman. It goes on to say:

'**Acumen:** The circumstances of our time will abruptly end and one cannot find themselves caught unprepared. Plans must be made well in advance.'

"Acumen, which means shrewdness and having keen insight. This must be Gerheardt's and Dr. Van Hoaf's part in Carl's life. The circumstances of their time will abruptly end and they had to be prepared the precise moment to move forward. They may have meant that the war would end, and they saw it coming and Carl may have been their ticket to a safe place—Italy, if he can get the wealthy Italian man to marry him.

'**Initiation:** Must begin before one feels it is time and as such, a critical part of this implies conjecture and sagacity.'

"Conjecture and sagacity. Logical thinking and making good judgments. There was no room for error.

'**Generate:** Put it all into action immediately, without hesitation.'

"Generate, which to them meant to produce, bring into existence, which would be Charlotte. They would produce Charlotte, made up of the former lanky, handsome, man Carl. They would put their plan into action immediately. What if Mr. Contrelli got well, or decided to be taken to Italy to another hospital? Their plan would have a kink in it. In order to make it all happen, to escape to Italy and have Mr. Contrelli's money, it was all counting on him being attracted to their invented female—Carl, who would now be transgendered into Charlotte. Carl would be no more.

'**Perpetuate:** Live that plan, never letting down one's guard.'

"Of course, perpetuate the plan. It was reality then and there was no turning back. It was all real life then, after the marriage and the new Charlotte, lady of the house, had access to money, could hide her friends, as well as hide her own identity. Carl was gone forever, and then the letter to Mrs. Von Barren was probably sent, saying Carl had perished in an automobile accident after the war, trying to get to Rome. It was written by Dr. Van Hoaf. Carl was finished now! And then endure.

'**Endure:** This will be the forever. You are not allowed to turn back.'

"Everything and everyone was in place. Carl, um . . . Charlotte was ensconced in the house on the lake. Ingrid was hired to be the housekeeper, so her new life began. And Adam, there you were living in close proximity to the house, so you were also part of this new life of Charlotte's. Perhaps this is when the surgeries began. Up until then, maybe Carl was just a man in drag as a woman, but soon he was going to change genders and then there was no turning back. He needed to be sure in the onset, before it all began that he would move forward and never look back. So, if he could not accept the first phases, he would not get this far, and if he got this far into the plan, this was it forever. No turning back. Carl was gone, and Carl's anatomy would not be that of a man. He was going to be Charlotte. And then finally, Abide.

'**Abide:** There is no past; only the present and the future and the more rapidly you remove yourself from the present, the future becomes immune. Yesterday is erased.'

"At the end of the letter are the simple initials: GS. This was Gerheardt's plan, of course with the assistance of Dr. Van Hoaf. Abide was the ultimate goal. It was like a pronunciamento, or declaration and he probably had to keep referring back to it to help keep himself on his future path. The sooner Charlotte entrenched herself into her new life, and became part of the social scene on Lake Maggiore, the quicker she became the person that was invented for her. She had no past; she was just a nice German girl that a wealthy lonely Italian man took for his wife because he didn't want to die alone. She was his prize, as they say. She was young, elegant, charming, and intelligent, I might add, but could still move a fully loaded liquor cabinet. She could run his house perfectly. Remember, in her other life, she was a very high ranking officer, so the task of running the house would be performed with utmost precision. Imagine how sad it is that poor Mr. Contrelli went to his grave never knowing."

I added, "And Vincinzo. How ludicrous and sad for him also. Not only did she fool him, but she probably did murder him. Imagine a man like him, a handsome well known race car driver, a playboy, married to a woman who was once a man. He would turn over in his grave if he knew."

"Or if his fans knew. He was adored as a celebrity. We are assuming he didn't know. Maybe he was beginning to catch on to her and that was why she had to kill him. She was safe with Pietro, but not with Vincinzo. He might have known something wasn't quite right," said Felix.

"This is all so incredible," said Frederick. "I am just so happy my wife never knew about this. She loved her brother, Carl. She loved him her whole life, even when she knew what he was doing and did not agree with him. She still loved him and worried about him. She remembered how they celebrated Christmas together as a family when they were children, and isn't it ironic that Charlotte enjoyed Christmas so much? My wife was devastated when she received the letter that he died in an automobile accident. And then she wanted to know what happened to his remains, and where he was buried. Until the day she died, she always wondered. Thank God she never knew the truth."

Adam spoke up quite adamantly. "Okay, this is all very interesting, and disgusting, I might add, but again, what proof do you have that any of this includes me? I see you have proof about Carl's surgeries, and I guess we can't dispute that, but about Carl being my father—you still haven't explained how you came to believe so strongly about that."

"Yes, I'm coming to that. I said that I found two pieces of paper in the rubble of the carriage house. This is a translation of the paper that looked as though it was taken from a journal or diary. I had to have this translated and deciphered also." Bjorn took the second sheet of paper out of his jacket pocket. "It was retyped from the original handwriting, which by the way was the same as Carl's handwriting. It matched the writing on the back of one of the photos, and also from a letter in Dr. Van Hoaf's files from Carl asking for a higher dosage of pain medicine. That letter was signed Carl. I'm quite sure if Frederick looks at the original writing, it is the same as the letter your wife received from Carl when he was leaving for Rome." He handed the letter to me. "Diana, would you please read it for us? I am becoming very tired. I've talked enough tonight, I think."

I reached over and took the paper and held it up near the light of the fireplace and began to read it aloud.

> "My life is a facade, a total illusion that I have unconditionally accepted knowing full well that this would be my ultimate existence. But then there is a part of me that wants to connect to my memories. I just cannot help it. If I don't have those little bits of memories, then it is as if I was just born, as I am now, as a duplicitous being, with no childhood and no trace of a lineage. I have trained myself to never think about it, but there are times that these thoughts creep into my mind and I fear that those thoughts can be read on my face through some expression I am not aware of and my face is telling a story. In the beginning I avoided mirrors, but then learned that the mirror was my reinforcement and I had to study my face, to get to know it as it is and as I am and try to look at my reflection and not remember my former self, but see me as I am. But sometimes it is so difficult and I have no one to talk to. I can never say what I really think and I cannot control my thoughts. I can never be natural or act without my own consciousness and being fully aware of my every move, every utterance, and every expression of thought. Nothing can be unrehearsed and it exhausts me. I have created a dark place where I can go and where no one will find me. It is the only place in the world where I can go and think freely, and

*let whatever expression dares to come to my face or emotion my mind wants to express to be free. There are no mirrors, no reflections, nothing that shows an image that looks back at me. I had the windows removed so there is no light, no reflection. I only allow myself small amounts of time for this liberty, but if I cannot have this freedom and privacy, I think at times I may go mad; maybe it is too late and when I am alone, in the total darkness, I think about this and wonder if indeed I have gone mad. I am never allowed a moment to think as I really am, so I must at times recoil and pull back and just sit and think. I will never allow myself to think thoughts of remorse. There is no purpose in regret and wishing I had done things differently. Nothing will come of that and it is a waste of brain power to let my mind go there. I have sealed off the pantry and had the windows bricked over and made the entrance private so I can go into the room and be totally alone, with myself, my thoughts and not allow anyone to find me. I sit in the dark and just think about my childhood and imagine myself innocently playing in the sun. There I was just a child with no worries, nothing to take me away from just having fun as a child should, being certain that I was loved and taken care of, and being able to laugh freely and just be myself. It was another's life when I think those thoughts. Everything about me after that was not me, it was being what someone wanted me to be, doing as they expected, or me striving to be something else. Somewhere I got lost, and only in this very dark and silent place can I begin to try to reclaim that life so long ago. It is the only thing about me that is real. There is nothing else. I sit here writing this note, and look down at my legs and feet and think they must belong to another. Those are the legs and shoes of a woman. They cannot belong to me. But none of that matters. The vessel of this soul is nothing that matters and will dissolve one day into nothingness. My offspring are gone and now are someone else's children. The only one I have ever seen more than once is also gone and there is no trace left of my life. I will never see him again, and this room now serves another purpose. I remember him sitting here with me, my own flesh and blood and my creation and yet, he was so distant I could not allow myself to touch him, or to love him for fear I would not be able to let go. I amazed myself that I could have created such a beautiful human being. He is so perfect and I created this with my own being. But now, there is nothing left. So I sit in the dark and I forget what my face now looks like, and what my body looks like and I try to get in touch with my soul and wonder if that is still the same soul I had as a child, or if it too has been transferred to something else, somewhere else where I will never again be part of it. I try to connect, but I am an empty vessel and it is an exercise I repeat each time I am in this room, alone, and each time I find I cannot connect. I have no soul."*

Silence fell like a wet blanket over the room. The only sounds were heavy sighs, soft breaths escaping and the crackling of the embers in the fireplace. Finally Felix broke the uncomfortable silence. "That says it all and certainly explains the reason for the closed off room. Maybe she wrote this after the death of one of the husbands, or after you left to go to school in France, Adam. Or maybe this is her suicide note. It appears it was written in one of her most desperate moments."

"Yes, it could have been written near her death. She was obviously quite despondent when she wrote it," said Bjorn. "She enjoyed her new life as a wealthy woman living in a villa and was happy then and probably proud of herself; she pulled one over on the world. It was written later on when she was becoming beaten down and then forced to reflect on herself and what happened to her and probably when you left for France, Adam. At that time your family probably wasn't getting paid by her anymore and they wanted to get you away from her. All that might have happened about the same time she had the windows bricked over. It could have been a suicide note that she was leaving for Gerheardt in the garage while he still lived there, before their marriage and then she chickened out. We will never know how it ended up in the garage. It could very well have been just before she died. There was no date on the page and there is no way to tell when she wrote this, but this alone helped me put the truth together. Felix and I were speculating up until that part. I just got this back a few days ago. I believe everything happened as I said. Felix had some facts about what happened during the war. The doctor in Switzerland had some hard facts that told us what this person was and what she became. It is a real stretch of the mind to think people could have gone to such great lengths to hide, but they had plenty to hide from. They would have faced execution or at least life in prison had they been captured after the war. Instead they spent their life looking over their shoulder, losing their own identity and becoming someone else and probably living in fear of being found out. It was much like imprisonment. They were never free of that threat. They probably didn't trust one another and maybe that is why she kept Gerheardt near her all through the marriages so she could keep an eye on him. She kept him in the carriage house, and then gave him free range to roam around the house, sneaking around between the kitchen and the library through the pantry during the day and probably the entire house at night after the servants were gone, and Pietro went to bed. Just like some kind of rodent skulking around in the dark. Both Charlotte and Gerheardt held something over the other's head. They could control one another and threaten one another and they probably did. There was no trust right from the beginning of their so called marriage. And that may be why Gerheardt had to die and even then, Charlotte had no assurance that he hadn't disclosed her somehow. They were each vicious enough to have disclosed one another; however, in doing so they would have put themselves in harm's way. They were in an impossible situation.

*The House on Lake Maggiore*

The plan worked for a while, but then when the money ran out, their options also ran out. What could Charlotte do? She was still young—only about thirty eight or so, according to her death records. Could she marry again? She would have had to have someone take care of her and then there was the risk that he might find her strange or not put together right, with her bits and pieces askew. Maybe she was losing confidence in her womanhood. Could she take that chance with a fourth husband? She had no profession or means to take care of herself. She knew the police were suspicious and she was probably very worried about that. What future did she have? She had to end it, so she did the world a favor and grabbed a rope, took a trip to the attic one rainy day and lassoed a beam and that was the end of it all," said Bjorn, as if it were the prosecution's closing statement in front of a jury, and we were the jury.

Adam stood up and walked over to the fireplace and stood quietly for a moment. Bjorn got up from the sofa and went over to Adam and put his hand on Adam's shoulder. "Are you all right, Adam? I am sorry for all of this, but I felt you needed to know the truth. If I was wrong in doing so, please forgive me. I didn't know, honestly, that all my digging about would uncover all of this or that I would find things that affected you." Bjorn was very sincere and could see that Adam was a bit shaken.

"I know. You had no real choice. I realize this was all important for you to find out about all of that. I am sorry for your brother and your parents. What a tragic life you had! It is hard to imagine living with those horrible memories. But I think I've heard enough. If this is true, it's a very sad story, and it sickens me to think this vulgar, fallacious person could have been my parent. Say no more. I don't think there is anything to be gained by trying to understand them. He, she, whatever this person was, disgusts me. So he did his duty so many years ago, fathered his required number of children for the sake of his God-damned fatherland, while rounding up other children destined to die probably in the same day as his escapades to Lebensborn. It was all in a day's work for him. It was just my misfortune that I was the one to have to hang around and be accounted for. It sickens me to think that this person was responsible for my life, for my being born. How fortunate for the other three if they never knew how despicable their father was, or their whore of a mother. This person that took other people's children from their homes in front of crying mothers, this person that did horrible things during the war obviously was more heartless than caring. All my life all I knew were my adopted parents and they gave me a good life and a good home and it was the foundation on which I built my life. I never questioned who my real parents were. My adopted parents told me that my parents died in the war and they adopted me. That was all I needed to know. I never allowed myself to think about who my real parents were. It just didn't matter to me. Then, every now and then this strange person passed through my life and there were a few uncomfortable moments, but once I left the pantry, my life continued on, normally, like any other child's life. All the years, all the decades of my life, I knew only one set of parents that I loved very much. And when my wife and I had children, my parents were my children's grandparents and they were kind and loving and my children worshiped them. Our life was very happy and wonderful and complete. And now at this point of my life the truth comes out of where I really came from and who my real parents were, or might have been, and I feel shattered. It's as if my entire life was a lie. It shames me to know all this. How do you think I feel? What must I tell my children? That my life was a lie and I was the bastard son of this atrocious person, this cold hearted killer who believed in Hitler and all the horrible things he stood for? That it was all right in this person's eyes and mind to believe in eugenics and to take part in that? I can never be the same person now that I know this. I don't know how I will deal with this, or if I can even live with this. Now I see my adopted parents were part of her scheme and collected money from her to help support me. Even they deceived me. Who in life can you trust, if not your parents? I don't know what to tell my children."

By this time, there were tears running down Adam's face and for an instant I hated Bjorn for telling him all this and I hated myself for wanting to hear it all and not stopping him. It was a very sad moment to watch this poor man, who I had come to care so much for during my months in Stresa, just falling apart before my eyes. Knowing him as much as I possibly could in those few months, I know he was a very proud man who held his integrity in high esteem and lived his life with dignity. To have been so emotionally shaken in front of others, I'm sure was very difficult for him.

We all sat very quietly for a moment, a very long uncomfortable moment. It was incredibly sad to see Adam so miserable and I wanted to embrace him, but was afraid of how he would react. Bjorn stood there next to Adam with his head bent. I could see that he felt very badly and was searching in his mind for some words to make things better. Silence was all that could be. We were speechless, each trying to let all this information settle in our minds and trying to decide how to deal with it.

Finally Adam broke the dreaded silence again. "Diana," he said, just looking at me for a moment, as if he wasn't sure what to say. "I have come to care about you very much, but I have to say I wish you had never come here. I wish you had never found that pantry. All those horrible dark secrets were to stay hidden away behind bricks and mortar. None of it was supposed to ever be revealed. I think that bastard knew that too. All of you went digging for the truth and in the end, the truth was all about me." He began to walk towards the gallery and turned around to look at us one more time. "I have to go. I cannot hear any more." I stood up and tried to go after him, but he put his hand up and said, "No, Diana. Let me go. I need to be alone," and this poor broken man walked out of the room and soon we heard the big door in the entrance hall close behind him. We all just sat in silence and looked at one another, not knowing just what to do. I think we all felt shame and guilt in what had transpired that evening.

Bjorn went back to the sofa, sat down and ran his hands through his hair. He just sat for a moment on the edge of the cushion with his elbows resting on his knees and his weary head in his hands. "That page, maybe it was part of Charlotte's journal, but the fact that it was in the carriage house is a mystery. Perhaps Gerheardt found it, or she may have begun to use that garage as a safe haven in the few short days after his death and the days before her own death. We can only imagine when and why she wrote that. There was never evidence of a journal or a book that this may have come from," said Bjorn.

Ingrid said, "Maybe, um . . . she went into that carriage house to be near some essence of Gerheardt, after his death and wrote that note there, thinking about him. They may have hated one another, but he was all she had, it seems. Imagine how lost she must have felt after he died. He had always been there, near her somewhere, as her partner. When you think about the other document with those words spelling out the plan, it was not meant that she would go through that alone. He was to be there, going through those phases with her. Um, maybe it never occurred to her that one day she would be left carrying the weight of all that baggage herself. Maybe she was frightened thinking about it, and what her future would be. There she was, left all alone, sort of abandoned. There was no other phase on that plan to guide her along. He invented her."

We all looked at Ingrid and thought about what she said and how logical that all sounded. Having been the only person that had personal contact with Charlotte and spending so many years with her, all of these revelations must be almost as difficult for her to grasp as it was for Adam. She too was so deceived and the memory of the person she thought she knew and spent so many years with, was now a complete and total enigma. She too would have a hard time learning to live with this and moving on, without thoughts of this always creeping back into her mind. I felt sorry for her. I think Ingrid had a difficult life and worked hard. Sometimes the way she spoke, always pausing to search for words, one would think she wasn't very smart, but now I could see she was intelligent and a very sweet woman. Charlotte was lucky to have had her taking care of her so well and to have her now being so insightful and protective of her memory. Charlotte didn't deserve such caring.

We all sat quietly again for a moment. I noticed Ingrid was wiping a tear from her cheek. Bjorn spoke again. "Charlotte obviously wrote the page while recalling her youth and then decided the journal was too revealing, but she decided to keep selected pages for her own use in remembering her youth."

"Well," said Felix, "as we see now, Charlotte was never really friendly with anyone. She couldn't afford to let people get too close to her, even you Ingrid, yet in reality, in her heart you were more a friend to her than anyone, but she had no one else and at times she let her guard down without realizing it. She had no one to talk to, so she talked to a journal, perhaps." The room became quiet and somber again.

Ingrid sniffled and wiped her cheek with a handkerchief and her voice was full of emotion when she spoke. "Yes, she made it a point to keep everyone at arm's length. I think, um . . . she would feel friendly one day and then the next day she would turn to ice and start issuing orders again. She would tell me or someone else on the staff to do something or reprimand us for doing something wrong, and be sure to put us in our place and make us feel very bad. I think I felt closer to her than any of them and then I would once more be so hurt when she turned on me."

Bjorn said, "She was an SS Officer. She knew how to give orders."

"Yes, that's what she really was. All those years, she was not just the lady of the house, I guess. In her mind she was still a Nazi. It was a mixed bag, dealing with Charlotte. Perhaps she was mentally ill. How could she have been considered normal?" added Ingrid.

"How could a person be normal and live through what she went through, and make the choices she made?" My question, as with all of our questions, were quite rhetorical because it was apparent we were all struggling for logical explanations and at that point, thinking out loud. "I can't imagine being born into one gender, and then changing genders. How psychologically challenging would that be? And as she said in her note, always having to check herself, her thoughts and expressions to be sure she was acting the right part of her new gender. In her situation that was a matter of life and death. I can't imagine living like that and not being real. But we do realize now after hearing all this that Charlotte was a lonely woman and seemed to have no real friends," I added. "Only Gerheardt, who was always in the wings waiting. He wasn't her friend, but more of a partner in their transgressions. They could not leave one another. Obviously they could not trust one another and therefore, had to remain devoted, but always with one eye open. I can't imagine living like that. It was like living in confinement."

"No, her life was surely no walk in the park, but that was her doing. So many secrets. Not just the façade of her gender, but of her history in the war, before she came to Contrelli's house. She had much to guard and must have had to carefully think about every word she spoke for fear she would give herself away. I don't believe she was that malleable that she just let those things happen to her. She played a very active part and for all we know, she may have manufactured the entire thing. We will never know what could have gone on in her head and how could we possibly relate to this person. We can only surmise, because we are human, but we can never assimilate our own selves to someone like her. It is beyond our understanding," added Bjorn.

"In my little exploration and research, I also met with the police department here in Stresa. They had some record of a police detective who had kept his eyes on Charlotte, suspecting she had something to do with the deaths of her second and third husband. It was just too much of a coincident that they both died unexpectedly of accidents. They opened all those old records up for me. It seemed that their curiosity was raised when they discovered that Vincinzo was an expert sailor and it would have been unlikely that he would have been so irresponsible as to be drunk while operating the sailboat. He would have known

*The House on Lake Maggiore*

better, and also, his body had strange bruises, so it appeared as if someone had held him under his arms and dragged him. And as I said, there was no water in his lungs. He suspected that Charlotte first killed him and then dragged the body to the sail boat, took the boat out herself and then dumped his body and left the sail boat on the lake and took a small dinghy back to the shore. Also, the third husband fell over the balcony. Even if he was drunk and stumbled, the railing would have broken his fall. There was a little damage to the railing at the time, so his body may have hit it with significant force, which could have happened if Charlotte pushed him. He believed she had uncanny strength, much more than a woman might have had, so he suspected something strange about her. There were notes in the report that he watched her hands as he talked to her. They were large, and not as graceful as a woman's hands would be but looked strong and she didn't use them gracefully. She would sit with her hands folded in her lap, with her fingers intertwined. Her fingers were large and not very delicate. She fumbled with a small tea cup and holding a fountain pen. It appeared she had a hard time holding small items. She fumbled with her handbag to open it and get her cigarettes, as if this was a foreign object to her and she wasn't certain how to use it. He recalled that he couldn't seem to take his eyes off her hands because it was the only thing about her that didn't seem to fit her, other than her feet, which were also large. So you have to wonder about what Vincinzo felt about her. As everyone said, she was not pretty, but more striking in appearance. I think Vincinzo needed someone to finance him and Charlotte came to the rescue. She may have thought he loved her, but it was money he wanted. Whether he did or not, at this point, as I suspected, she was testing her new womanhood, seeing as the surgeries were complete. They lived the high life, and the spending got out of control and her money began to dwindle. Remember she may have had the body of a woman, but her mind was that of a man and Carl liked men. Charlotte, Carl, was probably sexually gratified with Vincinzo. She was able to perform sexually as a woman, and was also able to hide her scars, but after a time, this husband may have begun to suspect something was strange. Two years into their marriage, he died suddenly by drowning one night out on his boat on the lake, during a thunder storm, I might add. That's not usually when you would go sailing on a lake. The police said they knew this man was well versed in navigating a yacht and had won many trophies. It was not investigated, however and because he was known to have a drinking problem, it was assumed that he was intoxicated and just fell, perhaps hitting his head and was unconscious by the time his body hit the water. His body had washed ashore a few days later after the incident. The boat appeared to be abandoned after two days being spotted in the same place on the lake, and of course, Charlotte reported her husband missing. I think with what I found out from the police report, it was fairly easy to surmise quite a lot from their information," Bjorn added.

"I just want to say that I am sorry to have raked up this contorted, twisted, horrible story and to have dragged you all through it. I feel just dreadful about Adam," said Bjorn. He stood up again and walked to the fireplace and stood looking at the fading fire, with his back toward us. His voice became softer and full of sadness. "Perhaps it was selfish of me because it was really my quest and I should have left it at that. Ingrid, please forgive me for pulling this dark veil over any good memories you had about your experience in this house. I know it was not all good for you, having been through the deaths of her husbands and also finding her body as you did. All that was bad enough; I didn't want to make all that worse, but I'm afraid I did."

"Oh, no, Mr. Thorner. Please don't feel like that," said Ingrid, quite emphatically and almost pleading. "As bad as all this was, I needed to know the truth also. That day I came to the house and first met you, Diana, you remember how when I told you about the people here, I was full of questions also. I never understood them and of course, her killing herself like that. I pitied her all these years, and I no longer feel sorry for her. I was always curious and I needed to know the things you found out,

Mr. Thorner. Thank you for all the work you did in finding this all out. I think we all needed to know, even Adam. He himself said that he always questioned the mystery of Charlotte. It is very difficult to go through life with unanswered questions that just continuously eat away at you. I needed to know why Charlotte killed herself and now I think I have an answer to that question. Adam needed to know and I'm sure he will be fine. He just needs time and he will be fine, I'm sure."

"Yes, Bjorn. You must not feel like that," added Felix. "If there is any blame here, then I am equally to blame because I added fuel to the fire. None of this was intended to hurt anyone and it is not your fault that others were a part of Charlotte's life. That is just the way it was. There is enough information to close the book on it all. No one needs to wonder anymore. Closure is what everyone wanted."

I agreed and we all wanted to be sure that Bjorn didn't carry away any undue guilt. No one was to blame for this horrible story, but Charlotte and Gerheardt. They alone, in all their hate and exploitation of one another, deserved each other and for eternity remain culpable and no one should ever mourn their memory.

The guests all began to leave, but Bjorn decided to stay and help me clean up. We picked up all the dishes, glasses, cups and saucers and took them into the kitchen and as we worked in the kitchen, we continued to talk. I felt drained from so much information, but my mind seemed to stick on the thoughts about how Charlotte's surgeries could have actually made her perform sexually with a man, and that he would not suspect there was anything abnormal or different. Bjorn went back to his suggestion that maybe it was not all that perfect and maybe Vincinzo did suspect something, and that might be why Charlotte felt that relationship had to end. Or maybe it was at Gerheardt's prodding that she had to end it because he was getting impatient. Dr. Krantz described to Bjorn in detail about her surgeries, just as Dr. Dresden described it in his report, as he spelled it all out in such finite detail.

"Well, it's all very strange indeed. Dr. Krantz worked for Dr. Dresden and became his partner soon after graduating from medical school. He worked with him for several years and then after Dr. Dresden died, Dr. Krantz took over the practice. Dr. Krantz packed up all Dr. Dresden's files, but as I said, he was moving into different offices and was sorting through those old files before destroying them. Imagine his surprise when he began to sort through them and found those curious things. Dr. Dresden performed surgeries that Dr. Krantz knew nothing about. Dr. Krantz had no idea Dr. Dresden knew anything about such things, because the practice was mostly involved in common practices, such as pulmonary and vascular diseases and performed surgeries like repairing heart valves, that sort of thing. It was basically a cardiovascular practice. His surgeries documented in the files were far beyond that and Dr. Krantz had no idea he had such knowledge. He did indeed have a patient that lived in the house in Stresa on Lake Maggiore. There was no name on the file, only an address and a name of Case Number 3. There was however, that short note from Carl about requesting to up the dose of pain medicine. Dr. Krantz tried to read the reports to me, but I had trouble following him. Finally, he showed me the file. His records definitely did not mention a person by name. He named the person Case 3. That's all, just Case 3. His reports would say things like, 'When Case 3 entered the room, we discussed the next series of surgeries.' Or, 'Case 3 is not healing properly.' Dr. Krantz could not tell who this person was, but he had the home address in one place, just in one place, which made Dr. Krantz think it was an oversight on Dr. Dresden's part. It was obvious he guarded his activities with this patient carefully, for some reason or another. Dr. Krantz worked so closely with him for so many years, and after Dr. Dresden died and he found these reports, he realized he knew little about Dr. Dresden's clandestine work and what he was doing. Dr. Krantz did recall that Dr. Dresden did not talk about personal matters or who his private patients were, and it became obvious he was not to inquire, but just tend to his own patients. Dr. Dresden died suddenly of a heart attack, so he had no time to destroy any of his records, which he would have naturally done, if he had the opportunity.

"Your curiosity was the same as mine. It was pretty much spelled out in the case files, and it appeared that Dr. Dresden was very proud of his work, as well he should be, I suppose because his creation seemed to fool many people. As I said before, one of the most important surgeries was to invert the penis and make a vagina. This was one of the most serious surgeries, many more cosmetic surgeries or alterations as he called them, and then of course a series of hormone treatments took place. But along with all of this is the psychological work that had to be done to really make a man a woman and a woman of this stature. Imagine how one must recreate their psyche, the work that needs to be done in one's mind to make them think like the opposite sex, like opening a handbag with hands that were more used to throwing a ball or firing a gun."

Bjorn went on to explain the details of the surgeries, as he recalled Dr. Krantz's interpretations from reading Dr. Dresden's reports. His goal was to create as normal a vagina as possible, provide maximal clitoral and vaginal sensation, furnish a deep vagina allowing satisfactory sexual intercourse, and minimize disfiguring scars. The operations were both cosmetic and reconstructive. Bjorn said that the files included drawings Dr. Dresden made, at each stage of the surgeries illustrating the type of surgery he was performing. Because these were done gradually, towards the last years of Mr. Contrelli's life, the severity of each surgery was minimized and the healing process not excessive. By the time Mr. Contrelli died, the surgeries were complete and that is when Charlotte decided to put her womanhood to the test, and she found Vincinzo.

# CHAPTER 15

---❖---

After Adam's departure that evening we all felt helpless and depleted. We felt sad for him and talked about what we should try to do to help him. We believed he needed time alone to think about it all and come to terms with it. No matter how dreadful the truth was, it was all true, we were quite certain and Bjorn and Felix did a lot of work to figure it all out.

I got hold of Adam the next day on the phone, while he was staying with his friends Mary and Paul in Stresa. I knew that he was clearly devastated by this. He told me in quite a long dissertation that he did not know how to handle this, what to make of it all or what to think, but it seemed to him that Bjorn had all his facts and seemed to be able to prove all of it. He spoke for quite some time about his boyhood dreams about life and what his life eventually had in store for him and how he thought he had found all the happiness he ever deserved by marrying his wife and having children of his own, and then grandchildren. He was truly blessed and now, it seems like it was all built on a lie and he wondered how he could have had a parent that was so horrible and did such awful things and wondered what thread of this parent runs through his being. How to deal with this truth was a tremendous quandary for him. How could he ever stop thinking about it? How could he ever sleep again because when he closed his eyes he saw Charlotte looking at him, as she did when they were in now infamous pantry? Her face had become much more vivid and etched into his memory. He was truly sad and devastated and I heard the pain in his voice. This dreadful man that was his father was an atrocious monster and he couldn't even imagine what kind of person his biological mother might have been. Thankfully she was just lost forever. He believed she was equally as dreadful because she was part of the Lebensborn program and just being a manufacturer of babies. It was all a horrible nightmare.

Adam said "What part of him is in me? What biological residue of him was part of my physical being? He was what 'she' was and I am what I am. Maybe that person's blood runs through my veins, and maybe my chemistry is made up of his genes, but that is all. It was just a biological connection—nothing more! I can't get the vision out of my mind that the woman in the pantry was a man, my father, dressed as a woman, trying to find some closeness to me. It sickens me just thinking about it, and I can't stop thinking about it. I am myself and I will not let anyone tell me I have any of his traits. Never in my life have I been anything other than a good person and I have lived a good life and I have never hurt anyone. Carl was a monster and I am ashamed to have any innate characteristics that link me to him. He was a soulless person. How could he be one person for most of his life and then throw that away and make some physical changes, then become someone else and forget the other person existed? How can that be? How many people suffered at the hands of Carl to make Charlotte come to be? How despicable to take children from their families because they had the right characteristics to be German looking and be part of Germanization. This person took parents to the train that led them to their death. Imagine taking children to be part of experimental surgeries and ruining the life of small children, murdering people, deceiving people, and still loving oneself. What kind of person is this? You think he is my parent? If so, then I am ruined forever. I cannot be me knowing he is somewhere in my biological self. I am truly physically sick from just thinking about what I am made of. How can I tell my grandchildren who their great grandparents were? How can I look in the mirror at my face and think now I see a resemblance to him, or her? I hate that person for what they did."

He told me I mustn't feel responsible, but the facts are as they are and I had to realize how this made him feel. He pleaded with me, "Please, Diana, go home and find your life. Your life is not here, and I wonder if my life is still here. Go home and be happy. We will meet again one day and I will try very hard to put this all behind me, but for now, I have to go figure out how to do that and I must do it by myself." He hung up the telephone and I was left in tears. I was so sad to have him leave me this way and I would have given anything for some way to help him, but I felt hopeless and so responsible. I decided to take his advice and go home. I think I had a bit of healing also to do.

Felix came to see me that morning at my hotel. He too felt terrible about what happened the night before and how it affected Adam. We talked more about evil Charlotte and what her life must have been like. What drove her to carry on her life and be oblivious to everyone except herself? Felix was also worried about Bjorn. They became good friends and worked hard together in their search for information. Felix believed Bjorn was glad his search had ended, but he also felt responsible for bringing so much sadness to Adam.

That morning, over coffee and pastries in the glassed in dining room of my hotel looking out at the lake, Felix continued my education on the horrors of the war, which he for many years could not talk about. This is why whenever I was with him, I had the feeling he was holding information back. It wasn't that he was being secretive, but more that he was uncomfortable talking about it, since he was German and in the German army. Many memories were trapped in his mind and he had to live with the horrors of the war for all the years of his life. He reiterated what Bjorn said about Germanization and Eugenics. It is a sad reality of that horrible war.

The reality of Carl's life was tragic, even at the beginning of his youth. He was destined for unhappiness. From what Frederick told us, when Carl as a young boy joined the Hitler

Youth, it began his journey away from his family and closer to his entrenchment into the Reich, and laid the path for the destiny of the remainder of his short life. Children were removed from private homes where old ideas, books and traditions formed their character and loyalties to church or local customs could conflict with this new order. Boys went into the Hitler Youth and Girls went into the Bund Deutscer Maedel, or BDM. The boys joined the Jungvolk organization at age ten and then four years later, they moved to the Hitler Youth and there they stayed for four years being indoctrinated to the ways of the Nazi ideology. Then they were taken into the Party, into the Labor Front, and into the SA or into the SS. If they were there for eighteen months or two years and had still not become real National Socialists, then they went into the Labor Service and were polished there for six or seven months. It was a continuous indoctrination of being a good and fit German. Carl lost himself along the way and the matter of his becoming a woman was unimportant and anticlimactic because his essence was already lost.

After breakfast with Felix, I returned to my hotel room and called Adam again. He was going home to Lugano that afternoon. I begged him to stay and meet me for dinner so we could talk, but he said "Absolutely not. We talked too much already." His voice was weak and quiet and I could tell he was despondent and depressed. He ended the conversation abruptly and hung up the phone. I felt almost frantic because I had to begin to think about going home myself, but did not want to leave without knowing he was going to be all right. I wrote him a letter to send to his house in Lugano and apologized again for allowing this all to happen and tried to convince him that he must not dwell on all this and rise above it. He should look at himself and his life's accomplishments and realize that he is his own person and his origin only breathed life into him—nothing more. He must file it all away somewhere in his mind and enjoy himself, his children and grandchildren. I tried to tell him that he was important to his family and also to me.

A few days passed and I moped around the hotel waiting for a response to my letter, but it didn't happen. I became more worried each day and didn't know what to do. My work at the house was finished and I had no reason to stay. The house was listed with a realtor and there were several potential, serious buyers in a bidding war. Bjorn was anxious to get his profit and I just wanted to be done with the entire matter. I wanted to go home, but didn't want to leave until I heard from Adam.

Finally in my last attempt to reach him, I rented a car and drove to Lugano and went to his home, but to no avail. There was no sign of him anywhere. I panicked and didn't know what to do. Oh my God, I thought, what have I done to this poor man? He was so devastated and angry when he left the house and when he talked with me by phone. Bjorn and Felix also tried to locate him, but it was as if he disappeared. I rationalized the situation, trying to put myself in his shoes and realized he knew best and just needed to go away and think about it and once he reconciled himself to the reality of his childhood, he would be fine.

I returned to Stresa with a broken heart and a truck load of guilt. I felt responsible for Adam's heartache, but I couldn't fix it. It just was not in my power to make things right for him. Normally I never liked being alone in the house by myself at night. The shadows were just too ominous and I always thought I heard noises, but I felt I needed the quietness to just sit and think and be alone there to say a proper good bye. I would give those horrifying spirits one last chance to reach out to me. I sat in the big house that last evening, in the big room with only the fireplace lighting the room and the high ceiling swallowed up in the darkness. I was curled up on the couch with a glass of brandy staring at the fire and thinking about my little cabin in the woods. I had many pensive moments there in that cabin in front of the fire, sipping brandy or cognac and letting my mind wander. I ached for the familiarity of that wonderful little place, my sanctuary. I wanted so to be surrounded with something familiar, a small room with a feeling of closeness and something comfortable and the archive of my life. I was tired of this big

*The House on Lake Maggiore*

house and the work that I put into it. I was tired of the big room with the high ceiling and the balcony overlooking the room where Gerheardt lost his life. I was tired of living with the ghosts of that house and having them taunt me every minute begging me to just think about them, asking me to climb those attic steps to see where Charlotte took her life, the last scene of her theatre.

I could almost hear the voices screaming at one another upstairs, the arguments and the hatred that transpired between Gerheardt and Charlotte, perhaps a scream of threat and blame. I regretted the hours I spent thinking about these horrible people and their despicable lives and I was angry at myself for adoring her image, thinking she was such a lovely lady, envying her story book life. She was a deceiving opportunist seducing the unsuspecting wealthy Italian, performing her witchery on him, convincing the poor man to bring her to live in his villa and give her a life of riches. She was so undeserving and poor Pietro died never knowing what a perfidiously cunning person she was and how she used him. I thought about Pietro's first wife and this house that he built for her and how sad it was that the sweet memory of their life and their little daughter who lived there was washed away and overridden by the deceitful theatre of such disgusting people as Carl and Gerheardt. For twenty years of their short life together it was their beautiful home and they were probably much more deserving of it than Charlotte. The first Mrs. Contrelli was the true lady of the house and it was a shame she died and left Pietro alone, so lonely that he had to find himself a new bride and then ended up with someone he never really got to know, the she creature of Carl who became Charlotte, and oh how I even hated to say that name. The hours of my time she took from me, thinking about her, envying her, wishing I would have had her fairy tale. Thank God I am who I am and love the life I have. It has been a million times better than hers. She never knew what love was because of her all-encompassing narcissism. There was no room in her heart for anyone, if indeed she had a heart. She was an opportunist and spent her entire life posturing herself, and it didn't matter who she deceived, stepped over or killed. She didn't love Adam. She only loved the fact that she had something to do with the child's creation, as if an art masterpiece. It was all part of her ego. She amazed herself and it was always about her. And now, nearly sixty years after her death, she is still spreading her nefarious madness into our world. Had she just died and faded away, it would have been just. Then I think about her despair and her diary page where she had to go into a dark room to recall her childhood and try to get in touch with her soul. That was an impossible task because I'm quite sure she was a soulless person, and there in the weakest moment of Charlotte's theatre, she thought the same.

# CHAPTER 16

There was a firm offer for the house. In fact several perspective buyers present at the opening night's celebration, made offers. The bidding resulted in an offer higher than the asking price. Bjorn and his investors were very pleased and I was thankful the experience had ended and I was finally going home. The furniture loaned to us from the other villa was scheduled to be returned and our house was now ready for its new inhabitants.

The time came for me to say good-bye to the house. It was bittersweet because I loved the way the house looked and our hard work paid off, but it was because of this house that we uncovered such sadness. I just didn't know what to do about Adam. I hated to leave without knowing he was all right, but I had to go home. It had been a very long eight months.

Adam's son Andrew called me on my cell phone, just when I thought I had no hope of hearing how he was. He told me his father had come to him and told him everything. He was quite sure Adam would be fine and he assured me that Adam had no animosity towards me at all and did not blame me for anything and he was sorry for his harsh words towards me. Adam wanted Andrew to assure me that he was not angry and also to tell me I must go home and he would contact me by letter. I thought perhaps his family was angry at me also, but Andrew reassured me this was not my fault and no matter how sad the truth was, he had to know. I needed to be sure he was fine and that he would recover from his sadness. No matter how much Andrew tried to reassure me that it was not my fault and Adam did not blame me, I felt responsible because I dug up so many unpleasant things. I cursed the day I broke down that wall to the pantry, but it would have eventually been discovered.

Andrew assured me that Adam would be fine, but he didn't want to talk about this with anyone for quite some time. He had many times in the past expressed to his children his thoughts about the mystery of the strange woman that used to take him on a sojourn into the pantry. Now at least, he need not ever ask those questions again or wonder. He assured me it was not my fault that the answers were destructive and something so unimaginable. Andrew said none of this matters to any of the family. They all love Adam and believe he is a good man and nothing would change that. He told his father that he should live in the moment, not in the past. How many orphans are there in the world that never knew where their life began? Perhaps if they knew they would also be horrified. Life has no guarantees of happy endings, or in this case, happy beginnings.

I appreciated Andrew's call and his kind words and asked him to tell Adam once more that I was so terribly sorry and that I was leaving, but wanted to be sure he would write to me. I wanted Adam in my life.

I took one more last walk around the house to say good bye. It was a much more different walk than it was eight months earlier and I recalled that first walk. How it had changed! It was as if it was a different house and on the surface it was, but deep into the entrails and skeleton of the house, it was still the same place. Those ghosts may still be there. I would be happy to be rid of them. During my walk through I lingered for a while in the kitchen breakfast nook, where I spent so many hours when I first got to the house working at the old plank table and looking out into the yard, which was now a well-manicured elegant Italian garden with trimmed shrubs, fruit trees and sculpted topiaries. I walked into the library and also lingered there for a while, looking up at the story book moldings of the famous Doré illustrations. I looked at the shelves full of books now and the little molding entablature that opened the secret door into darkness to allow evil meanderers to be swallowed up and disappear in the night and to reappear again, perhaps sitting at the table in the kitchen nook nonchalantly sipping coffee and smoking a pipe, waiting for Charlotte to enter the room.

I walked up the elegant floating stairs and stood at the top balcony, again not too close and thought about Gerheardt standing here and falling to his death one dreary afternoon during a truculent exchange with his beloved she creature, here one moment, gone the next. Then I walked down the hall to the she creature's suite, elegant and feminine and I looked at the bed, now dressed in linen and satin and imagined it as Ingrid once saw it with the bedding all piled into a knot, but empty.

I stepped out onto the terrace and looked at the lake and imagined despondent Charlotte sitting in a lounge chair, wrapped in a blanket, smoking cigarettes and drinking brandy with her eyes fixed on the lovely lake, but probably not seeing anything beautiful in front of her because her eyes were focused inward into her own being trying to figure out what to do about life, how to deal with her lost loves, and her loneliness now that her only real partner in her life plan was gone and she was left alone and stuck in the "endure" stage of the plan so ingeniously designed by Gerheardt. They never wrote the next stage because it didn't occur to them there would be need for a next stage and without that written instruction, she may have been too pedantic to create a new destiny. Perhaps it would have been labeled Indefinite Sustainment.

It was over for the she creature and the only way out of this depression was down the hall and up the stairs to the attic where her ending would be all tied up with a neat little knot. I felt no need to take that walk again and with that believed I had enough and on my way out would look past the gloom of the house and appreciate the beauty Bjorn and I created and it was indeed beautiful and it sparkled. I went directly down the stairs through the gallery, placed the house key on the console and continued to the foyer. I turned for one last look and then left, pulling the heavy door closed behind me. I felt as if I had completed a circle and closed the loop. It was time to go home.

    I returned home to Los Angeles and it was a couple weeks of getting my life and business back together before I could clear a couple days and visit my little mountain cabin. The thought of the house on Lake Maggiore in Italy was beginning to find a place to settle deep in my cortex and it was all not as fresh and I was happy that I could stop dwelling on it. But I sat in front of my plain brick fireplace with the single timber mantel over which hung the painting with the mountain scene of the Alps. The simple little cabin was a far cry from the house on Lake Maggiore, but I loved it and felt that it loved me too. I thought about that horrible night in the house in Italy when we were all gathered around that fireplace and Bjorn told us the story of his life and then how Charlotte came to be. I had the photograph of Adam in my hand that was taken that first night in Milan when we went to the opera at the very beginning when we were looking for financing and were to meet Bjorn the following day. I couldn't shake the sadness I felt for him. I loved the smile on his face and the twinkle in his eye in the photo and wondered if he would ever smile again as he did that night.

    I looked around the cabin at the simple post and beam cathedral ceiling and the bank of clearstory windows above the loft with the black night and stars showing through and thought about there not being any columns with richly carved entablatures, or cartouche panels, or spandrels leading into the rooms and I thought about how far away all that seemed to be. There are no pediments, Churrigueresque designs running along the roof, allegoric story book moldings, or frescoed ceilings.

    It was my nature to never be complacent or pusillanimous, and to dare to be audacious and step out into unknown territory to seek adventure and explore the world. I did just that in my venture with the house on Lake Maggiore, and in doing so met people that I will never forget and became enriched in life experiences that I would never have dreamed were possible to be a part of. In doing so, I broadened my perspective of life and my scope of living and it was emotional, both in a wonderful way and also in a very tragic way.

I will never forget Adam and am so happy to have met him, but carry the guilt of causing him pain. Had I left that wall in place and never discovered the secrets within, the path may have remained cold for Bjorn and Felix. They would have had no reason to continue their quest and rouse their vexation about missing Nazis. Frederick would have never found the lost person known as Carl. Adam would have remained untouched by the reality of his early boyhood and would have just continued the life he found for himself watching his grandchildren grow up. Before learning of his parents, he ultimately would have continued his life with the pleasure of happy memories and the family life he knew and it was all very satisfying to him. Uncovering the truth of his beginnings overshadowed his happy memories and made his life seem like a lie to him. I would never have intentionally wanted to harm anyone and especially not Adam.

As Bjorn said, sometimes leaving well enough alone is what should be and I will tread every so cautiously from now on. Uncovering secrets that were meant to be left hidden is foolish, and those secrets were left hidden for a reason. It was as if Charlotte believed the truth might be harmful and destroy someone's life, and yet, if the truth must be known, she made it possible to not erase it entirely. She left it up to those that followed her to decide just how far they should dig. Having it become my decision was something she had no control over and it was her gamble as to whose hands her secrets would fall into.

There is no possible way for my thinking process to apply reason and justification to any of Charlotte's secrets and the way she lived her life. Perhaps it was the best she could do and even though it seems her choices were so horrific, I cannot begin to imagine what life was like in that time and place of history and it is impossible to relate to her. I don't pity her and I am not sorry for her and maybe one day I will come to terms with how much I really detest the thought of her and what she represented to the lives of Adam and Bjorn as young boys, and in my life even though I only really came to know her ghost. I will learn to rationalize it all by thinking that perhaps it was the best way for her to survive, and survival might have been at the heart of all her decisions, right or wrong. One can never know how their life decisions and choices may ultimately impact another. And most importantly, maybe the real objective in life is to survive and to succeed is only secondary and happenstance.

Charlotte's child was never conceived out of love and it was never love she felt for Adam, her son, I'm sure. It was her pride in her own ability to create and it seems quite clear that everything Charlotte did in her life was only for her. She lived her life self-indulgently and cared very little about others. Certainly, if she cared and loved her son, she would have destroyed all evidence of how she brought him into the world, and who she really was. The fact that she didn't destroy the truth proves that she thought she was worthy of someone finding out about her and she would not really be lost forever. She herself needed those reminders that she hid in the pantry, but maybe it was just for her and no one else was intended to stumble over them or delve too deeply into her archive, which was the narrative of her life. No matter what she went through and the many painful surgeries and emotional trauma of becoming someone else, she never really could let go of her past. Her mind was twisted and her endeavors were always short sided and distorted. Had she loved her son, she would not have wanted to taint his character in any way by leaving the horrible truth of her life and his beginnings to be discovered, and risk destroying his life, which up until the truth be known, was a life of goodness and pride. Charlotte, Carl, whoever that person was, did not deserve to be remembered or validated as a human being because of the things he did during the war. It seems inconceivable that this was Adam's parent. It makes one wonder if, had Charlotte lived and come to know Adam as an adult, would she have been proud of him as a person? I tend to believe she would not, but instead might have resented him because he was good and kind and everything she was not. I try to imagine what her life was like when she was a child. She, of course, was a little boy who loved Christmas and his sister. What a long and troubled road it was through that child's life to get to be what that person became.

The exploration of this enterprise turned into a phantom that began to grow tentacles reaching further than I could have imagined and brought forth a profusion of twisted circumstances consuming too many lives like an evil malignancy. When one became involved, they could not escape being wounded. All it took was just a slight scratch of the surface to unveil the nightmare and once it began to live, it was as if it could not stop its momentum.

When I returned from Italy, Los Angeles, upon my arrival, was its usual sunny, 75 degree weather and a total juxtaposition from the impending rainy winter in Northern Italy. That in itself was healing for a few days and I made an honest attempt to throw myself into my work, but to no avail. Somehow, I did not want to heal and I did not want to distance myself from my experience in Italy because in doing so I would be letting go of Adam. I needed what the mountain would give me. I needed to see the plants wilt in the cold air, and the finality of autumn descend over the mountain and I needed to smell the pine trees. I needed to be in the higher elevation, with the clouds covering the treetops and filtering the sun. I wanted to feel what it would be like to be in Northern Italy and the Alps, just to keep my memories alive and Adam's voice still fresh in my mind. I did not want to let go and now I sit in front of this fire with the smell of cedar in the air, and the sounds of snapping wood from the embers, and I look at the amber cognac in the crystal glass and as I sip it, I imagine I am sitting in front of the ornately carved fireplace in the house on the lake, and my new friends are there with me and we are engrossed in interesting conversation. I can almost hear them and I can hear Adam's laugh. I can hear Irene telling stories about what her life was like when she had a big house on the lake and I smile when I think about her getting tipsy from the wine.

The best times were wonderful, and it was before the truth began to obliterate the event and turn the good times into somberness. At that turning point, it became impossible again to enjoy the friendships and avoid the subject, each of us searching and wanting to know more. How would we have known at that time that there would soon be a time when we could not endure the melancholy of our acquaintance, which became doomed because we shared this horrible secret of what went on in the life of one person and the house on Lake Maggiore. From where I sit now, it seemed like someone else's life experience. Did it really happen or was I dreaming? If only it were just a bad dream.

The more the truth became unveiled, the more everyone knew we were destined to have to carry the burden of that truth forward and it would create a schism in our relationships because we would be a constant reminder of this secret each time we were together. My advice to Adam of leaving what was in the past, in the past, was even difficult for me to believe. Sometimes the past can find a way to continually and surreptitious creep forward and with Adam, he became overwhelmed with searching his memory of the woman he once knew in the moments in that pantry and trying to recall every detail about her, once he discovered she was his parent. What were her mannerisms? Did he move like her, speak like her, use the same hand gestures as he spoke, as sometimes children do just from innateness and their parallel genes? He searched his memory trying to assimilate to her, hoping in his heart he could not, and then disprove the theory and reality of her being and perhaps being part of him. Was Charlotte a monster, or was Charlotte just trying to get through her life as best she could in order to survive? In reality, I believe Charlotte was many things and did many things for different reasons, but it was always about her. I don't believe Charlotte knew how to love, but used the love of others to her own advantage. In the end, she was not happy and her constant search for survival became too much for her and she knew when it had to end, and she took it into her own hands to bring her life, her sad tortuous life, to a conclusion, just as her own son would contemplate many decades later.

Andrew wrote to tell me that Adam's depression took him to very dangerous territories, but with the watchful eye of his children and the help of a therapist, he was recovering. He realized his life was full and he loved his children and grandchildren too much to end his life. But he was driven to the brink and luckily his son stepped in and got some help for him. He still was not ready to communicate with me.

Learning of the severity of his situation made me feel even worse than before, and just imaging how much he was suffering mentally. I will mend and I will overcome the feeling that I caused someone great harm, but it will take time. I know I am not the same person as I was before I met Adam and before my work with the house. One can only hope that every life experience makes us stronger and invests something in our character.

Now in my mountain cabin waiting for the snow is where my story began. It is winter and the air is brisk and I relish in the warmth of the fireplace and sitting here staring into the flames, I cannot tell how I will live with this, but I know I will find a place deep inside myself where these thoughts will stay with me forever. I know I will never act as though nothing happened or that my life was not really so critically impacted, because even now as I remember every detail, every conversation, I am emotionally moved and fight back the tears. The memories will stay, but I will become hardened to them and learn to live with it. Life will go on, in one way or another.

There are many kinds of wars, and too often those who suffer the most are the children of those wars, because they live the longest and those memories must travel through life with them. This was an old war, but a war so devastating that volumes and volumes have been written about it and is still being written, but those that witnessed it are leaving us and all we will have left are their stories. Millions of people perished and too large a percentage of them were children. They were thought to be worthless because they were just one more mouth to feed and were unable to work and therefore looked on as useless. Any that survived are now in their golden years like Bjorn and Adam. If they speak at all about their memories of that war, they recall a youth tainted by the ghastly manipulation and strategy of others, who were completely unaccountable and had no regard for the ramifications of their actions and they are long gone, but these "old" children who survived still suffer the consequence. They are nearing the end of their strife and will carry those memories to their grave. Their youth was taken from them and in their most impressionable time of life when children explore and witness new things, these unfortunate children learned that beyond the weapons of war, the artillery, the bombs, the never ending bloodshed, the forbearance with mankind was overridden with hatred, which was the most vicious of all weapons. It is instilled in the character of man and does not end.

Still in this world today wars are born and fueled by hatred, the fundamental deep rooted cause of most wars and evidenced by vicious abhorrence, indifference and disregard for others. It has been the state of life from the beginning of recorded history and will always be, and it makes one wonder where in the world at this very moment are children still suffering and what war in the future will harm, divert or take the lives of more children? These are the wars of old men, but it is the children that suffer. As vicious as man's nature is, some of those children will grow up to become the executor of new wars and one would wonder if it is that old vengeance that besets their nature. It is the nature of humans and history will repeat time and time again and our children will become more lost with each war.

Printed in Dunstable, United Kingdom